NEAR HAVEN

Matthew Stephen Sirois

BELLE LUTTE PRESS

Near Haven is a work of fiction. Names, characters, places, and incidents are the products of Matthew Sirois' imagination, or are used fictitiously. Any resemblance to actual events or persons is entirely coincidental.

Published by Belle Lutte Press. www.BelleLutte.com

ISBN 978-0-9973260-4-8

Library of Congress Control Number
available upon request.

Printed in the United States of America

Cover Art by Antonio Mora
Cover Design by Michael Patrick Dudding

BELLE LUTTE PRESS

While today's media maximizes profits by force-feeding the populace cheap and unoriginal thought, Belle Lutte Press is fighting the good fight—hell-bent on publishing original, high-quality novels.

NEAR HAVEN

For Dad.

I.

I can calculate the motion of
heavenly bodies, but not the
madness of people.

—Isaac Newton

~~305~~ 304

Of the dozen buildings slouched riverward in Near Haven shipyard, only Stearns Fiberglass let on that it might be occupied. The bait company, canvas supply, machine shops, and all else sat dark under their corrugated aluminum roofs, while at Stearns a floodlight watched the empty yard and a dull blue flicker lit the windows.

Tom paced the stained production floor, a beer can hanging from his arm like a clock weight. The motionless air of the boat shop still tasted of epoxy, though nothing had been built here in months. Abandoned hulls lay keel-up on scaffolds, soaking in the television glow with matte-grey flanks. A little black-and-white phased in and out of service, offering reflections, restatements, redactions—but just one story. Like everyone, Tom had come to imagine the forecast events of next May from his own solitary vantage. An abrupt flash in the eastern sky and the five-hour wait that would follow. Five hours to smoke, jerk off, tie one on for good. Five hours, and the few molecules known as Tom Beaumont would be ripped westward in the shockwave. Thrown in with the damned of every backwater shit-hole on the worried edge of Maine.

Tom fished another can from the Coleman chest and turned a chunky dial through the network channels. Most were out by now, folded. On 4 he got a signal, wafting up the coast from a carrier station in Portland and tracking badly. Tom worked a rude semaphore with the antennas until finally the picture gelled. He lit a cigarette and backed away from the set, watching it as a cat watches a dark crack in the wall.

"These are bold accusations," said the television host, more to the camera than to his guest, "which you're leveling at the executive office and its appointees." He held his chin in his hand and spoke over thick, pale knuckles—eyelids hanging as if sedated. "You've essentially accused the United States of fraud, and now murder," he said.

The interviewee sat stiff, facing him in her molded plastic chair, haloed with a glowing CBS logo. Three carpeted risers separated her from the cameramen, giving the impression of a studio audience somewhere. "Whether my colleagues were murdered is beside the point," she began, clipped and acidic. Her hair and clothing were all clean lines and calm tones, but an insomniac's worry shivered in her eyes.

"The science community is almost unilateral on the Fletcher issue. We have independent data from observation points all over the world showing a flyby." She paused, swallowing as the camera tightened on her. "I don't believe that you or the interests you represent can suppress that data."

At this, the host pushed back his chair and raised his open

palms, feigning surrender and letting her turnabout die in silence. He gathered some papers before him, never glancing at the text, and cracked them into alignment on the edge of his desk. The strike sounded through the microphones like a starting gun. "Ms. White, does it surprise you… having been labeled a *shomee?*"

"What's surprising is that certain figures in the media are using such a childish term in the first place." Her response gave the question no air, no time for a viewer to even parse the epithet. *Show me.*

"Yet," his voice rose in pitch, "here you've implied that a commercial airplane was knocked down intentionally—without there being any evidence to that effect or any clear connection to Dr. Fletcher. How should we characterize these statements?"

"Some of the top minds in physics and cosmology died on that flight, and all were scheduled to testify against Mr. Fletcher's claims. If that's not a clear enough—" she let go of the bait, seeming to probe some space beyond the cameras for guidance. "For the last time: I did not come here to discuss the crash."

"Of course. You're here to deny findings corroborated by DARPA, the State Department, the Federal Emergency Management Agency—this list goes on. But what I want, Ms. White, is for you to tell us just who and what brought down that plane." He extended a hand, raising his eyebrows, to demonstrate the simplicity of this request for the camera lenses. "There's a certain… demographic… who'd like us to think it was an inside job."

She closed her eyes just for a moment, maybe to gauge

the rhetorical checkmate she'd been backed into. Acquiesce or accept the brand of extremism. America is no cowardly assassin. She looked at the host. Her face pinched reflexively, as if his self-satisfaction had an odor. Lowly, from her throat: "I'm sure I wouldn't know."

He turned to the camera, again speaking to it rather than to her. "No. I'm sure you wouldn't." Having held the loose pages for those few seconds, he slapped them back on the desk. His grin, barely formed, evaporated the moment his interrogation began anew. "Ms. White..."

"...You can't pretend there's only one possible outcome here," she cut in. Whatever violence she'd pent up now surged along the conduit of her speech. "That's not how science operates. Your network—these networks—are just cheerleading Fletcher's doomsday narrative for ratings. You're making reality itself a partisan issue—inciting the same panic you use to fill headlines. And to question any of this, you've decided, with these divisive little slurs," she gestured toward her own person, "is treason."

The host returned his hands to their position beneath his jaw, knitting the thick fingers together and frowning with theatrical patience. "The Fletcher Report is, of course, not the only source one must consider here." He went quiet for an uncomfortable span, letting his next question appreciate in perceived worth. "Ms. White," he asked, and the tone was punitive, magnanimous, fatherly, "do you believe in God?"

The response that came was only a whine of feedback and a confused jostling of the cameras. Calm as ever, the host looked on as his guest tore the microphone from her lapel, dropped it to the floor, and exited the frame.

An electric crackle sounded at the far end of the shop. Tom turned an ear toward the handheld ship-to-shore, but his eyes remained fixed on the television screen. They'd gone to a station ID.

"Tango, Oscar, Mike..." came a voice, shredded by the wire mesh of the radio speaker. *"Time fa Yankee Whiskey, Foxtrot."*

Tom smoked and considered the radio. Its squelch circuit opened again, the same rough voice saying, *"C'mon, Tommy. I know ya jus' drinkin' alone in there. I can see ya lights."* He finally picked up the rubberized black box with its waggling antenna, digging a thumb and forefinger into his eye sockets and releasing a lungful of anxiety. He pressed the transmit button. "Hey, Nev. Be there in a minute."

Tom walked back to the TV and flipped it off. The black-and-white picture went—*zap*—as it collapsed into itself. He fed his cigarette to the beer can's mouth, hearing it sodden with a hiss.

Muscle memory guided him over the iron marine rails, fixed him to each foothold across the wet concrete slabs of the boat launch. Threading a shortcut through the marina, he loped down gangways and over gaps between pontoon docks, past a floating trailer park of cruising yachts in low-rent slips. Tom emerged on the far side of this wharf-rat's maze, damp and winded, only to double back for two more cans and to kill the forever hum of his generator.

Neville Bradford sat on the old tavern pier, a fifth of Allen's beside him, watching as a half-dozen drunks shuffled out the tavern door. The restaurant hands were closing shop, carrying black garbage cans down and spilling their contents over the beach. Here, where the St. George River met the sea, its half-salt water licked indifferently at the refuse. A hand-painted sign recently nailed over the tavern entrance said, "Normal Day Pub—Come As You Are." The place was a soup kitchen, plus booze. The cooks hauled back the empty cans and took them dripping into the gaslit building. They'd been running it this way since whenever the last garbage truck rolled through, each morning's sun finding new breadth in the rotting piles.

The gulls loved it.

The tavern would be a ruin eventually, gull-shat and windowless. The town's sewage pumps had already chugged to a stop, a reeking backflow flooding the streets and creeping toward the river, killing off a season's worth of hatchling fish. Snow would pile eight feet high on sunporches and dormers and gables and just crush them. The river itself would gnaw at every seawall, every pier and pylon, bringing them down in roughly the same order they'd been put up. The roads would freeze and buckle, and saplings would root themselves in the cracks, drilling like maggots into a wound. The human labor of centuries would fall to nature's reclamation in a matter of years.

"Was jus' talkin' with Dexter Hannah inside," said Bradford, not wasting a hello.

Tom took his customary seat and handed over a beer. "Yeah?"

"Course, Dex is the fucker who'd finally get me jittery 'bout this thing." Bradford didn't identify it by name because there was only one "thing," and any pains they now suffered in their waning lives here were collateral to *it*. Radiated from it like sunlight. He stared at the night sky with a slack, stoned look on his face. A big man sitting kid-like on the pier's edge, broad shoulders slouched and work boots dangling over the water. His belly strained at the snaps of a flannel shirt, and a mesh ballcap hovered perpetually about his ursine head. "Told me a diesel driver come through town on 'is way north. The rig was all shot through with bullet holes. He come up 95 from Hartford, an' the pike was one big warzone."

"You think that's true?"

"Ya think Dexter Hannah's a liar?" Bradford challenged, coughing and indignant after he'd hit his spliff. "Goddamn Feds a been seizin' gas all ovah. No imports since, when, March?"

Tom sniffed the coffee brandy and then took a quick pull. He'd known the auto-garage owner his whole life. "I need to talk to Dexter about that backup generator. Tried feeding it cut methanol, and it won't start."

"Y'oughta stick ta oil lamps an' wood heat. Them lights'll draw the wrong crowd."

"I'm not concerned with lights, just need power for the tools. I want this boat in the water by next summer."

"Right. 'Cept, yer supposed ta be dead by next spring."

"I'll burn that bridge when I come to it."

Bradford laughed and tried to pass Tom the brown roach, stuck there to his big, gnarled thumb. Tom wouldn't take it from him, never had, but felt a bit of the tension in him shift and dislodge.

"This shomee attitude a yours might make ya feel smart," Bradford said in a fraternal whisper, "but if ya get shot for a couple gallons gas, it won't make ya any less dead." He looked pleased with having tied this rhetorical sheepshank. "Same dif'rence if Fletcher's rock spreads ya bony ass from here ta Detroit."

Tom hit the bottle again. "Did I show you this?" he said and offered Bradford his middle finger.

The foghorn at Osprey Head Light brayed its wide, flat tone, somewhere out there in the soup. They'd gotten their generator up.

"Well, Dexter's probably holed up at the garage with a shotgun in 'is hands. Them underground tanks are right full, an' fuck knows who might come up the pike lookin' for fuel." Bradford took two parting puffs and flicked his roach into the dark. "Gonna tell me that don't make ya nervous, Tommy?"

Tom rolled a cigarette and lit it. He spat at the water below, where it lapped at the pylons. He thought he saw a bass come up and gulp at the phlegm bubbles riding the surface, but it was dark and he was drunk.

"I just want to finish out my contract," Tom said.

The reflection of his cigarette cherry shone in the oily, black water. Its red glow could have been a traffic light at the far end of a dark road—miles away, down under the George. It was like his own damned ghost, winking back from the great whatever beyond.

Four years prior, standing in the Portland quad on a slushy February morning, the entire UMaine student body seemed to flow past Tom like a river around a stone. The payphone receiver crackled with rushing air, the sound of Hank Beaumont letting go the smoke of a Winston 100. "You're gonna give up your grant," he said.

"So. It's money. I'd be throwing it away anyhow. My program's full of idiots."

The black Bakelite earpiece was cold, and silent for an awful stretch.

"You've got the same answer for everything, Tom. Your mother and I are idiots for going to church. Your professors are idiots for believing in education."

Another white-out of exhalation, and Tom looked up at the crowd milling past the payphone. The few who met his glance wouldn't hold it, and he realized how he must look, shivering and wet eyed.

"You know, I was always proud to have a smart, sensitive kid," Hank said. "What happened to him, Tom? 'Cause somewhere along the line he turned into an angry, arrogant prick."

"Dad."

"Come on back to town if you want, but don't bother comin' home for a while. I'd hate havin' to live up to your standards."

Tom skipped breakfast and then lunch, unable to shake this last sentence from his ear. By mid-afternoon he was smoking just to quell his hunger, watching the sun go down, and waiting on a northbound bus.

Abel Stearns was the biggest boat-building name in Near Haven harbor at the time, named into the business it might seem, when Tom approached him for work. The shop master had looked him over briefly, this strangely wearied young man, raising a dubious eyebrow. "Do you have any qualifications?" he'd asked. "Have you done fiberglass work before?"

Tom tried to meet Abel Stearns' eyes with some measure of confidence. They were chilly blue and steady as a cat's. "No," he said, adding, "I'm a fast learner."

Mr. Stearns pushed some forms in his direction and said, "Food and lodging, such as they are, shall be provided to all apprentices. Five percent commission on finished projects. Schedule is eight to six, Monday through Friday. Weekends, when there's a launch. If you smoke, do it on the beach. Every damn thing in here is flammable."

"Five percent?"

"That might sound small, but for a kid your age, it's a good-sized piece. We build real boats here."

"What are these papers for?" Tom scanned over three pages of pidgin-legalese.

"That's a contract of apprenticeship at Stearns Fiberglass and Marine Construction. It outlines my expectations and the length of your appointment."

"And how long is that?"

The old man might have smiled, but Tom hadn't known

him long enough to tell. He spoke very deliberately, as not to be misunderstood. "When you can take a vessel—on your own—from the drafting table to St. John's Harbor without taking on considerable water, then you'll have served the contract in full."

"St. John's? Newfoundland?"

"I've a brother there, Robert, who's harbormaster. He'll check your bilge and sign your papers, should you be successful."

Tom looked down at the contract lying on the table, thumbed through it again, and imagined his life in two or four or six years. He'd walked in looking only for a job, and here, he was facing a career. As Tom reached across the table toward a coffee mug of ballpoint pens, he asked, "And what if I can't learn to build sailboats?"

Mr. Stearns raised both eyebrows, as though admitting the possibility. "In that case, Thomas," he directed Tom's attention to the far side of the shop, "you'll spend the prime of your life dry-patching rowboats with Neville."

Tom followed this gesture across the wide concrete floor to where a goliath in denim coveralls crouched under the hull of a Boston Whaler. The man called Neville straightened up, his ballcap rising over the skiff's gunnel, which itself was elevated on scaffolds some six and a half feet from the ground. He pulled the carbon-filter mask from his face, adjusted his balls with one mighty paw, and said, "Go fuck ya selves."

This was how he'd met Neville Bradford and how they'd shortly become a close, if asymmetric, contingent. The pair of them spent that summer in matching respirators, taking turns running the disk sander or laying fiberglass cloth, the crusted epoxy drippings turning their blue jeans solid and exoskeletal right on their bodies. They were mollusks together.

Bradford ribbed him for being the scrawniest, greenest motherfucker in the shop. Abel would pull Tom aside, though, to assure that he appreciated Tom's meticulous nature, the way he spoke his mind and had a genuine care for what he did. No matter how much Tom felt he was holding up progress, Abel seemed to approve. There was an air of solicitude, even, in Abel's criticisms.

Abel's sons, Brian and Eric, had grown up to become lawyers or proctologists or whatever, and left Maine. Abel was disappointed, wanting someone of his blood to someday take over the business. Toward the end, his boys just stopped speaking to him altogether. By the second year of his apprenticeship, Abel had altered Tom's contract. He was giving Tom a controlling share in the business. He'd long been a widower, and without his sons around, there was no one to protest. Abel had something that he needed to teach, and Tom, to his own surprise, had proved a bright and eager student.

Abel died on May 25, 1987. Tom couldn't say for certain, but he suspected the cause to have been pneumonia or congestive heart failure. Abel was an old fellow, certainly—"Just this side of a century," he'd liked to say—and the years of labor and glass dust had eventually dragged him down. He refused to see a doctor and passed away quietly at home. Abel said he was ready for it and warned Tom not to make a fuss. He was that lucid, that stubborn until the very end.

The Stearns shop—and every other in the yard—had shut down a few weeks after they'd buried him, Tom and Bradford and the other apprentices. The electrical grid went dark, and it seemed he was never to finish his apprenticeship. He'd overseen work on plenty of beautiful, seaworthy boats for clients over the years, and Abel was always pleased with his work. But Tom had never done it single-handedly, and he'd never taken one out of sheltered Muscongus Bay and into the open sea that lay between it and St. John's.

Here, a pestering thread of memory: there was a night that spring, a warm night, and he'd just seen the old man to bed. As Tom walked back toward the shop, he noticed a shooting star, and then another, and another. He stood out in the yard for hours watching them. Hundreds falling low over the harbor like a slow rainstorm. The *Aquarids*, they were called.

~~304~~ 303

A breeze whipped through the shop, bringing in the smell of the mud flats. The clinging emulsion of ocean spray and spoiled eggs woke Tom from a dreamless, blackout sleep. He stretched and cursed and clawed at his eyes to loosen the crusts. A cat pawed through Tom's garbage bin and hardly flinched as Tom stood and growled out a yawn.

"Morning, Buck," he groaned at the cat, as it regarded his mouth, his hand.

He pulled a ballcap low over his brow and walked out the door into a sun-blasted morning on the George and across the gravel of the boatyard. The glare off the water and the white shore rocks and the pitched aluminum shop roof lanced his eyes. Summer's heat was closing in, a smudge of agitated particles in the west. Tom scooped a panful of rainwater from the drum, picked it clean of pine needles and mosquito larvae, and set it on the propane burner to boil. He dropped in a fistful of stale Folgers Crystals and stumbled to the brush for a piss and then just waited—for divine inspiration or for his bowels to get moving.

He happened a glance at the chicken coop. Stared at the five birds there. Marveled at the massive, clumsy stretch mark someone had left when they'd broken through the wire.

"Fuck's sake," he said to no one.

Tom had taken on six bantam hens in June, thinking to forestall the coming privation of winter. He found them scratching at the sunbaked earth and eyeing one another hungrily in a backyard coop off Wadsworth Street. They were mostly scrawny and pecked to tatters, with the exception of a sturdy old matron, but it was clear they'd been bred as show birds. The owners had fled, like so many other old-money types, in the first noticeable post-Fletcher exodus. Right after the "epicenter" or "ground zero" or whatever had been decided, a North Atlantic coordinate somewhere east of the Grand Banks.

The white-haired population of Near Haven dropped by half, quite overnight, leaving the general population down a heavy third. The Grand Banks fishery had originally brought most of these families, their estates built on haddock and pollock and cod. Only their God, or maybe their brokers, could say where they'd all gone. To Aspen in a flock, was Tom's guess. To Johannesburg. To Brisbane. What a boon for the travel industry. Tom imagined them packed into cramped turboprop rigs at Portland jetport, arriving to week-long queues at a dozen terminals, camping out of their luggage with a million other fortunates. Stuck as anyone else.

He'd found no other signs of life in that small Victorian mansion above the marsh and purloined its more useful stuff with impunity. But he'd puzzled over the chickens for a while.

Tom had never stolen anything living.

Using bits of his lunch to bait them, Tom managed to catch each bird individually and then bind their twelve legs together with bailing twine, as they flapped and squabbled in the dirt. He marched home slowly, his rucksack loaded with domestic implements and this living mantle of claws and feathers and eyeballs slung around his neck. If Bradford had caught him at it, the fucker would have died laughing.

Not a month had passed, and already the chickens had begun dwindling in number. Tom poured some coffee into a plastic travel mug and returned to the shop, where he found the cat kneading his sweat-stained pillow and eyeing him expectantly.

"Hungry?" he asked.

Buck jumped down from the cot, gravity forcing a cat noise out of him like a dropped concertina. Tom fed him a sardine from the Coleman box, taking two chicken eggs for himself.

A curling-edged wall calendar hung above the drafting table, appointments scrawled here and there in the boxes, none of which mattered any longer. The photographs up top were of vessels built in the Near Haven yard. Yachts, mostly. The *Mary Day*, the *Pride of Arcadia*. A cabin cruiser named *Severance Package*. Tom shook his felt-tipped Sharpie to loosen the ink, then drew a line through the box labeled July 3 and the number "304" he'd marked it with yesterday. In the next he wrote "303" and put the marker back in its cup.

Sitting at the drafting table, books and makeshift ashtrays

and reams of drafting paper and so forth strewn around, he could hear Buck still crunching tiny bones. A spider scuttled past, disappearing under a *Farmer's Almanac* for the planting season of 1986. Tom picked a pencil stub from the clutter and scratched incoherently on a pad. The doodles could be taken for whales or airplanes, but he knew what they really were. Curved, finned, and swept—these nautical forms were his hand's default in the spaces between thoughts. After them came a list that read: WD-40, BIC LIGHTER, 12V BATTERY, KEROSENE, DRY GAS, HONEY. Tom scratched out "honey" and allowed some space and began again: HEMINGWAY, ASTRONOMY, BIBLE.

On bright mornings like this he'd raise the eastward hangar door of the boat shop and let the sun paint his shadow long on the concrete floor. When Tom finished his list, he tore the sheet from its gummy binding, folded it in eighths, and slid it into his pocket.

Walking up Fox Street and then along Main, Tom made a list of neighbors he thought ballsy enough to steal a chicken from him, but the tally grew unmanageably long. He poked around behind the old office block, where some displaced riffraff were recently making camp. A few bearded faces appeared, long enough to note his passage, and then returned to idle dozing. Tom hooked and laddered through the residential backstreets: long, quiet stretches of unmown yards and boarded windows and freshly painted crosses. Crosses had spread, in those months, over every vertical surface like a strain of geometric mold. As if a few slaps of house paint here and there would be enough to keep the vampires out.

Lindy Bly caught him sticking his nose between the chain-link fences on Green Street and waved him down. She wasn't specifically worried about Tom hanging around, but everybody was stockpiling something and trying to keep mum about it. Foodstuffs and ammunition and petroleum. Toiletries of every kind, especially feminine. Car batteries and cash and insulated boots, the practical and prudent, right on down to chewing gum in vendor's cases and pallets of Diet Coke. Anxiety was the mother of hoarding, the sibling of theft.

"Hey, Lin," said Tom, as if minding his business.

"Tommy. You lookin' for somethin', hon?" Lindy wore a V-neck undershirt that showed sweat stains in the armpits and her breasts hung free behind the thin fabric. She was a pert twenty-four, as stormily attractive as she'd been when they last fucked in high school, but middle age seemed to crouch like a wolf in her periphery.

"Lost one of my hens. Just figured I'd take a walk, maybe see where she ran off to." He took a long, easy drag and blew it out again. He looked at her bare feet on the worn porch boards. "How's Dar?"

"Dar's fine, so long as he ain't sober. Wish he'd come home once in a while, instead a messin' with the boat or whatever the hell." Lindy put her hands on her hips, stretched her back to tell him she'd been working at something, she was tired, take notice. "You hungry? You look about post-thin, as usual." A big powder blue cross on the white clapboard behind her. "Peace on Earth," someone had written above.

Darwin's not home—the thought flared like a struck match. "No, that's good of you. Really. I should be getting on." Tom could have been more neighborly, he supposed. He could have offered a hand at whatever. She let her ponytail out and tied it back again and watched him smoke. If Tom were ever really hungry, Lindy would know it. "Give your old man my best, Lin."

"Okay, sweetheart."

Tom felt a need to move on, a kind of guilt that pushed at his eyeballs.

"God bless..." said Lindy, as Tom turned his back to her and stepped into the street.

He threw a hand up behind him, a slack farewell. "Yup."

Off Green Street and toward the harbor, some freight rails bisected Near Haven, with homes to the west side and defunct waterfront businesses, like Stearns Fiberglass, to the east. Tom cut away from the street, favoring the train route, which lead diagonally toward the water. The train bridges and trestles were popular camps for drifters who now moved mostly southbound along the rails, like ants trickling single file from a trampled nest. Tom hopped along the ties and crunched through the gravel shoulders for a mile or so, nodding at the men he found slumped under bushes or squatting in the ditch.

Two-Buckets hunkered over his campfire by the train trestle, a vision in rags and mismatched tennis shoes. Tom noticed his bicycle leaned there first—actually the two white plastic ten-gallon pickle tubs, by which he was known, slung over the handlebars—before he saw the tinker himself. These other beggars and freight hoppers, they were all new to town, and they'd be gone within days, just human jetsam in a massive, outgoing tide, but Two-Buckets was their own son. A kind of village idiot who'd been living off the waste and charity of Fox County ever since Tom could remember. He'd achieved mascot status, rattling around Near Haven like a dud kernel in a popcorn bag, his moniker spoken endearingly, and though no one could recall his given name, they'd all thrown him at least a couple handouts over the years.

Sure enough, the cheeky fucker was cooking Tom's hen.

"Two-Buckets!" Tom yelled, running down the embankment. "That's a laying hen, you damned fool."

The man-child turned slowly, searching for the noise like a bird overhead. He gave that look of his: an open smile with his eyes pinched tight and a spittle string hanging, his features goopy-nebulous within the bristled pork chop of his face.

"T-Th-Thom!" he said, all fucking surprise. "Um cookin' dinnah now, Thom. Buh… I'll let choo stay." His speech was mostly tongue, as though he hadn't had a drink of water in days.

Tom hid a grin behind his fist. Two-Buckets had been camping more or less regularly on this river inlet over the warm months, just a stone's throw from Stearns, and they'd gotten a bit neighborly. Tom was poor at enforcing boundaries. He glanced at the ill-fated chicken hung above the fire pit, half-plucked and stuck through with a dirty length of rebar. "It's all the same to you, bud, I think I'll pass."

"Okay, Thom! Mo' fa mee!" he coughed up the words and spat to his side, still giggling hoarsely. The imbecile's happiness was bulletproof.

Tom walked to the bicycle and inspected the contents of its buckets—all the scavenged artifacts Two-Buckets had accrued in the small circuit of his nomadism. Some useful and some just curious. He pulled out two cans of "she-crab soup," a kind of chowder made in Louisiana. Tom used to see it at Fale's General, now and again. Some local had evidently developed a tooth for this stuff in their travels.

"You really should buy local in this economy," he said. Two-Buckets laughed, Tom assumed because he knew what sarcasm was supposed to sound like. After finding nothing else edible, Tom held up the cans and said, "I'm having these, Two-Buckets," without looking at the man. "I'll consider us even." This was not an even trade, but nothing would come from trying to haggle. "Listen, bud, if you're hungry…" Tom looked at the old tinker in his moldy, ragged layers. Two-Buckets had no idea what was happening here, of course. Could he comprehend it, would that change anything about his relationship to the world? Tom wasn't about to rob Two-Buckets his ignorance, and hoped no one else would, either. "Just don't steal from me, alright?"

Two-Buckets busily scraped at some charred feathers with a cattail switch. "O-Okay, Thom. Okay."

Tom schlepped up Fox Street, past the abandoned sea captain's houses that stood like unkempt museum pieces and turned on Gleason, his rucksack heavy with chowder cans, a pipe wrench, and a car battery he had no means of testing. He hastened through the barren parking lot of St. James Catholic Church, despite the weight, and crossed onto the library grounds. In the four years since his return to Near Haven, Tom had avoided these buildings the way a smoker withers from the gaze of a child.

He set his pack in the feral, untrimmed grass and lay beside it, panting as the sun climbed over the easterly rooftops of Main. The post office, closed as of June, caught the rays on its flaking, gilded trim. A bleached flag hung limply from its pole. The mouth of Beechwood Street held Near Haven's only traffic light between its curbs, the same as always but for the weeds now shooting through the cracks; Tom thought of his parents' little saltbox house, only a few miles distant along that road. The stubborn, ungiving apple tree there and his father's boat in the yard. He thought of the last visit he'd made to the house, the argument with his mother, the way Hank hung by, unspeaking. Some ideological chasm had divided Tom's family ages before, and as yet, no one seemed willing to cross it.

Bolted into the stone façade of the library was a black-and-yellow sign that read FALLOUT SHELTER, with a circular fascistic symbol painted in its center. The ground-level windows were all nailed blind with sheets of plywood, and Tom wondered if he'd be able to get in. He wondered how long it had been this way and why he hadn't stopped to notice before now. Surprisingly, the rear entrance door had been kept open with a little wooden shim. As he pushed through the door, the sunlight cut out and he found himself blind for a moment while his vision recovered.

The same familiar creaky steps. The same community bulletin board hung on the left, now empty or tattered here and there with the remnants of old news. Plays, potlucks, dances—grey as obituary pictures. He climbed to the first-story landing, pushed the massive wooden door open, and saw his childhood sanctuary, despite all odds, intact. The brightly painted covers of children's books adorning a shelf to the foremost, the broad officialdom of the desk in the center of the room, with its Rolodex sorters and stamp pads. The vaulted ceilings and towering windows and tall shelves waiting.

"Hello?" There was no answer, and he realized he'd barely made the word audible. Tom set down his pack by the desk and winced as its metal hardware clinked in the still, open room. He moved slowly, walking the rows. Fiction A–C. Fiction D–F. The soles of his topsiders floated silent along the carpeting.

Tom heard a low whine, like wheels inching forward, and then a voice from somewhere among the dark shelves. Just a whisper. Incantatory, unaware of his lurking. He took a few more paces and wiped the moisture from his palms, trying to make out the repeated phrase. He rounded the next aisle. Louder, Tom said, "Hello?"

"Thomas Beaumont," she said, knowing him by voice alone.

"Miss Neary," answered Tom, more sir-yes-sir than a greeting.

She emerged from the corner tentatively, clutching a half-dozen hardcovers against her delicate form. "You're home."

Tom stiffened as Neary put a cool hand on his cheek. He didn't mention that he'd been "home" for years; he'd only been living as somebody else. Somebody she didn't know. Her eyes in the half-light flashed like garnets. "My god, look at you…" Her smell was deathlike, floral and damp, yet her dress was clean, and he thought he could even detect a hint of makeup grouting the creases of her face. "You're a man, Tom. It's so good to look at you."

"I…" Tom faltered and smiled. "I wasn't expecting to find anyone." A lock of his black, oily hair fell across his face and she replaced it behind an ear. He was nervous and pacified, pulled in opposition to himself. "How are…"

"Well, the library budget was cut, just before the schools, you know…"

"Yeah, I can imagine," he said. The budget was cut, the government went into hiding, the streets flooded with shit. What an awful bother.

"We're all closed down now, no electricity." She sighed long, made a gesture of, what? Futility, he supposed. "I just keep them dusted and dry. Keep the windows sealed; patch the leaks where I can. Winter will be here before we know, Tom."

Tom could see that Peg Neary, Head Librarian, the fairy godmother of his lonely, bookish youth, had not spoken with anyone in some time. He couldn't imagine how she'd been feeding herself, how she'd keep warm through the coming seasons. She was like a person held long in the darkness, desperate for touch and talk.

"Yeah, but why are you," Tom waved a vague hand at the stacks, "here?"

"I've been here for thirty-five years, Tom." Neary let her hand reach out, of its own accord, to straighten a Longfellow anthology on a wire stand. She pulled it in again to smooth her dress. The collarbones stood out from her chest like a rope laid across it. "Where else should I go? I'm comfortable here, at least, and no one bothers me. When the workmen come to do their business downstairs, I wait in my office and read poetry. If I'm hungry, I trade with the neighbors. You'd be shocked at the demand for romance and cozy mysteries." She winked conspiratorially, giving him an effortful half smile.

"Okay, but still. Where's your house?"

"There's nothing for me there. And it's too far to walk."

"You can't just live on old routines."

She wouldn't abide his concern. "Tom," she said evasively, parroting the book-matron from his past, "what can I do for you?"

As Neary shuffled through index cards, Tom poked around the building, taking in the familiar. Too much here, in this old brick relic, for one person to keep tabs on. The innumerable volumes did look well attended, as she'd said, dusted and Dewey-decimaled as always. The carpets were so clean that he imagined Neary on hands and knees, plucking offending crumbs with her fingers. How else? Even the potted rubber trees and African violets were thriving, occupying the corners still touched daily by the sun. But something was off. The sounds and smells and substances of life were gone. The warm moisture of teenagers necking in the basement lounge. The greasy, moth-wing flutter of children's fingerprints. The assuring thud of stamp-pad and boot-tread. Missing.

Neary slid the wooden drawer into place and beckoned him to follow between shelves that stood dark and close. A stout, petrified forest. The aisles seemed too narrow. The space too little for them both to occupy, the air within too scarce. Miss Neary's scent consumed him. Tom didn't think he'd ever get it off.

She found him a King James Bible, as per the list, with cross-references and footnotes. She said nothing about it, just handed it over and kept walking. The science section had always been broad, but Tom was surprised to find more volumes on astronomy than he could span with his arms held wide. Some estate donor must have been a space buff. He pored over them for several minutes, eventually settling on a book entitled *Comets: A Detailed Catalog* by someone named Harvey Mint. What a friggin' handle, he thought.

In the fiction section, Miss Neary couldn't seem to locate *A Farewell to Arms*, but suggested they check the original editions kept in a glass case behind her desk. The case had a steel latch with a lock and keyhole. Neary slipped in the key that she kept covertly on her person, turned and lifted the hasp, and opened the door. It was obvious that the case had admitted a certain amount of water, which it maybe hadn't been designed to keep out. What issued was a smell of leather, old leather, old paper, and a hundred additionals that could only be described organically. It smelled like death, or like Neary herself in some more wet and concentrated form. The unearthing of something that had died long ago, and a hint of something else trying to cover it. She handed him a Scribner's hardback and shut the case.

Tom admired the book, turning it over in his hands. "There's a house on the corner of Wadsworth and Hyler, big house set off the street behind a wrought-iron fence. Nobody's there. It has a guesthouse or a mother-in-law or whatever through the side yard, past the chicken coop. There's a small woodstove, and cordwood outside. There's a pantry in the big house with some canned goods and flour. The basement's been flooded, but that shouldn't bother you. I want you to go there, Miss Neary. The library can wait 'til next year."

"Listen to you, Tom. Next year. And the one after? A real agnostic, just like when you were a boy."

"I've already busted the lock cylinders, but there are deadbolts on the house and the mother-in-law. It's safe."

"And what about you? Who's swooping in to rescue you, Thomas Beaumont?"

He tried to find the sarcasm on her face, but it wasn't there. "I don't get it," he said.

"You're reading up on astronomy, helping an old lady get by." She backed off a couple steps and squared herself to him. "You're not wrong to question what's happening, Tom. I know you can't help it." Was it guilt he saw then? "Just be mindful of the company you're in when you admit to disbelief. The things you doubt are, for a lot of people, the only assurances in this world. They could get very hostile should they feel someone tugging at the rug beneath them."

When the phone lines went dead, it came down to DC power and the ethereal chatter of the shortwave. Mostly just folks entertaining themselves, talking about their pets or singing off-key ballads that floated out patchy with fuzz. There were armchair preachers at ten cents a dozen on the radio those days. Turning the dial, he'd hear them wash into each other and overlap indiscernibly. Liturgical slush. There was talk of an election season that would come and go without a vote cast, rumors of a federal government gone underground. And every so often, Tom would catch a shomee on his tirade. He had never heard the term self-applied, but a shomee was anyone who rejected Fletcher's prediction, for any number of reasons. They were conspiracy theorists and retired Washington insiders. They were economists and atheists. Mathematicians. Astronomers. Theologians and historians. Of course, most of them were just crackpots. All blacklisted for apostasy, all shouting into the prevailing wind of Fletcher, Reagan, and God. The short wave was the shomee's forum, wherein he could only be touched by anger: an anonymous, disembodied counterpoint. Curses and rebukes cutting in from a hundred handsets, attempting to drown him out. Electric siren sounds zapping across the channel, heat seeking his voice in the night.

Sometimes a transmission ended abruptly, with a mechanical bang or electric crackle, but often just amid the radiofied surge of human wailing. Tom could never tell whether from pain or just sorrow, and he never ventured to ask. He kept his receiver off except on the loneliest nights, unnerved by these dispatches from Limbo.

The noon sun watched him cross the low-tide flats, heard the mud sucking at his shoes. These dog days on the George were a stifling affair, and the seasonal shift happened as usual: abrupt, unceremonious, and unpredictable. A certain bulk added itself to the atmosphere, hanging in sinuous vapors over the condensing water and sitting thick on the sweating land. A changeable breeze, cool by night and relentlessly hot by day, when there was a breeze at all. Any tiny current felt on the back of a damp shirt, in the pits of elbows and arms. A wreath of biting flies perpetually darting in the skirt of one's vision, drowning themselves in the moist canals of the ears. The harbor was a giant bowl of moldering blue flame, stirred by seals trying to roll free of their fatty coats.

A fist beating on the Stearns Fiberglass entrance carried through the shop, across the yard, and to the water's edge, jarring Tom out of his quiet labor. He heard the little-used door hinges screeching, the clangor of a knocked paint can. The intruder would, of course, be Bradford, who'd find the shop interior dusky and spread with evidence of Tom's comings and goings. A thousand books, in a hundred locations, precisely squared and stacked. A dozen cans of cigarette butts, all neatly lined against a wall. A ragged folding cot, crisply made, with stained pillows fluffed, and a moth-eaten blanket tucked under at the corners. The floor, an expanse of well-swept concrete, interrupted by only a spread of newsprint and the rust-eaten fittings of a two-stroke generator that lay upon it. There was a can of WD-40, and a flathead screwdriver, but there was no Tom. Bradford would be turning himself around. He'd be seeking his companion somewhere closer to the river.

"Tommy!" yelled Bradford, "Beaumont! Ya home, guy?"

Tom was squatting over some crab pots and wiped his hands on his jeans. He closed the baited pots and prepared to throw them by their ropes into the river. The six wire boxes were tethered to a post in the ground, each with about thirty-five feet of slack. Tom cranked each one through the air, helicopter-fashion, and then flung it out into the peak tide.

Bradford rounded the corner of the shop and ambled toward him, holding a sixer of PBR tallboys above his head and shaking them as though they'd jingle. "Brought drink," he yelled over the wind as he approached.

"Where'd you get those at, Neville?"

"Gettin' place. Happy Fourth."

"Cute."

Bradford pulled a couple of deck chairs to the water and eyed Tom quizzically while he threw in the last of his traps.

"Ya catch many that way?"

"Enough."

Bradford yanked two beers off their plastic rings and slid the others into the river to cool. They cracked the tabs, foam bursting out over their knuckles, and crossed their legs the way old men do, pulling them up by the knee.

Gulls fought for a time where the crab traps had gone in and bubbles still pocked the surface. A lone boat came tooling slowly out over the water, heading around Hawthorne Point and on to open sea. From where they sat on the shore, it appeared to barely move at all, and they watched in silence but for the small, far-off chug of its engine. The fishermen had taken to brewing methanol in lieu of diesel, the latter being increasingly dangerous to procure and impossible to keep secret—the smell of petroleum exhaust a dead giveaway. Wood alcohol ran clean, but gave these marine engines a choppy, coughing sound. An anonymous human figure in bright orange coveralls moved at the boat's stern. The boat's wake gradually crossed the still harbor and lapped at the shore, at which point Bradford said, "A bit late in tha day there, Hupp."

"That Old John Hupper going out this late?"

"Nah, not John. Christ, he'd a been up, out, an' back ta bed by now. That boat belongs ta his son. What's-his-name. Fuckhead. Mikey. Ya prob'ly went ta school with 'is sistah."

"Oh, yeah. Mike Hupper. Little pencil-necked bastard."

"Yuh. Jus' like you, Tom."

"Don't challenge the skinny guy." Tom lit a smoke, shaking his disposable lighter and flicking it three or four times before it caught. "He's hungry."

They drank their Pabst, Tom thinking about the Huppers and other fishermen, that enclave of society he was never allowed to enter. No love for the awkward French-Canadian and his college vocabulary. Still, Tom admired them. Plugging away, feeding their families, keeping a candle flame of trade lit.

Truth be told, Bradford hadn't worked lobstering either, not even as a sternman, and would never have talked shit about members of the fishery in their presence. He enjoyed having a buddy he could do that with: stomp his sour grapes. Seeing Mike Hupper hitting the water late during softshell season was a great opportunity for this.

Bradford's family went back a ways in the area, enough so to have claimed some fishing grounds and made a good living at it, but his father had never been very well put-together and had squandered this birthright. Reputation heavier than gold, here. Collin Bradford had been a regular at the Harpoon Tavern and the Fox County Courthouse alike. Never got out of bed early enough to keep any traps. Worked for many years alternately driving a garbage truck and making a poor name for his family. Bradford had never completely forgiven the old man and likely just used his father's memory to scapegoat his own shortcomings.

"Mikey probably doesn't see much use in it anymore, fishing. He's one of them," said Tom.

"One a who?"

"Fletcherites. Sheep. Grazers."

"I'll hand it to ya, Tom. Yer cocky for a little bitch."

"What did you want to be, Bradford?" Tom asked, not losing the beat, just sipping at the warm, flavorless beer and widening his eyes to fit the sky. The sun had retreated further westward above their heads and the harbor danced like a mirage.

"Whassat mean, Tommy?"

"I don't know. When you were younger, maybe. I mean,

before the rock. Let's just say it never happens: wasn't there something you always dreamed about doing?"

"Ah, Christ... Really?" Bradford shuffled uncomfortably in his seat and squeezed the last third of his PBR down his throat. He threw the crushed can out to the weeds, where it rattled over several dozen of its predecessors. "Tha fuck did *you* wanna be, Beaumont?"

Tom thought of the grad students in his workshop, gathered at a broad table, each tombstoned with a spiral-bound composition book—solemn as toddlers building a block tower. It hardly mattered that they aspired to write novels and not practice medicine or design airplanes; any ambition was, from a certain perspective, meaningless. The decision to become something seemed to require faith, or just ignorance. "I used to think I was a writer."

A sputter and hiss from the ship-to-shore saved him having to continue.

"I'll check 'er," said Bradford, reluctantly stalking off to answer the radio.

Tom had spent his years at Stearns Fiberglass learning how to keep his hands moving, which brought a kind of peace. He'd once thought that writing was the profession for someone so full of frustrated energy, but then tried to harness it and found nothing but a roaring hollow.

Bradford returned from the shop, moving with uncharacteristic haste. He dropped a pistol at Tom's feet. "Put that in ya belt," he said, running off in a different direction.

"Wait, Nev? Why?"

Tom stood and did as he'd been told, then plucked his deck shoes from where they lay on the bare earth and pulled them on. Bradford quickly returned, having procured two bolt-action hunting rifles from where he'd hid them in the woodshed.

"What the fuck, man?"

"I ain't sure, Tom. Road gang, I s'pose. Andy an' Dex jus' called from Crick Hill."

"You're kidding."

"Hope so."

They climbed the hill without talking, pockets full with the glassy tinkling of loose shells. Bradford kept his rifle in an over-the-shoulder hunter's rest, while Tom trailed a few yards back, gun held away from his body like a live animal. Tom struggled to breathe around his swollen tongue, his constricted throat. His body went mulish, like it knew what it was he marched toward.

Pops and crackles from a half-mile distance. Smoke rising in snake coils of black, first here, then here, and here. Soon what had been far off and small was sky-big and ringing in his skull, and the air was tight with explosions, shouts. He and Bradford were a tiny militia, minutemen, as if the history of this town were an enormous slowly rotating sphere and they'd come again to that peculiar island in time where guerilla fighters slew one another in narrow New English streets. Tom saw Bradford stopping, saw him leveling his rifle. Nothing but deliberate movement. No hesitation.

CRACK!

Tom's guts went queasy with what seemed like too many

revelations to absorb at once. He'd never seen anyone killed before. The man's body slapped dumbly against the door of the home he'd been forcibly trying to enter, and his weapon clattered on the wooden porch. Tom hefted his rifle. It felt cold, heavy, and utterly useless in his hands.

The dead man's clothes were not unlike Tom's, and he'd also been young, been white, been a little starved and harried looking. Tom could imagine himself with that same wound in his neck, its stubble and sinew wetly interrupted, slumped against a door.

"How do you know who's who?" he begged Bradford.

"Ya recognize that motherfucker?"

"…no?"

"Me neithah." He ejected the spent shell, stuck another in the chamber.

Tom noticed Bud Andrews, in his weathered blue vest, crossing Wadsworth Street at a frantic clip. Bud turned to check behind as his two grown sons followed, and they made eye contact. "Andrews!" Tom yelled, his voice dying somewhere in the smoky street. Bud cradled a shotgun in one arm and, with the other, indicated a direction Bradford and Tom might head. He didn't bother trying to shout. Tom waved back an acknowledgement, just as a middle-aged woman in sweats tore around the corner, clutching her own arms as though straightjacketed, chased. A broad-shouldered man rounded the corner, half a beat behind her, a woolen balaclava hiding his features and a baseball bat gripped in both hands. Tom and the woman brushed shoulders as she passed, and he caught her face long enough to recall that she'd started teaching at Near Haven Elementary a few years before. A pretty, unwed brunette named—fuck, what was her name? Bradford dispatched her pursuer with a sudden shot through the guts, another in the back. Tom shut his eyes to quell a wave of dizziness. He opened them, searched for Bud and his boys again, but they'd already run ahead.

They approached Main Street amid a campaign of looting and window smashing. A frenzied grab at anything of worth. Pickup trucks and flatbeds were heaped over with goods from towns further south along U.S. Route One. More than looting, though. Tom's ears were overwhelmed with the sounds of black-powder explosives blowing doors apart, rifle fire crackling, lead hitting flesh, the shrieks and silences of ambush and murder. They crisscrossed the area like a swarm of ants. Their vehicles lined Main Street in an idling convoy, the exhaust of mongrel fuels rising and coalescing where balloon strings should've twined and the sky should've been blue.

Maybe in Jersey City, in Hartford, it had been different. Maybe these same guys had tired of hunger and austerity and started pushing their neighbors around, traded jewelry or motorcycles for guns, made some brazen threats, gotten a crew together. Maybe they'd said things like, "We're taking the lot of it, your dried goods, your valuables, your livelihood, but we'll let you *live*." It had grown rough on the I-95, working their way through the overpopulated bedroom communities and strip-mall districts of the sprawl. They'd run into others with similar intent, others who'd jumped ship on their families to push out where the land was a little fattier. Maybe, when it started, it was about staying alive. Holding momentum. Maybe. But at some point they'd found themselves in this happily ignorant province where the trees outnumbered the yokels, and Fletcher's doomsday was just behind the sunrise, and any consideration for the lives of the pallid, stubborn few had gone.

The narrow intersections were shakily held by armed men and boys of Near Haven, but the fight had no real front and the corners were difficult to defend. Tom stood there feckless while Northy Ames, the harbormaster's deputy, got shot down running west on Green Street, and a moment later, Rory Chamberlain returned fire, heading east from Main. Lindy Bly knelt by her dying cousin Northy long enough to eject the spent shells from his gun and begin venomously blasting rounds into the choked street herself. Her eyes scanned the area where Tom stood, but he avoided them. Some species of organ was creeping bulbous and purple from under Northy Ames' jacket hem. In the film version, Tom would look on Northy all stoic and think, "He was a good man," but a spinning bullet sung past Tom's ear like a terminal hummingbird and his legs went bandy.

"C'mon, you gangly fuckah," said Bradford, grabbing Tom's shoulder and throwing him into a run. "No standin' still in the open…"

At the southern terminus of Near Haven's Main Street, they found a temporary shelter of abandoned cars, very near the Maine State Prison which stood empty and slowly crumbling, an edifice that could barely have held every murderer now loose in the rural streets. Bradford and Tom crouched with their backs against a boxy white import sedan as projectiles whizzed overhead. A nearby windshield exploded in a shower of imitation jewels.

"You bettah start shootin'," Bradford directed in a deadpan shout. Tom looked down at the rifle he'd apparently been holding all the while. If it weren't for Bradford, he'd likely have met the cold eternal back on Green Street with Northy. "Breathe even," said Bradford. "Fire on the exhale." This was just basic hunting advice; Tom knew it well enough already. But he was open to instruction, as his own inclinations weren't exactly tending toward the heroic. Tom turned and put his gun up over a rusting front fender, wishing his eyes were on stalks instead of buried in the center of his head.

Fighting waves of bone-level terror, he shot. The street was thick with moving targets. Bradford, thankfully, picked away at these like so many crows on a wire. Tom's first several attempts were swallowed into the chaos, their trajectories warped by his nervous anticipation of the blast. With active war ripping over and past him, Tom tried to make the rifle's scope his world. He exhaled, he pulled, the gun bucked, and a red rose blossomed in his scope.

A shout came from the far side of Main Street, and this one clearly pronouncing his name, otherwise he'd not have noticed Darwin Bly. The guy Tom knew as a goofy drunk and a floundering charter boat captain was crouched behind a vehicle there, much as Tom was, but his eyes were sober and hawkish. This is a husband and a man my age, Tom thought, and his time is limited and he cares what he does with it. Dar shouted

"Tom!" again, and made a cautious wave of the hand. Tom returned the wave and elbowed Bradford, who momentarily glanced, nodded, and shucked a spent shell.

Tom loosed another round into the fray, heard the resultant shriek, and ducked back within his shelter. Dar was trying to communicate something with a hand gesture, bunching his fist and working his thumb over it repeatedly. Tom realized he was asking for a lighter, as if none of this were happening, and they were just two guys hunkered in the green glow of a pub entrance. He shrugged back in annoyance, but Dar raised an index finger at him: *Wait.* In another moment, Darwin had produced a plastic fuel canister and shaken it to show that it was mostly full. Tom dug through the ammunition in his jeans pocket and located his disposable cigarette lighter. This he waved in evidence.

What happened next was communicated silently, which negated any opportunity for quibbling or rehashing of plans. Dar pointed at the long row of idling vehicles that dominated the street—mostly expensive pickups and Jeeps with obsolete license plates from Rhode Island, New Jersey, New Hampshire. "Live Free Or Die." *Okay*, Tom nodded. When he was sure that Tom understood, Dar elucidated the rest of his idea with clear hands:

I: Run along that line of vehicles

I: Pour gas, starting THERE

YOU and BRADFORD: Cover me

YOU: Ignite gas HERE

...BOOM...BOOM...BOOM

Tom related the plan verbally to Bradford while Dar Bly

waited. Bradford gave the man a quick, incredulous look, but then shrugged as if to say *Alright, hero.* There was no count of three, just Darwin ducking out into the street with his gas can and no other weapon. He stuck close to the tires and ran straight, despite the latticework of caroming bullets, dispensing a shimmering slick behind him that flowed unbroken for nearly a block. Tom trained his gun on one and then another man, carefully, while beside him Bradford's rifle pounded a steady rhythm, as if drawing and thrusting the bolt were just bothersome encumbrances to his ability for shooting.

Darwin Bly was killed near the intersection of Main Street and Beechwood. His head came up, maybe to see if Tom had followed, looking in that direction, but suddenly jerked sideways as part of his jaw was removed by one bullet. The second bullet dropped him to the ground, where a puddle of gasoline then widened, waiting for Tom to act. Tom looked out over the five yards of open ground that separated him from its wick.

Flashes. Little bright flashes, he thought. We're lightning bugs in a jar.

Tom's first and second tries went nowhere. He couldn't convince himself to move. He white-knuckled the lighter, saw the gasoline pooled at the back end of a GMC, its edges beginning to soak into the pitted surface of the street. He knew how little this would take, but his legs were as heavy as sandbags.

"Oh, for fuck's sake, Beaumont…"

Bradford's eyes narrowed as Tom set his rifle on the ground. He was apprehensive about the plan. Still, he grabbed Tom's shoulder, pulling him close enough to shout into one ear:

"Jus' be quick. I'll keep an eye on ya."

I could slink like a housecat, thought Tom, or walk out and have done with this. As he stood he felt the hilt of the 9mm against his back, stuck tight under his belt, and this gave a bit of confidence. Three or four quick strides and a half skip got him in position behind the monstrous truck, its gritty tires glistening providentially with splashes of fuel. He felt a superstitious hint of warmth rising from the spot where Dar had passed only seconds before. Bullets flew, many of them Bradford's, but a dreamy singularity of person and purpose enveloped him, closing him off from the sounds of gunfire and screaming in the outer chaos. For a quiet, boundless moment, there was only Tom, the lighter in his hand, and the river of gas.

He leaned in, held his breath, and rolled his thumb over the striker.

Nothing.

The fumes made his eyes water, and he hadn't yet taken a breath when he tried a second time.

Nothing again.

He shook the lighter hard, felt maybe a milliliter of liquid splashing around in the empty tube. He'd dealt with this problem a thousand times, but never when it really mattered. Tom thought, I just need a spark. He shook the thing some more, said a little gambler's prayer, and struck it again.

A tiny lick sprung up and caressed his thumb. Not thinking, Tom pressed his hand into the sun-warmed gasoline and touched it off. The heat-greedy pool of it was flaring up blue before his thumb left the flintwheel, and soaking into his cotton sleeve. He dropped the lighter, and its plastic cylinder exploded with a quick, vicious pop. Tom staggered backward on his heels and realized that he was on fire.

"Tommy!" yelled Bradford from somewhere in the periphery, and Tom knew he had to get back there, to get away from the truck before the mounting flames reached its gas tank, only feet away. But some idiotic reflex kept him planted in the spot until he could beat out the evil tongue of fire consuming his arm. He slapped his hand against the fabric of a pant leg, but in the end had to hug the blackening limb close to his core and choke it out like a wrestler. He saw Bradford hammering rounds into the air and only then understood that he must run.

The first of the GMC's rear tires ruptured with a blast of rubber flatulence and the entire vehicle slumped back in Tom's direction and he moved. Such a short distance: two body lengths and a couple of extra feet. Just a few hops, but he wasn't quite allowed to complete them. Tom was so close to safety that he could see a calm sweeping Bradford's face, could see his gun stock lying where he'd left it. Two paces away. One pace away.

Suddenly, Tom collapsed. Heat and pain flared above his right knee, and then his face was inundated with gravel and road dust, and he heard his throat emitting a queer mammalian squeak, and then Bradford's fist was clutching his shirt collar, dragging him to the curb.

"We gotta go, Tom."

"My leg…"

"Yup. Ya been shot."

Tom fumbled with an already torn pant leg, managing, with seared fingers, to rip a piece of the fabric away and expose his knee. He sat in a cellar bulkhead where Bradford had dropped him like a duffel bag and gone ahead unencumbered. The cold cellar air, still rank with the memory of upwelling sewage, bit into Tom's raw flesh, and probing in the dark for his wounds proved too much to stomach. Explosions shook the house under which he hid, beginning with that massive GMC, and a shower of metallic debris pinged against its clapboard siding. Two more vehicles blew almost simultaneously, then another, and another. He abandoned any attempt to tourniquet the leg and just sank back into the dark and the hypnotic throb of pain. Some time passed, probably only minutes, and then the hatch flew open, the sunlight rushed in, and there stood Bradford.

"A'right, let's go."

"Ghhh…" said Tom.

It was much quieter in that outer world now than when he'd been stuck down in the cellar. He tried to do better than guttural noise.

"How'd we do?"

"Guess they wasn't in the mood. Jus' beat hell outa here in whatevah still had wheels." Clots of whirling, black opacity stalked the air around Bradford's shoulders. "Come on, bud."

They picked out a three-legged path back toward the harbor, the blood on Tom's leg, slow as cooling sap, gradually filling his shoe. He watched Main Street as it burned, twisted metal limbs growing from a swamp of melted asphalt, washing in and out of view through the smoke. Something nagged him.

A feeling of something forgotten.

"Wait, Nev."

"What?"

They stopped two blocks from the building flames, and Tom squinted through the murk.

"Tommy, what?"

"I don't know. I don't know. Nothing."

~~303~~ 299

"*. . . is Dexter Hannah. Lookin' for Stearns Fiberglass. This is Dexter. Tom, you on this channel, son?*"

Tom opened his eyes and turned reluctantly toward the radio. He'd been lying on the cot for three days, mostly sleeping, eating only when Bradford came around to heat up a can of chowder or toast a cheese sandwich on the propane stove. Bradford had removed the gauze wrappings from his leg, but the makeshift sutures would have to remain for another week or more. Tom's lower right thigh was inflamed like a red grapefruit, and he had to carefully sponge salt water over it twice a day. There were some pills lifted from Pottle's pharmacy, a bottle of Darvocet that grew airier each time Tom shook it, and these he chewed like chalky sunflower seeds during his short waking hours.

Abel's walking stick—or "Abel's Cain," as Bradford had joked—lay beside him on the floor, and Tom reached a hand over the edge of the cot to pick it up. He swung his legs around and gingerly planted his bare feet on the cold concrete.

"*Aaeooow,*" said Buck, hungrily.

"Catch something," Tom told him. "Be a cat."

"There Tom? Hannah's Auto…alling Stearns Fibergla…"

"Just a moment there, Dex," Tom said to the radio.

"Aeow."

"Jesus Christ."

Putting his weight on the smooth handle of the cane, Tom pulled himself up from the cot and took his first steps in days. The leg was like a Christmas ham wired for lights. He couldn't seem to move forward without banging the cane against it, pain flashing white against his vision. Finally, Tom eased down onto a barrel and picked up the handset.

"Mr. Hannah? I'm here. Go ahead."

"Christ, Tommy, where've you been? I seen Neville about, but I ain't gotten to ask if you was okay. Good to hear from ya, son."

"Been laid up at the shop, but I'm okay. How are things looking?"

"Things are lookin' right shitty, to be honest with ya. Tryin' ta round up some boys for a cleanup today."

"Not sure I'll be much help," Tom said, searching for something to follow it. He glanced out the window and saw the river sparkling, a few ownerless sloops being rigged and unmoored by resourceful survivors. "Has anyone heard from my folks?" he asked.

"Not that I'm aware of, Tom." Several seconds passed. *"Be happy to bring ya out there, if ya wanted to look in on 'em."*

"If it's not a bother," Tom said before he could change his mind.

"See ya in two–three. Out." The channel went to static for a

moment, followed by a loud click, and then silence.

When he hobbled out into the noon sun, everything was still and quiet. No wind. Even the birds seemed reticent. He took a survey of the yard. The shore, where his crab pots were still tethered and waiting. The latrine, its door hanging open. The chicken coop.

"No," Tom said to the chicken coop.

The four remaining chickens cocked their heads abeam when he spoke.

There was no stretch in the wire, no burrow dug under its frame. Just a couple brown eggshells split open, their contents licked clean. A rusty tattoo of blood in the sandy floor of the coop, and some drag marks in the dirt outside. Tom limped around the enclosure and found more blood and a few feathers and eventually put his finger in a viscous lump that was stuck to the wire. In the gore and pine tar, there were several short, wiry brown hairs, and he lifted them to his nose, winced at the smell, and said, "Fisher…"

The diesel rumble of Dexter Hannah's tow truck grew in the quiet and soon it was rounding the turn onto Water Street and slowing to a stop. The truck sat there for a few ticks before Tom tried waving, tried waving his stick, tried shouting. The rust-pitted hulk of it, trembling under its own power, waited idle at the top of the hill.

"No time for chivalry, Dex," Tom said.

He shuffled up the gravel drive, backsliding and stabbing the cane, cursing with every belabored step.

"Sorry 'bout all the shit on the floor," said Dexter when Tom opened the passenger door of the high cab. Paper coffee cups and empty beer cans clattered down to the street as Tom tossed his cane in, hauled himself onto the running board, and vaulted his body into the seat. "Ah, Christ, son. I shoulda come down there to meet ya. What done it?"

"Bradford says two-twenty-three Remington, but who the fuck knows. Whatever it was went straight through." Tom shut the heavy door with a yank of the handle and then turned to shake Dexter's hand. It was then he noticed the large, stained bandage fastened against the man's ear. "Are you okay?"

Dexter Hannah said nothing, just softly hummed to himself as he put the truck in gear.

Slowly, they wound their way along Fox Street, Dexter piloting the tow truck like a patient elephant driver through the blackened cars and other objects littering the road surface. He put two tires over the curb to avoid a dented and broken Harley-Davidson that lay on the centerline. "Ain't that a shame," said Dexter, the old gear head.

Tom raised a hand to the few people he saw milling about their properties, each looking enervated and aimless. Some waved back, without friendship, closed-mouthed. They carried shovels and axes.

"I don't know how much you seen the other day," began Dexter, and it was obvious how gently he tried to broach whatever the subject was about to be. "Well, somebody had the bright notion to set those trucks afire, and they all just begun blowin' up, right down the line."

"Yeah, I saw that," Tom replied, shifting his weight to the left buttock.

"Well, those city boys all took off. And most left out heading east on Route One. But not all of them."

Tom waited.

"I don't know if it were just all the confusion or if they'd been plannin' it from the start, but five or six of them vehicles cut north and went inland. I seen 'em go and thought to chase after, but there was fire spreadin' quick, and I got them diesel tanks to worry over..."

Dexter wasn't being intentionally cagey, but Tom could see there was a dark center that his words all tended to orbit. Some knowledge he didn't want to own. "Cut north how?" Tom asked.

"Up Beechwood, Tommy."

The turn onto Beechwood Street from Main was completely impassable, a sculpture garden of twisted metal and charred asphalt. The air was still thick with petroleum fumes and the tang of burning vulcanized rubber. Dexter grunted slightly, leaning over the wheel and examining the scene. "Eee, Christ," he mumbled. "Guess I shoulda figured on this. The boys was supposed to get rid of all this shit this mornin'." He jockeyed the gearshift, parking the truck where it sat straddling the centerline, and shut off the engine. "Gotta scout a way through."

A dozen men milled around the intersection, circling the

demolished trucks, pointing and talking, crouching low to assess the sunken chassis like triage medics. Some of them Tom recognized, but had never really met. He got the impression that each of them would be sitting in a dark corner, nursing a whiskey, if someone hadn't bound them together and kept them on their feet. Dexter moved off to talk with them, leaving Tom free to hobble about and do his own assessing.

He crept through the rubble, taking it in, vaguely aware of his own culpability in this mess. Peering through window frames without glass, Tom saw hands, boots, ribs—just pieces of those who'd been incinerated. The smell was thick as tobacco smoke and smoking was his best shot at breathable air. Tom lit up and pondered the remains of a man who'd died breathing smoke as well, his bones frozen in place where he'd been clawing at a narrow crack in a door. There were truck chassis upended by gas-canister explosions, free-spinning tires reduced to just radial coils creaking slightly in the wind. Steel passenger cabins blown open in odd directions when the flames had discovered mortars and hand grenades and other small armaments hidden inside. Tom spent some time examining a windshield, the safety glass fragmented a million times, the omnipresent black soot staining its exterior and a clump of hair caught in the upper-right corner of its frame. He wondered how that hair wasn't burnt away.

A spot of color caught his attention, a bright cartoon-pink something wedged between two bumpers. It was furry, and a browned wad of cotton batting poked out from one of its torn seams. With a little work he pried the thing loose. A rabbit. Plush, flop-eared, a little larger than his palm. A kid's toy. Tom thought of the cigarette lighter exploding in his hand, of shrapnel lodging in shingles and flesh as he hid in a basement. His heart momentarily lost its rhythm. I've murdered a child—the thought forced its way in and flooded his mind with grisly iterations of how and where. Piercing, burning, crushing—I've murdered a child.

Tom stuffed the rabbit into a back pocket and spun around, but nobody was there. It was only his own superstition, his guilt, eyeing him from some hiding spot in the wreckage. He couldn't shake it. Every hair on Tom's scalp stood electrified, and he picked Abel's cane out of the muck and made himself move.

The bodies of some thirty-five or forty men had been pulled from the vehicles and laid out on the sidewalk, in case anyone might be identified and claimed as a local. So far, only the crows seemed interested. Later, they'd all be hucked into a mass grave, spat on, cursed over, and buried for good. Tom moved slowly down the line of them, reflecting on the faces conveying no sense of rest, fabricating little histories for each in his mind. This is Bob, and he'd been a plumber, once in Queens. This is Martin, day laborer, never got outa Manchester until a month ago. Dave learned how to fire a weapon when he shot his own neighbors…

All the faces smeared black with creosote. All the faces agonized with the death they hadn't expected, these aggressors who'd been consumed in Dar's fire. Tom's fire. Whatever. The pot-bellied, the flat-footed, the heavy jowled. Lying in a row like fish at the market. Tom couldn't make sense of it, couldn't figure what had moved these people to leave their homes and set out on the road, hell-bound, heedless, in a roar of stolen vehicles. To arrive here, of all places, when everyone here was so desperate to get somewhere else.

Tom checked the street, saw no one looking his way, and reached down to pluck the wallet from a singed jeans pocket. This one corpse had piqued his interest, glaringly different from the rest. The thick neck—*roughneck* was his initial thought—the close-cropped hair, the overall look of health and worked-on musculature. Tom opened the wallet. Inside were a military ID for one Adam P. Murphy, USMC—interesting that this wanton criminal had been a Second Lieutenant, a ranking officer—an NRA membership card, and a shocking amount of cash. It had been months since Tom had found any use for currency. This guy was either deluded, Tom thought, or he knew something I don't. A Connecticut driver's license. A photograph of a young blonde woman. A photograph of a young blonde girl, probably six years old, same freckles and cheekbones as the woman. An old scratch ticket, worth a dollar, from the Rhode Island Lottery. And lastly, tucked behind the ID cards and such, a calling card with nothing printed on it but a phone number, a four-digit extension code, and a date. The glossy off-white cardstock betrayed nothing of its origin, but the date gave Tom a shock. He read it three times, not trusting his eyes: *5/2/1988*. One day *after* Fletcher's date.

Voices. Tom dropped the wallet beside the Marine's body, but pocketed the calling card and pushed himself into a standing position, wincing. An old instinct told him to grab the cash as well, but he ignored it. Dexter shambled up and said, "Them poor bastards never knew what hit 'em. Good riddance, I say."

"Agreed," said Tom, still looking down on the Marine, perplexed.

"Cousin a yours?"

It took a moment for Tom to register the joke. He broke out a self-conscious smile and said, "Clean-cut for a shomee, right?"

"Takes all kinds," said Dexter.

A man approached them, the weight of unwanted authority troubling his face. Cleanup crew leader. He wore a stained grey hooded sweatshirt and an old baseball cap with the Boston "B." Maybe just ten years Tom's senior, but enough to seem weathered. He spoke low through a heavily stubbled mouth.

"Hey, Dex," said the man.

"Andy," said Dexter. "No good getting a truck through just yet?"

"Nah. We ain't got the horsepower to move any a this shit. 'Bout ready to call in a fuckin' ox team, ya know? But, if you guys go back down by St. James an' cut up Erin Street, you'll get through."

"Thanks. Andy, you know Tom Beaumont?" Dexter jerked his thumb in Tom's direction, and Andy followed, squinting. He lifted an appraising eyebrow, scanning down the narrow figure bent over its walking stick.

"Nope. Hey, Tom. Say, are you Hank Beaumont's boy?"

"That's right."

"Hell of a nice guy." Andy tossed the phrase back, reflexive as *amen*. "Say, Dex, any chance we might get ya truck out here soon? Be a big help."

"Yeah. I'll come by later with some chains and whatnot. We'll clean 'er up."

"A'right, Dextah."

"Alright, Andy."

"Hey—Beaumont," Andy then said, like an afterthought, as Dexter and Tom turned to leave. "I run into Lindy Bly this mornin'."

"Okay?" said Tom.

"Said she's lookin' for Tommy Beaumont. Wants to have a word. About Dar."

"Right." Tom put a hand in his pocket and straightened over his cane. "Well, I'll be down at Stearns. As usual."

"You won't be runnin' east with the wild dogs, will ya?"

Tom tried to meet this man Andy's challenge, tried to exude something bigger than a broke-wing coward with a lot on his mind. Andy's lip curled, his eyes smiled with taunting. Violence hung in the gaps between his words. All Tom could push past his throat was, "I'll be at Stearns."

Andy nodded without breaking his gaze. "A'right, Dextah!" he said again and walked away.

The heat had grown oppressive, so they cranked down the windows as the truck crawled along quiet side streets. Tom offered Dexter one of his hand-rolled cigarettes, and Dexter accepted, and they smoked quietly, the noise of the tow truck echoing back off houses and work sheds and into their ears. Tom counted twenty-five front-room windows in a row that had been sealed up with plastic and duct tape and cardboard and framing lumber. Front doors, as well, were nailed shut, probably barricaded on the inside. He thought he'd better secure the boat shop in some way, soon.

"Andy's kind of an asshole," Dexter offered finally, as though it'd been weighing on him. "He works hard, but he's always been mean fa no reason."

"It's okay," said Tom, surprised.

"I just don't want you ta think I was…" Dexter pulled on his rollie. "Anyway, I know you're a good guy."

Tom considered what that meant.

"You happen to know what a two-o-two area code is, Mr. Hannah?"

"Yeah. That's where my son-in-law's from. Fuckin' asswipe. Why?"

"It's where that shomee came from, I think." Whenever Tom uttered the *shomee* epithet, his guts churned. He felt his skin getting hot.

"Well, that figures. District of Columbia, son."

On Erin Street, they made their way past the ancient Near Haven Cemetery. First and closest to the town were the very old, very grand plot markers and mausoleums of the founders, the Fox's and Wadsworth's and other prominent English families who'd taken a besieged and ill-fated naval outpost and whittled it into the cozy seafaring village that Tom knew today. Had known, anyway. He'd laid eyes on these monuments so many times, rubbed at their lichens and drunk beer among their windbreaks and kissed girls on their moonlit altars during that time of low poetry which was his teens. Some of the birth dates there reached back to the seventeenth century. They'd been familiar to the point of irrelevance, but now offered something deeper, maybe about the role of an individual death in the history of a larger whole. That history itself was just an endless shift from peace to cataclysm and back again.

These markers eventually gave way to an expanse of smaller stones, the more recent graves of contemporary families, many of whom Tom recognized personally. Ames, Black, Howe, Anderson. Even Bradford. The Irish and Scotch and Scandinavians who'd come later, to fill in the gaps, to tap the resources and round out the small society of the town. And lastly, among the tiniest of the headstones, a few French names either chiseled-out or chiseled-in, though Beaumont was not yet one.

Beyond these graves stood a row of sweeping willow trees, and beyond the trees lay acres of new land.

"Christ, look at 'em all..." said Dexter in a hoarse whisper. He flung the last of his smoke out the window and slowed the truck even further. The ground was broken in hundreds of spots across the unmown field, down in that hard New England clay, and piles of it peaked like anthills everywhere. An infantry of shovelers, men and women and teenagers stripped down to their undershirts in the sun, picking at the land like so many prospectors without a lead. The new graves were arranged roughly into rows, and Tom saw in the far corners that many of them had already been filled. The planted dead seemed to have germinated quickly, each oblong mound of packed dirt sprouting a tiny white cross. Just a little wooden strip to bear a name, like a label in a vegetable garden in spring. So that survivors could walk among the dirt piles and remember: Whose father was this? Whose daughter? Whose wife?

As the truck passed, many of the diggers stopped, standing waist-deep in their individual pits and leaning on their tools to watch. Sweat glistening in the creases around their eyes. No one waved.

"Tom," said Dexter as they rounded the corner, back onto Beechwood. "If you ain't ready… That is, if ya want me ta go ahead."

As a boy, Tom had once struck a chickadee with his air rifle, after hundreds of unsuccessful attempts. He was stunned to see its feathers explode in a cloud, the little body dropping from its branch like ripe fruit. Tom had poked at the tiny thing and turned it over in his child hands and cried for hours over his own great, ignorant power. He'd expected some type of cosmic retribution for years after, feeling the thing appreciate in value for each day he went unpunished.

"No, Dexter. Mr. Hannah. It's okay. I'll be okay."

The truck hummed along beneath them.

On this stretch the houses were set wide apart. Some of them handsome, with cedar shingles and little gardens. Others were just mobile homes that had been hastily parked on freshly cleared lots, garbage bags and dead automobiles serving to obscure the now rust-frozen wheels that had once delivered them. All manner of in-betweens, too, from log cabins to A-frames to prefabricated mansions with vinyl siding and PVC duck ponds.

A wide spectrum of social class, spread thinly enough to lend privacy to each family's pride or shame or indifference.

A thick forest, much of it predating white settlement, carpeted everything that wasn't paved or tended. Conifers and oaks and maples, white birch that soared fifty feet before branching, these dominated the land even at this late hour of human occupation. Between properties some of the tree trunks had been dashed over with neon spray paint, an indication that the land was purchased but as yet undeveloped. It was soothing, in a dark and quiet way, that those trees had been given a stay of execution.

"I'd always figured somethin' like this was comin'. I heard things on the radio," Dexter was saying, as Tom half-listened. A hollow sound had built in his ears, a kind of seashell tinnitus, and the sentences reached his brain disassembled. "I was makin' money hand-over-fist, there, for a few months. Repairs, fill-ups. The till was just bustin' with paper, folks being scared and wantin' their vehicles in good condition, a stockpile a gas at home. Folks blowin' outa town. Spendin' cash like no tomorrow."

Dexter laughed under his breath and then checked himself, crossed himself.

"But I knew it weren't gonna last. Here I am, bags fulla money. What good does it do me? Nobody cares about money now. It's a barter market now, right? So instead, they brung me things. Microwave ovens. Gold chains. Baseball cards and tea kettles. The hell am I s'posed ta do with them things? I ain't a thrift store. But still, I got all this goddamned fuel. I just started givin' it away..."

They came to the familiar bend, the creek and the culvert and the primrose bush.

"Mr. Hannah, slow down."

Tom could see his father, even from the road. Dexter eased the tow truck along the narrow gravel-lined drive. The grass of the yard had been recently mown, the tool shed repainted, Hank Beaumont's aluminum fishing boat rigged and ready. Everything in order. Except both of the family cars were missing. And the limey-white gravel had been kicked in all directions, deep gouges showing where tires had exposed the earth beneath.

Hank was slumped over the porch steps, arrested in the act of climbing them. Tom's breathing got fast and shallow. The truck came to a stop, and he wrenched open the door and jumped out of the cab. Tom's right foot touched the ground, and half of him went electric with pain, and he tumbled, landed on his shoulder, and ate gravel. He spat and yelled, and his cane clattered down after him, and he hollered and shook with anger.

"Tom..." he heard Dexter saying, a small noise somewhere outside his head.

It'd been a long time since his old man quit hunting, but apparently Hank Beaumont had kept the rifle. An ancient single-shot model from Sears and Roebuck that sat high away on a shelf for the past twenty-five years, evading spring cleanings and tag sales. Tom could remember, as a kid, catching glimpses of its wooden stock, a chestnut gleam behind suitcases and ski masks and gloves with no match. He'd never touched it. It had been some kind of totemic item, back then, though Hank himself never seemed to remember it was there.

The story of how Tom's father had given up hunting was a family parable, the particulars always changing but the basic moral intact. Tom had never really let it go. He could always hear it humming in the white noise of his conscience, shaping him in small accumulative ways.

One morning in winter, maybe a year after Tom's birth, Hank had driven his pickup to the general store on North Pond and purchased a box of Springfield shells, his annual doe license, a thermos of black coffee, and a ham and egg muffin that slowly spun in a glass case by the door. He spent the ten-minute drive home eating the muffin and then perfunctorily smoking half a Winston, his big orange coat and his cigarette fire the only colors brightening a county road at dawn. He pulled the truck slowly past the big house, where Tom's grandparents slept, past the mobile home, where Hank's young wife slept, and his son had likely just begun mewling in the dark, past all the standing man-made things and onto a logging trail for another mile before he killed the engine and simply sat. A few breaths worth of time in the quiet.

The family property in central Maine was wide and wooded, the preferred hunting ground for Hank and his brothers. And it was customarily with these brothers, by blood and by marriage, that Tom's father had gone hunting deer. The season which brought them together from disparate lives, away from work and wives and all the other silhouettes that waited for them on brotherhood's retreating horizon. But on this morning, for whatever reason, on this last morning, he was alone.

Hank left the pickup unlocked and his keys on the bench seat, checked that his thermos and knife and compass and watch were all where and as they should be. He slid back the bolt of the rifle, well-oiled and obeying his cold red hand. He slipped a cartridge in the chamber as he walked, his boots sucking at the mudsickles of the logging trail—an even, unhurried pace out from under the quickly blueing sky and into the dark, close trees.

He walked for hours, noting tree bark and tree limbs. Hollows in the ground and anything still bearing fruit. He detected pathways where most anyone would see only brush, and then, in a moment, he doubted himself as most anyone might. When the silence grew so complete that his pulse was audible and the woods could not possibly be less alive, Hank leaned the rifle on a stump and pulled out a Winston and held his thermos between his palms and spat. The early snow had told him nothing in these hours of tracking. Nothing, as he swallowed the last drops of coffee. Nothing, as the noontime sun carved half-dollar cavities into the snow beneath his feet.

And then, a doe. Tom's father had already relented, turned to track his own footprints back toward hot water and meals wrapped in plastic and the Patriots at Chicago. The doe skittered into his life, completely unaware, out of that panoply of vertical lines and slouching boughs. He stopped still and watched the tiny animal mirror him, suddenly frozen and achingly conscious, the both of them bristling with the shock of having overlapped worlds. His thoughts were on the one shell in the chamber of his rifle. Hank weighed the situation quickly, too many factors to dwell on any one. The doe seemed to occupy some in-between space of fortuity in that moment. She was small, and she was distant, and she knew that he was there. But the hunter was un-moneyed and recently wed. An infant son at home. A meager wage to earn tomorrow, and the next day, and the next. He took the shot.

BANG, the gun shouted, a brick through glassy silence. The doe, a hundred yards away, felt the strange fire bite into her flank before hearing it. Without thought or hesitation, as Tom's father squinted down the hot barrel, she bounded. Over the leafless blackberry tangles, over the fallen trunks of last year's thicket. Into the dark parts, the sanctum, the place where coyotes are bamboozled and men only poke around the skirt of, wondering. She jumped and kicked and danced through these obstacles, fleeing the fire, fleeing the bang.

He had to follow the doe. Having winged her, blundered the shot, he was bound to follow. The hunter's mistakes do not go unnoticed. He feels the world's breath on his neck as he watches his quarry spring, leaving a red sentence behind her in drips and splashes. Hank cursed softly, shucking out the empty shell, digging with stiff fingers for another, and running.

Spoor traces in the snow pack, frantic hoof marks, snapped branches, and fading light. For hours this was his life, dizzy with minute concentration, as the doe used her last great reserves to flee. No discernible goal, only away, away. Deeper and deeper into the twilight he found himself drawn, until he could no longer be certain that this was still the family plot, until landmarks and the sun's declination stopped informing his search and he, like the doe, followed a path of pure and hectic struggle. Hank was exhausted and hungry. He'd thought many times to curtail this insanity. But the tiny stains of her blood before him, showing black and oily in the gloam, insisted that she was close. The doe had run as far as her blood would carry her, every explosive leap a rejection of the cold earth below, and costing her another ounce. Unable to run any longer, she reluctantly hid.

There were coarse brown hairs caught in the evergreen needles and hasty scratch marks in the snow. If sunset were any nearer, he might not have seen these. The doe may have spent her last hours alone, with only her defeat and a black chill crawling toward her heart. Hank approached the tree slowly, a sort of holy torpor weighing on his limbs. He reached out to a low-hanging bough and pulled it aside, ice crystals in his palm going liquid, shedding wan light on the cavity where she was curled and panting.

Dark, wet eyes. Big, pretty eyes, in his own words. They'd haunt him, holding the root of all hard lessons in their depth and blackness. The doe did not move from the spot, did not move in any way, and returned Hank's gaze, unblinking. For several minutes they considered one another, themselves, their shared—if uneven—circumstances in this forest, far from either of their kin. Hank may have sworn, or prayed, or wondered what his own father might make of all this.

Hank fired the second shot. The second of the day, the last of his life, he'd decided. Or maybe she had decided. He'd think about that question, from time to time, as holidays brought Tom's uncles together to swap hunting anecdotes. When someone said, "Why don't you come out for once, Hank? That doe still got yer goat?" The life he'd shed, which came cloying back at him through the lips of his brothers over brandy and beers as Tom sat there, wondering what his father might say. Hoping he'd rebut those middle-aged boys for poking a long-dead fire, extinguished by larger factors than just the doe. Tom wanted to see them shamed, but Hank would only smile. He wasn't bothered. He seemed whole.

Hank placed the muzzle over her neck, probably because of those eyes. Or because he believed in the abstract that's called "sin." Or for fear that the memory of this shot would come to him whenever he spoke to his children or sat down to dinner or watched his wife sleeping or drove along a winter road. The doe, for her part, never flinched. Frightened beyond fright.

He turned his head against the sound. He squeezed until he felt the recoil, until the explosion shook him and shook the snow from the pine branches down to the ground.

The rifle lay on the wooden steps. They hadn't bothered to take it.

Hank Beaumont was shot twice through the back. Tom stood there, transfixed. He stooped and touched the body. It was neither cold nor warm, just the same temperature as the air and the ground and the cracked wooden planks beneath it. There was a third wound in Hank's shoulder, from a shot that grazed him. Three bullets.

Tom tried to piece it together, just to know. Hank had come out the side door when he heard them. The door was still open, and the storm door rested unlatched against its frame. Did he shoot first? But no, this wasn't right. Tom could see the side door lock housing had been blasted away.

Hank had walked out the side door, locking it behind him. He'd met them face-to-face, and there'd been shots fired. There were sapling-white holes torn out of the cedar shingles all around. He'd been struck in the shoulder. Outnumbered, outgunned, he had turned. Toward her. They hadn't let him go any further.

Tom picked up his father's rifle and slid back the bolt. A single cartridge fell out of the chamber, intact, unfired.

The windows and furniture were largely undamaged, but the closets were all torn apart, ransacked. Tom had to wonder if anything, in the end, had actually been taken from the house. His folks hadn't owned much. The wooden floors were filthy with a crosshatch of boot marks, maybe eight or ten individuals represented in total, and a few shell casings glinted from the corners. This is what happens to civilians, he thought. Fifty years of labor, just to love someone and share their bed, to spare a couple moments of the day for appreciation, and all of it gone in minutes. All lost to boots and guns and somebody's twisted ambitions. Five, maybe ten, minutes of shouting, terror, and brutality without words. That's all. That's what it amounts to.

The kitchen looked as though a wind had blown open every door, every cabinet, and sucked out the contents. Almost comical, the effort that went into this petty looting. In the absolute quiet, there was something that jeeringly clung to this place. Something timeless that mocked Tom's pathetic, impotent grief.

A breeze licked at Tom's neck in the same moment that Dexter walked through the door, rustling some of the debris at his feet, giving a false impression of life. Dexter stepped carefully into the kitchen and put his hand on Tom's shoulder. Tom had never thought of Dexter as being particularly familiar, never paternal or close. But he was glad for Dexter, for his living presence in the house.

"Mr. Hannah…"

"Don't say nothin', son."

Tom went to the basement while Dexter checked the upstairs rooms. The wooden stairway creaked as he worked his way down with agonizing slowness. Tom's leg went gummy under any direct pressure. He could only narrowly make out the bottom landing in the darkness. Trying an Eveready torch on a shelf to the right, Tom clicked the rubberized button and smacked the casing with his palm until the bulb flickered and then glowed, a weak but steady yellow.

Hank's woodshop was essentially as he remembered it, albeit dustier from disuse. There were cloths draped over many of the free-standing power tools, ghoulish looking in the dim light of the torch. It seemed Hank held some hope that the power would one day be switched on and he could simply lift the shrouds and continue where he'd left off. Hank had built much of the furniture in the house, and the house itself, salvaging lumber wherever he could. Gnarled grey planking from shipping pallets and burnt-down barns somehow became oak tables, maple cabinets, honey-toned and solid. Tom's father was a builder.

With his cane, Tom swept everything off the wide workbench: all the half-full glue bottles and minor hand tools and stacked drafting materials. It all fell to the floor, and he hoisted himself onto the bench and lay there for many minutes, with his arms around his knees and his eyes open to the dark.

"I want to go see her," Tom said to Dexter. Having come from the second-story bedroom, his face as pale as the bandage that obscured it, the garage owner was now standing at the foot of the stairs, intentionally blocking his way. "Let me go."

"No," Dexter whispered, shaking his head slowly. His eyes were pleading.

His mother was dead. He'd known it before they arrived, before that slow drive past the cemetery, when his last hope broke on the faces of the diggers. "Dexter," he said flatly, trying to sidle around the big man. Tom came from the opposite side, pushed with his negligible weight and was easily deflected, Dexter still shaking his head sadly and saying, "Tom, Tom, Tom…" Finally, taking the cane in both hands, he reared back and jabbed Dexter Hannah savagely in the gut.

Dexter took the blow but refused to budge. Instead, he snatched the cane out of Tom's grip and, swinging it in a wide arc, cracked the solid maple handle of the thing against Tom's good knee. Tom yelped in surprise and fury as his legs crumpled beneath him. Dexter caught him under the armpits and, while he wrenched and fought, began to drag Tom toward the door. As they moved back into the daylight and thick July air, Dexter spoke slowly and deliberately into his ear:

"Son, I understand. You wanna meet this head-on." They stumbled together over the porch steps, past his father. Tears muddied Tom's face, spit hanging in strings from his mouth as he cursed. "But it's done already." Tom writhed and kicked, but his feet still trailed through the gravel of the drive. He watched the white door of the truck swinging open, felt himself heaved upward, into the cab. "A lot a people died, Tom. You ain't one of 'em."

There came a loud groan of hinges, and the heavy passenger door slammed shut.

II.

All the world is made of faith,
and trust, and pixie dust.

—J. M. Barrie

~~299~~ 257

It was precisely the sort of object that any professional in the field might call a *planet killer*. The phrase made a suitable lay term for enlivening a sleepy tribe of molecular spectroscopy postgrads, or threading a TV news blurb with a tinsel of drama. Just hyperbole, almost playful dysphemism, to suggest the object was large—ten miles large—and fast, to the tune of sixty kilometers-per-second. It hadn't been seen before and, at the point of discovery, remained perfectly invisible. No optical telescope or human eye would ever catch the thing, not before it had gotten much, much closer. But on the comet's size and speed and existence there was a consensus, from the JPL guys doing radar analysis out in Pasadena to NASA headquarters in Washington, D.C. to all the variously affiliated observation points throughout Europe and Asia from which someone tirelessly watched or listened or otherwise probed the sky. And though the general population would come to feel quite differently, the size and speed of object *C/1986-Fletcher* had most in the cosmology set describing that summer's atmosphere as "very exciting."

Understandable, then, the confusion and dismay when Caltech put a stop to all telemetry work on *Fletcher*, citing orders "from above." You must cease tracking the object. You will turn over all data. Noncompliance is termination. If this sounded like divine dictate, then the implication was *don't ask why or who.* It happened all over the country—astronomy departments learning that the orbital work would take place elsewhere; the observations would come from other observers. The once-buzzing international discussion of *C/1986* died, as work got pulled from universities and given to privately funded research facilities—Skunk Works, Groom Lake—who weren't talking. There was clearly something unique about this comet, something that turned occult, mythic. What began as a popular, upbeat news item, a piece with unifying, global import, "our prodigal cosmic sibling, returned," became suddenly taboo. It was driven underground, and when the floodgates of media opened again in November of 1986, Daniel Fletcher himself, credited with the great, dark discovery was the first to step through and hand down Revelation.

"Eighteen months, to be succinct," said Fletcher, a nondescript man in a dark suit whose shoulders just fit the screen, whose face flashed in the memory like a sunspot and quickly faded. Grave and impersonal as a doctor—his title was "Doctor"—he exuded an authority that made his eyes and mouth and gestures immaterial. His credentials were as lofty and arcane as spangles on a General's coat. Fletcher had done pioneering work in gravitational theory at Cambridge and mathematics at Yale. He'd written two books on near-Earth objects and currently lived the seldom-imagined life of a science advisor in Washington. He spoke calmly of utter destruction, and didn't seem to mind that the god-hammer bore his name. He would speak for five minutes, but the televised address would live on for months.

Only yesterday, it had been Communism and nuclear holocaust. The cinderblock bunkers and water jugs and waterproof matches of some other cataclysm. Simple, black-and-white fear. And then communication modernized, the news cycle sped up, and candid images complicated the long-standing engagement, muddied the "us versus them" of it all. Vietnam did that: made apparent the fact that Earth was a complicated place, full of actors and agents. A world of spectra, of colors. The twenty-first century was shaping up to be a gradient world, with a lot of uncomfortable nitty-gritty you'd never find in a Superman comic. After Gorbachev's *perestroika*, it became clear that Soviet power was crumbling faster than the graffitied concrete that lobotomized Berlin.

The trade was effected quickly, seamlessly. All broadcast news would now be apropos of Fletcher. President Ronald Reagan—an aged Hollywood B-lister by trade—at once solemn and sparkle-eyed in his way, but his was not war talk or peace talk any longer: "Making our every effort… Our thoughts turn to God…" The television was awash with *cometalia*. "Expert" interviews. Oversimple animations in bright, childish colors. Telemetry and orbital periods. The Book of Revelations. The Mayan Prophecies. New Agers and the fate of the dinosaurs and rock bands and ancient engravings and upstart, tax-exempt faith-based organizations. An explosive, orgiastic cultural phenomenon, seemingly without irony, inaugurating itself with a celebration of its own demise. It was dumbfounding and boring at the same time. Repulsive in its familiarity. *Your world that dies perpetually. Your world that fetishizes death.* For all of their digital gadgets and concrete talk, how were these people any different from those Mayans, cowering under a solar eclipse?

Tom once asked Abel what he thought of the man, Fletcher. This was early in the affair, and Abel wasn't one to dwell on televised dramas.

"All the world's a stage, Thomas," Abel answered.

"And all the men and women merely players," Tom quoted back. "So what?"

"Not all. What we forget—what we're meant to forget—is that every play also has a playwright."

All clients stopped payment on their Stearns Fiberglass contracts. "Who needs a boat?" they said. Tom doubted whether half of them were even still kicking, the yuppies. They should have stayed, finished their boats, and lived out at sea while the world set itself on fire. The other shop masters left the harbor, just left everything, buildings and machines and all. Left to go check off their "bucket lists" or whatever. Tom was glad that Abel didn't live to see it. A man like Abel couldn't be put level with that sort of defeatism.

C/1986-Fletcher darkened headlines through the spring of '87, until circumstances pulled the entire publishing industry to the ground. But for Tom, and the other laymen of the country whose lives were crushed under its gravity, it was simply "Fletcher's rock."

The rain cut in horizontally, an atomized spray needling his eyeballs between the ballcap brim and slicker. He dragged the handtruck another few yards, into a windbreak between dumpsters where the asphalt looked half dry. Tom fixed the bungees holding a tarp over his goods, pulled his hood back, and squatted carefully against a redbrick wall. He lit a cigarette and rubbed the knuckles of his right hand against the palm of his left. Switched. Repeated. Exhaled and watched the wind ripping smoke from his lips, casting it out in ribbons against the passing microburst.

Three cans condensed tomato soup, he thought. Five pounds dry paper. Stove matches. Two blocks of paraffin wax. Fishing line, one spool. Glove liners. Four panes Plexiglas. Five pounds potatoes. One small block and tackle—wait, what is that?

The sign was nailed to a dead utility pole on the corner of Wadsworth and Main, cardboard and hand-lettered in paint, fifty yards from where Tom was crouched. He could only make out the first two words, but it was enough to get his attention. "Town Meeting." The cardboard buckled and flapped in the wind. Tom crept to the intersection and checked both ends of the flooded street. No one was about; a few crows danced hopefully around a sealed garbage can. He saw another sign painted directly on a fractured shop window. A third was fixed to a molting birch trunk in the Main Street Commons, rooked with bird-shat war monuments, a hundred yards east. Tom pulled the yellow rubber hood over his cap and tugged the dolly behind him.

The signs were of various shapes and sizes, but all were lettered in the same hand, with the same brick-hued house paint, from the edge of the same flay-bristled brush:

TOWN MEETING
St. James Church
Sat. 15th, early afternoon
Coffee + Sugar

There were at least twelve of these signs posted in the most obvious places along Main Street and Fox. Anybody who was mobile would come across one in time. Summer was bound to hold for at least another month, but this thunderstorm was a reminder of changes to come. Whoever'd called this meeting, their timing made a certain kind of sense. Gather the survivors.

The discovery hit Tom like a sunburst, melting a few layers of his glacial numbness. Maybe someone had devised a plan, something with trajectory and purpose. To do what, he didn't know, but anything would be welcome. A plan to stick feathers in their assholes and run around squawking would be more productive than sitting in darkened rooms with loaded shotguns, quietly waiting for oblivion.

There had once been strength in this community, an ambition to keep the gears turning, despite the odds. But now, there was no "Normal Day Pub," no growers bartering vegetables in the parking lots. No fishing season to offer a happy distraction, something to gather around. The events of the Fourth had not only robbed lives, but also some essential element—will, identity, maybe just naivety—from those that survived. As grass and clover worked to hide the graves, Near Haven was already beginning to pace and mumble to itself, a recent widow paralyzed by the heartbreak that would eventually kill her.

Maybe a milk delivery again, he thought, or a garbage pickup. Anything to counteract the entropy, however small. A food pantry. A mail service. His mind reached for something beyond biological necessity for the first time in six weeks.

These things could help, the little things like mail. Even the weekly inserts from the druggist, full of coupons for aspirin and snack crackers, used to remind folks that the world was still turning. That someone somewhere was running a press of some kind, and someone else was stuffing the bags, and a man or a woman had visited at some point during the day to deliver it whether you'd noticed at the time or not. The idea that this person had withstood barking dogs and maybe a thunderstorm or snow, and then went home, cooked dinner, made love to their wife, to their husband. It was something. Reminding oneself that other people are living life was one of the best self-preservatives that Tom could reckon. He promised himself that he'd bring all this up at the meeting.

The church meeting.

He turned this phrase over in his head. Tom was dimly aware that the St. James Catholic Church was, in a feeble, shadowy way, still functional. His mother's old priest, a man Tom remembered having an uneasy rapport with, even as a kid, had kept its doors open when so many other institutions sat shuttered and crumbling. A handful of ragged townspeople could be seen gathering there on Sundays, or just coming and going at odd, unscheduled times to meditate, or beg forgiveness, or weep, or whatever it was that they didn't feel as anointed doing in their more private worlds. Tom could grant, without his usual smirking sense of charity, that not all of these people were craven Rapture-awaiters. He knew that many of them were only seeking the familiar or a shared experience. It might have been the only one available to them, and he wondered if they couldn't be offered something else.

Tom tore down one of the cardboard signs, sure to check that others were nearby and it shouldn't be missed, and stuffed it under his tarp to show to Bradford.

Every now and again, the gas lamp flickered and the whole room seemed to shudder and Tom looked up, startled. The windows were now tacked over with roofing felt and sheets of Tyvek, anything that kept the light in. His cigarette burnt down to his knuckles, and he dropped it on the floor, swore aloud to no one, crushed it out with his heel, and rolled another. A tackle struck its mast, somewhere out among the occupied slips, and a negligible lip of water broke over the beach rocks. These tiny noises evaporated quickly, unable to withstand the enormity of Near Haven's silence. This was a silence not of peace but of tension, the sound of several hundred red-eyed citizens collectively holding their breath. The cacophonous silence of a million heart-stopping, paranoid thoughts.

Tom fought these nights with whatever was at hand, desperate to foreshorten the hours between sundown and sleep. When the painkillers ran out, he simply drank himself unconscious, but even this took time. He filled it with chores and talking to the cat and intermittent pull-ups from the exposed rafters. He masturbated often in a stupor and felt self-conscious about the spotty, pearloid aftermath. Scraped it off the concrete with rags, threw these in the stove. It felt like a way of dispelling dreams. As if someday the font would dry.

Tom put away the goods from his afternoon's scavenging, and wheeled the handtruck back to the rear loading dock. There he found his rucksack slumped against the shop wall, untouched since his visit to the library.

After boiling his water for the evening, he pried open a tuna can, tipping half its contents onto a plate with a handful of stale saltine crackers. "Hey, Buck," he called out, setting the remaining tuna on the floor. He took his first pull off a liter bottle of Canadian whiskey. The cat never materialized.

Tom pulled three volumes from his rucksack and placed them on the green steel cabinet that still housed all of Abel's books. There were manuals here on the construction of every conceivable seafaring vessel smaller than a hundred tons. Sloops and schooners and catamarans, all types of small craft, trawlers, lobster boats, cabin cruisers, yachts. Pages dog-eared or plain folded, notes and sheets of drafting paper stuck all through them. One ancient college-style notebook with pages hard and yellowed like mummy flesh and sketches of a dory inside. He began spreading books on the concrete floor and brought a lantern over. Tom went from one to the next and back again, flipping through schematics and comparing hull draft, keel depth, and stern construction. Silverfish woke from their nests in the bindings. He smashed them with a handy boot as they scuttled to escape the lamplight.

Tom eventually pushed the blueprints aside and glanced at the volumes he'd been given by Neary. Staring him in the face with its dull brown academic cover was *Comets: A Detailed Catalog.*

Tom flipped through, acquainting himself with the book. The first thing that struck him was its artless, pragmatic font. Tiny words mashed into the marginless pages, no room to breathe. In general, the book seemed amateurish in design and printing, as though a university, maybe, or a private print shop had produced it. It was divided into sections, each one representing a specific category of comet. Tom hadn't known, of course, that such specialization existed. The televised media, as last he'd known it, had only focused on the one comet.

Within the sections were mini-articles on each individual planetoid known to science. Most were named after their discoverers, or the dates on which they were discovered. The articles described orbital periods and visible characteristics, and any anecdotal information from history. It was a dry read, to be sure, but Tom became immersed in it nonetheless. Just the persistence and curiosity required to compile this sort of book was impressive. He checked the cover again; *Harvey W. Mint*, it said there. It occurred to him that this peculiar expert was actually out there, somewhere. Or he hoped that Mint was still alive, thinking about comets. It seemed that the world should have some questions for him.

Tom had been briskly scanning a section entitled "Long-Period Comets" when his eyes landed on a specific article. If he hadn't been so media-conditioned to notice the date, he'd have missed it entirely. But there it was:

Next predicted perihelion date for 109/P-Clarke/Isaac, May 1988.

Fletcher's date. "Perihelion," as he'd read, was the point at which a comet makes its closest pass to the sun and, therefore, the Earth. The odds against two objects sharing the same perihelion had to be literally astronomical. He pulled away from the text and glanced nervously around the room. Everything was in its place. Everything was just as it had been left. Tom was himself, the world was unchanged. An evil tingle crept over his shoulders and stuck in his throat, as though a ghost had just passed through his body. He poured himself another generous swallow of whiskey and went back to read the entire short article several times over.

Discovered independently in July, 1855, by Asher Clarke and Arthur Isaac. Rediscovered by Japanese astronomer Tsuruhiko Koto in 1985. The comet has an estimated nucleus of 26–27 km in diameter. Orbital period: 133.28 years. Likely seen and documented by the Chinese in 143 B.C. and again in A.D. 122. Next predicted perihelion date for 109/P-Clarke/Isaac: May, 1988. This object, with a perihelion distance of 0.9 astronomical units, has been called the "most potentially dangerous object in the Solar System." It is expected to be visible to the naked eye for several days in early May, 1988, but will ultimately pass.

He checked the title page and found, "First printing,

March 1986." The *Detailed Catalog* had likely been born in obscurity, an academic labor of love, but some months before Daniel Fletcher had attached his name to any comet at all. It was possible that Fletcher had published better, later data—but also possible the Fletcher Report was a plagiarism, and a lie.

Tom sharpened half a dozen pencils with a utility knife, shavings gathering in his pant cuffs. He rolled as many cigarettes and spread a draft sheet over the table. He began to draw hulls. Just hulls. Over and over and the cigarettes burnt, the pencil tips broke one after another, and he re-sharpened and rerolled and drew. His hand seemed almost autonomous, greased with booze and driven from within by some genie of ecstatic anger.

It was a genuine human noise that finally pulled him out of this trance. Tom's head shot up, spooked in the small hours, searching for the pistol. The stove fire had gone to embers, and one lantern wick was dying of thirst. Something bumped the shop wall again, someone groping under thin light for the door handle that Tom hadn't locked. The gun was somewhere. You idiot. You drunk. Do you have a death wish? They rounded the building; he could hear their boots squelching the invertebrate mud. There, on the sawhorse, under that glove. Casual as a set of keys. Pick it up.

Tom stood opposite the side entrance and put the gun in front of him. The door handle turned and the door opened and the wind brought a few rain splats down from the gutters and a figure with blowing hair and hunched shoulders showed in the frame, just darker than the night behind.

"I'll fucking kill you," Tom said.

"Tommy?"

Tom cocked his head like a lizard and checked both his shadowed wall clocks. 1:50, 2:35.

"Lindy?"

He pulled the woman inside, taking a one-eighty survey of the boatyard. He shut the door hard and locked it, dropped the 9mm on the drafting table, and only then noticed its clip lying nearby.

"The hell are you doing down here?" Tom asked her, the blood pounding in his ears. "I almost shot you. I could've shot you."

"Tom…" Lindy Bly absorbed the Stearns Fiberglass shop with a knit brow, questions accumulating behind her dark eyes. "What are ya doin' in here?" she said, finally.

Tom couldn't begin to answer, just relit the oil lamp and retreated to the drafting table. He took a shot with his back turned to her, and then sat to roll a smoke. It occurred to him to load the pistol and keep it within reach. The cartridge went in rough and bit his palm as he slapped it home. He put the gun back on the table.

"What do you want, Lindy?"

She was wandering, examining the sketches now littering the shop floor. "God, I don't know, Tom. I was lonely."

"I heard you wanted to talk about Dar."

"From who?"

Tom took a drag, hitching his bad leg up and over his good one. "Andy? I don't know. Andy somebody."

"Andy Waits? He was one a Dar's buddies from the cement plant."

"Must be how he knew my dad."

"Knew?"

Tom had another shot and set the bottle before him, but didn't offer. He watched as Lindy removed her hooded sweatshirt and dropped it on his cot. A black tank top showed her freckled shoulders, glowing like fruit in the lamplight. "Andy spoke to me after the..." He stood and pulled on his cigarette and tried to walk off the growing bother between his legs. "What did you say to him?"

"You're hurt," she said, following his movements closely.

"I'm fine."

"You can't hardly walk, Tommy..."

"I can walk," he said, standing in place. "Just can't run."

"You were with Dar when he died."

"I guess so. I saw it happen, if that's what you mean."

"And you didn't stop him. I heard you didn't stop him."

"Heard from... How was I supposed to stop him?"

"You and him had some kind a... what? A scheme or somethin'. And now he's dead."

Tom didn't explain that the scheme was Dar's. Lindy took his hands, pulling him down to the cot and fixing her eyes on his. He felt like she was inspecting something on the inside of his skull.

"Are you—do you believe, Tommy?"

"Believe." A glottal-stop laugh escaped him. A punctuation of air. "In what? God?"

"Are you a shomee, Tom?"

He made some space between them. His busted knee and buzzing head, both needing far more space. "Lin, I don't know why you woke me up at two in the morning, but don't sit here and call me names."

She sat back straight, laying her boyish nail-bitten hands symmetrically on her thighs. "Dar was workin' on some kinda plan before he died. He had the boat half-runnin' on ethylene or somethin' like that. I thought he was just trying to keep busy. Or fish. But he was loading it up with all kinds of dried food, and he was always lookin' at charts at home. He wouldn't even sleep with me some nights, just stay up with a lamp and a pencil, or listenin' to the damn radio. He wanted to take me somewhere, I don't know. He thought the army was coming. To kill us. He thought those bastards on the Fourth were *soldiers*. He said a lot of strange things. He wouldn't go to church any-more. Did he ever say anything?"

"No." Oh Christ, Darwin, why didn't you talk to me? "Not a word."

Lindy Bly clawed at her face with those red, raw fingertips, a low diaphragm noise boiling out of her. "I'm *alone*, Tommy. I'm alone in this fuck-all..." She pushed herself on top of him, something between falling and shoving, pinning Tom's bad knee. She came up to bite his neck, and he could smell the rosemary leaf she'd chewed before coming here. A mask over stale breath and inflamed gums, same as his. Breasts held tight against him, warm, drawing Tom in as guilelessly as sleep. "I don't care if he was crazy," she said into his hair. "I just don't wanna be alone when it ends." Her hands clawed into whatever they could find of him, rib and shoulder blade. They dug with the certainty of having buried something here long before.

"What if Darwin was right," it wasn't a question, really, and he let it fall from his mouth with careless inflection, "to feel the way he did."

She froze, and her fingers came away from his body, hanging suddenly in doubt.

"Lindy," he said.

She pushed herself up, off of Tom and off the cot. She took four backward steps, as though this were the prescribed amount, and then turned away. She bent to take her sweatshirt from where it had fallen on the floor.

"Lindy," he repeated. "Just because everybody believes something doesn't make it true."

She smoothed herself and didn't look at him again.

"Lindy," it was beginning to feel like a mantra, "I think you should ask yourself why you believe."

"What you *think*," she said, moving to the door, sizing up the deadbolt switch before having to actually touch it, "is like a sickness. There's peace, Tommy. It's there. But you have ta let it in." She opened the door and spoke through it, to the night air. "I lost my husband to your way of thinkin'. Lost 'im even before he died. It's contagious, your talk. And if I catch ya tryin' to spread it..."

"Lin, I never even spoke with Dar..."

"I'll expose you, Tommy. God help ya, I'll do it."

~~257~~ 256

The ground shook and his waking caught the very last of it, just the foundation of the shop settling back into position after a firm jostling. With his eyes still partially shut to the night, Tom could swear that he heard the remnants of an explosion echoing around the harbor, over the calm water that amplifies even the smallest percussion like a mile-wide timpani skin.

He turned in his cot and tried to recapture the where and when he'd woken from, but a moment later all the empty boats moored outside pitched loudly in the roll of some sudden swell, their metal parts striking, and then the bulk of the swell hit the beach and Tom heard it pound and then drag the small round stones of the land back with it.

There wasn't much night left. Tom pulled on some deck shoes and grabbed a pair of binoculars off the wall, hobbling to the end of the Stearns Fiberglass pier to see what could be seen. Small waves still kicked at the rocks around him, radiating from the explosion. Through the lenses he tracked a red glow on the downriver side of Hawthorne Point—deep, slow water—and flames licking up between trees in silhouette. Within seconds, the light disappeared, swallowed up by the river. He could have untied a skiff and rowed out to the point, navigating by memory in the dark, but once there, he'd just have a black mirrored surface and an oil lamp to gaze at his own reflection. It wouldn't be any use. Tom made his way indoors. He didn't sleep again, and soon it was dawn.

The shore was torn up, bits of driftwood scattered by the crashing swells in the night, as though there'd been a hurricane. Apart from this, the harbor gave up no evidence of the preceding event—flat and amnesic as quicksand. It was that sort of late summer morning, grey roofed with dirty cotton, but as Tom dressed and splashed water on his eyeballs, the cloud cover drew back like a curtain out to sea. A wan blue daylight replaced it, and he figured it was alright to let the chickens out to soak in the sun. He pulled up a trapdoor in the wall and stomped his feet and waved his arms and watched them file, one-two-three-four, out to the muddy coop. They wouldn't lay without sunshine. Tom wondered how many he'd lose to predation, knowing there was a fisher out there, prowling even now. Foxes, too. Bobcats and coyotes. As the countryside grew quiet and deserted, he could imagine a whole host of malevolent spirits emerging from the dark places, eager to stretch their legs under the sun.

Tom sat himself down in the dirt and spat. Nothing to be done. Having discovered a weakness, the fisher would likely take every hen, one by one, and not a goddamned thing to do about it. Suddenly, almost despite himself, he thought of Buck.

"Buck! Ahoy, Buck..." he called out in no particular direction. A few moments passed, and he expected to hear the lid shift on the kindling drum, Buck's scratchy, atonal yowl announcing his approach. No such reassurance came. Tom scanned the crab grass, the open woodshed, and Buck's sunning rock, but the cat was absent.

He threaded the heavy brass loop of a padlock through a hasp on the shop door. Tom hung it just so, stepped back to look, tapped it a quarter inch sideways, and nodded. The lock had no key, but a decoy lock was better than none. He left the gun inside on the table and the hens outside in the mud.

Tom hitch-stepped the length of the Near Haven shipyard, an even quarter mile of mud puddle parking lots, still criss-crossed with the impressions of half-ton pickups and fork loaders. Commercial boats sat dry-docked on cradles here and there. Walls of stacked sixty-pound lobster traps, frosted white with guano accretions. He passed the main buildings and scattered outbuildings of six or seven independent businesses, all of them dark and abandoned but for Stearns Fiberglass, back at the end of the row. Rainwater pattered through rivulets and low points, eroding the shipyard from under these tenants and sloughing it into the river. Tom's feet were soaked with it all by the time he'd reached the Mortenson Bait Co. with an empty bucket in one hand and a garden spade in the other.

He swung open the heavy outer doors to let in the light, propped them with some steel pipe lengths that had long been used for this purpose. The glass of an inner door had been punched out from its frame and spread glittering across the floor.

The bait house was as rank as ever, a menagerie of rot that had sat largely untouched since spring. Tom wasn't aware that anyone had been here in that time but him; the smell alone would keep most outside by two hundred yards.

"Hello?"

No one answered. Just the rats, but Tom was used to the rats. Someone at some time had simply come and gone. No worries. He crept over the springy wooden floorboards, past holding tanks that once teemed with live shad, alewives, and big-eyed squid that ink-blackened their enclosures each time the net was dipped. Now, the tanks held only carcasses and slime, tiny fish bones pricking through the few inches of stuff as it outgassed and fermented. Tom heard the claws skreeking on glass as he approached, saw the oil-black rumps and wormy bare tails fleeing his path. The rats jumped from tank rims and slapped against the floorboards, greasy with residue from their meal.

The last familiar face Tom had encountered at Mortenson, actually, was Buck's. The cunning little opportunist ate here twice daily, for all Tom knew, lazily ambushing this overfed stock of vermin.

Past the lobster-bait coolers—solemn vats of guts and chum—Tom came to the ladder, briefly cursing its ladderness. He hooked his bucket handle in the crook of an arm and began a slow, painful climb to the bait-house loft, his right leg dangling and the air growing thicker on his tongue as he ascended.

Of the feed bags he'd found in June, only four remained, and these fifty-pounders were punctured all over by rodent teeth. It wasn't chicken feed—actually, a cornmeal-and-cannery-byproduct mix that Mortenson's guys fed to the live bait—but Tom's chickens didn't seem to mind. When these bags were gone, the hens would be left to their own foraging, and he didn't think they'd fare long after that. Tom moved to the emptiest sack and beat it several times with his spade, hoping to scare off anything that dined within. He scooped away the rancid brown meal from the mouth of the bag and then began filling his bucket.

Snap.

The tiniest noise, but so clearly un-rat-like that he dropped the spade and crawled to the edge of the loft. Sunlight cut across the first story in a broad trapezoidal frame, but the rats and the felines, and whatever else was down there, moved in the dark corners, out of view. There was only a brief gleam as its oily fur caught the light, a sudden spot of gold like the flash of a dust mote, and the creature bolted out through the loading dock exit.

"Hey!" he shouted. Tom dropped the half-filled bucket to the floor beneath and threw himself too fast down the ladder. The floor rushed toward him and sent a crackling jolt of fire up his leg. "Fuck…"

Tom snatched up his spilled bucket and cantered lamely to the open doorway.

The fisher was already a quarter mile down the row, making good time, humping otterlike over the rutted muddy lot. Tom watched it go, amazed, and was left once more with only a few hairs and its little hard-dug claw marks on the ground before him.

"These fuckahs was on my bait like crazy." Bradford stood

in the open doorway of the shop, grinning and cursing with self-satisfaction. He dropped a cotton sack of dead perch on the floor, and it made a sound like thirty pounds of wet laundry. "Stink on turd, Tommy." He'd made a morning run to Seven Tree Pond, an hour's ride on a borrowed Polaris fourwheeler. He'd left before sunrise, fished for a few hours, and come back with this haul. "You ever been fishin' up ta Seven Tree?"

"Yeah," Tom answered distractedly, "Dad used to take me there."

"You evah catch much?"

"Not that I can remember." Seven Tree Pond had notoriously been overfished, but Tom and his father had usually caught enough to bring home for dinner—enough for his mother to make a meal of. Tom very carefully pushed these memories aside. "That lake was always fished out. We'd just troll around in circles."

"An' can you believe *this* shit?" Bradford hefted the bag of fish again and dropped it again. *Splat.*

Having not shown his striped face for several days, Buck suddenly appeared from somewhere among the machine tools to sniff at it.

"Nev, you know anything about an explosion by Hawthorne Point last night?"

Bradford made himself comfortable at Abel's desk and began unpacking the makings of a joint. "Old Jay-Cee Carver gone and scuttled 'is boat out there. Hell of a thing. Took himself out an' the vessel with 'im."

"Jay-Cee? A suicide? Where'd you hear it?"

"Pete Hastings. He leant me 'is wheeler last night."

"The fuck does Pete know?" Tom had spent four years accruing reasons to believe that Hastings, the harbormaster, didn't know shit.

"Well, he knew Jay-Cee."

"Well."

"We got talkin' down at the Harpoon. Carver's boat was unmoored as of sundown yestahday, an then I seen the fire from up the hill. Pete says he'd been gettin' into some old pills he'd found, been talkin' a lot a dark nonsense..."

"What kind of nonsense?"

"Oh, your kind, prob'ly. What else is there?" Bradford struck a match and lit up. He took a tentative hit off the joint, ran a wetted finger down the seam, under the cherry, and hit it again. "Pete hired me to do a salvage dive out there today. Hopin' you'd come along."

"Okay." Tom nodded and mulled. "What's in it for Pete?"

"Two-hundred-horse-powah Evinrude. Says he'll gimme somethin' for it."

Tom thought about dropping himself into the cold harbor, just to pull up an outboard motor for Pete Hastings. The asshole wouldn't piss on him if Tom were on fire. "Okay. So what's in it for me?"

Bradford smiled. "Pete's got a diesel generator. Three-phase, two-twenty volt. It'll run anythin' you got here. Help ya finish that contract, Tommy."

Tom stalled and lit a cigarette. "Let's take a look at those perch."

He built up a fire in the outdoor pit and brought a skillet. They passed a bottle of tepid white wine as they gutted the fish. High-humped backs of shiny black that gradated gently to the fat pale bellies. Tom put his mind to the task: knife into belly, head down to tail, slide out the guts.

He and Bradford ate and smoked, sitting by the water in folding chairs and watching the tide retreat. Tom speculated aloud on rumors of a barter ship sailing north from Portland, whether they'd have tobacco or Kentucky bourbon or flashlight batteries. Bradford morosely commented that any flashlight batteries would be drained and useless, and that every ship he saw leaving their harbor he figured to be the last.

"What do you miss the most?"

"What, ya mean jus'… stuff?" Bradford mulled it. "I dunno, prob'ly soap."

"We got soap, Nev."

"Nah, not them yellow lumps. I mean *real* soap. Smells like chemicals. Stings yer eyes."

"I miss ice cubes."

"Yuh!"

"And not just ice. I miss the whole fucking concept of refrigeration."

"This shit could use some ice," Bradford agreed, holding up the all-but-empty bottle in his hand.

"If we could make ice, we wouldn't be drinking this shit. What about air conditioning?"

"Nevah really used it, 'cept in my truck. I miss my truck."

"TV?"

"Nah."

"When was the last time you flew in an airplane?"

"I nevah been in no airplane."

"You've never flown?"

"Guess I nevah needed to. Is 'at weird?"

"I guess not. It's kind of strange we never see any airplanes, though. No helicopters. All those puddle-jumpers at Osprey Head. C-130s out of Brunswick…" Tom had been expecting military or police forces and the attendant jets, choppers, and armored cars of those organizations, but there'd been none.

"I ain't really noticed," said Bradford.

"I'd think there'd be jets."

"I'd think there'd be oceans fulla blood an' Jesus blazin' hellfire an' dead people walkin' around. But they ain't shown up eithah."

"I take your point," said Tom, but his thoughts outran Bradford's easy dismissal. For the first time in a while, he thought of Lieutenant Adam Murphy and the anonymous telephone number he'd carried. All those blackened bodies on Main Street.

Tom got up stiffly and excused himself to the shop. He returned with the cardboard sign he'd found and handed it over. Bradford took it in his mitts and held it up like a grandpa would, extending his arms and then retracting them for focus. Tom looked at him expectantly, though all he could see was the backside of that big piece of cardboard. "Well?"

"Well what?" said Bradford, as though he'd been handed a blank sheet.

"You wanna come to church with me tomorrow?"

Bradford took good aim and launched his empty wine bottle toward the shore. It struck his target rock, a granite wedge jutting chisel-faced from the lapping surf, and the glass burst into happy green shrapnel. "Sure," he said, after a time. "Tha fuck else I got to do?"

They spent the afternoon out-rigging Bradford's stolen dredging barge with new winches and tackle. Tom felt certain that there could be almost nothing left of Jay-Cee's vessel, but he didn't mention this to Bradford. With the sun at around four p.m., they were motoring slowly out of Near Haven harbor and toward the spot. "You sure it was Jay-Cee?" Tom asked, one last time.

"Or my name ain't always John," said Bradford.

There were two rebreathers and drysuits and enough oxygen for an hour, split between them. The air tanks had the words *Portsmouth Marine Supply* stenciled in a circle around their pillar valves, and Tom wondered what Bradford might have traded for them without his notice. It would be wise to inventory the boat shop soon.

Bradford being the more experienced diver, Tom let him go first and followed a few seconds later, feeling his mass sucked down into the strata where lobster and dogfish hunt. The sonic world went GLOOMP! as his ears filled. Everything here both loud and dull, somehow. An alien world of wavelengths long and deep. Tom felt the numbing, heatless pressure against his neoprene and was scarily lulled by the grip. Death by python must feel something like this, he thought. Tender.

They each carried a long winch cable, so they might secure it to any intact part of Jay-Cee's vessel and haul it up above the waves. Jay-Cee, however, seemed to have planted explosive charges all over his boat, along the spine and stern and gunwales. Nothing was left but splinters. There was nothing to salvage at all, and Tom wondered again if he should have spoken up, told Bradford that morning how the shockwave had rattled the land with finality. Maybe saved them the trip. But then, for what?

In the murk, they exchanged hand gestures for a time, suggesting to each other *check under the skeg, there... put your lamp on this...* Daylight came down to them in long blades that constantly switched and jumped as the movement of waves dictated from above. The sun barely dragged its fingertips through the organic mush of the river bottom, never usefully and never for long. It became clear that they were not here to salvage, but to simply appraise the thoroughness of a tragedy.

In his headlamp's beam, Tom watched a single clump of rockweed as it twisted slowly in the current, picked at by tiny bass fry that flashed silver and then disappeared. His limbs floated out from his body like a sleeping astronaut's, all motion slowed near to freezing, but his pulse thumped away.

It struck Tom that Daniel Fletcher might not really exist, may never have existed. Tom couldn't recall his face. The voice in his memory was ordinary, replicable, the voice of a late-night ad for Quaalude. He could have been anyone—pressed into an expensive suit and talcum-powdered and handed a script. They could all, on the television, have been actors.

Tom was underneath his own world, some Dantean correspondent, and from here, that place above became highly suspect. Filled with tabloids, card tricks, sardonic comedy… He was respiring more quickly and tried to keep his focus. Tom could see only so far across the murk, but he knew it went on and on. He was sucking air. Bradford swam close and took hold of Tom's cable, shaking the trance out of him. Bradford checked his pressure gauge and then signed before Tom's face with his thumb: time to go home.

At the surface, blast debris still clustered in the wave troughs, and a throng of gulls circled above.

~~256~~ 255

As promised, the smell of coffee permeated the cool interior of St. James. With breadline solemnity, Bradford and Tom queued up to fill their little Styrofoam chalices at the urn. Tom passed over the sugar, though it had been months, and he couldn't say if he'd ever get the straight processed white stuff again. But Bradford laved it into his cup like a perfect junkie. Tom began to laugh and Bradford elbowed him to shut up. There was no milk.

They took their seats at a comfortable distance from the pulpit. Bradford moved about the fixtures in this building in a noticeably self-conscious way, a bull that knew it was in the china shop. In Tom's eyes, the church was no different than the post-office-cum-pigeon-coop, or the two village banks, turned anachronistic jokes overnight. Bradford, though, likely hadn't once set foot in a place of worship. The artwork seemed to captivate him, the structure itself channeling all attention forward to the tabernacle, the vortex of manufactured history contained primly in a little gilded box.

Tom instinctively recognized the peaked brow and parted lips. He'd once felt the tug of divine authority, the gravity of this same man-made pile of stone, but that was during childhood. Tom now endured the church experience with boredom and mild annoyance, as though it were a patronizing advertisement or instructions on a box of toothpicks. He trusted that the wonder would soon wear off for Bradford as well.

Glancing around at the figures intermittently occupying the pews, Tom saw many heads that he recognized and a few he didn't. There was Charlie Howe, who used to run the gun shop down the street; Mark Jameson and his wife, Annie, who owned the grocery store; and an older couple by the name of Anderson, whom he'd met at Near Haven Café when he lunched there in high school. They'd always been pleasant and interested to hear about his teenage exploits. Now, Mr. Anderson looked aged beyond his considerable years as he stood in the dim church. When did they start attending church? Tom had never seen them, or many of the others present, under this roof before. Mark and Charlie looked unshaven, tired, and thin. Annie Jameson was like a caged thing with its wing-tips cut: a steady, dull anger in her eyes. Tom wondered if his mother would look just that way.

Bradford nudged him and pointed across the aisle, where John Hupper stood next to his son, Mike, who they had seen a few days before, motoring across Near Haven harbor. John gave them a short solemn wave, while Mikey just thrust his chin upward in the not-quite-friendly acknowledgment used by the young fishermen. Tom nodded back, surprised to see the Huppers had come up the peninsula for something like this. John had infrequently attended mass in the old days, to state it liberally, but he held a lot of sway in the community. Undoubtedly, he'd come with expectations.

When the last comers had filled their cups, the assembled all sat down and brought the already minimal chatter to a halt. No one wanted to ask after their long-time neighbors, Tom supposed, because they didn't want to answer questions themselves. Quiet died to silence, a side entrance opened, and in walked Father Val Gilbert, whose church this had been since Tom left it as a boy. That was fifteen years ago, and the lines of Gilbert's face were now graver, the white patches at his temples the only remaining hair on his head. Tom's throat clenched at the sight of this man, a known embezzler of collection-plate offerings and a thoroughly bigoted old-guard Catholic. Thinking of Northy Ames and Darwin Bly and a dozen other local sons he'd seen cut to pieces, it was difficult for Tom to accept that Father Gilbert still ate and breathed, and even proselytized, in this town. He didn't wear his robes, but the neat black suit and white collar of his station made Tom grind his teeth involuntarily. He's grifted us for decades, tax-free and easy, Tom thought. What could he ask for now?

Father Gilbert was followed by a younger man named Robinson, a sheriff's deputy. The cop was dressed in a buckskin coat and wool cap, a holstered pistol dangling black over his officer's slacks. Robinson shut the door behind himself and stood to the left of the altar, hands clasped before him like a bailiff. A guy who Tom remembered from school as being slow to speech and quick to hallway brawls. The glassy lack of presence in his eyes, like a shark's. When Robinson had taken his place, the priest began:

"Thank you, everyone, for coming today." He spoke in a measured, serious way. His watery eyes glistened from the pale folds of his hairless face, giving him an almost sympathetic air. "Timothy and I," he said, gesturing toward the cop, "have called this meeting in an effort to address our concerns for this community, and hopefully some of your concerns as well. I'm sure I don't need to tell you that God's plan affects everyone and that many in this world are grieving right now. But perhaps some of you have lost sight of His love and mercy and so are grieving more than the rest."

Tom braced himself, biting hard into his own cheek. This was standard rhetoric, and he'd told himself to remain open. Tom turned to Bradford to gauge his reaction, but Bradford's face was blank and he simply stared ahead.

"There's been a lot a deaths, recently," Robinson cut in, "and the majority have been suicides. You might a heard about Jeremiah Carver, just yesterday mornin'. Now, I'm not an officer of the law no more, and I ain't tryin' to enforce the law. But I think it's up to all of us to watch out for our neighbor. Try and keep 'em on the path, so to speak. Why, if I'da known about Jay-Cee and heard the kinda things he'd been sayin'..."

Tom's leg trembled, and he tried to massage the quake from it, his thoughts growing fevered. Carver said the wrong thing, to the wrong people. They shut him up with dynamite, the poor bastard.

The priest took up where the policeman left off. "I'm hoping this meeting will be a chance for dialog. Many of you are still congregants, and I don't have to explain my stance to you," he said, to a brief fluttering of hand claps. Someone said, "Amen" from the back of the nave. "But we've opened this meeting to the community at large, to also hear the concerns of those who are not yet members of the Church."

"Not yet?" Tom said reflexively.

"We need a proper fuel depot!" cried Mike Hupper, already fed up with the soft pitch. "We've had enough squirrelin' around for basic necessities."

"And a real methanol distillery!" came another determined shout from the wing.

"Alright..." said Father Gilbert, trying to mitigate.

"Yer greed'll land ya in Hell!" someone offered back, from near the pulpit.

"Aw, fuck off, Skip! Ya wouldn't know hunger if it kicked yer fat ass!"

"Don't tell me about hunger, ya godless mongrel..."

They stood on pews to harangue one another, the factions unknowingly mingled and suddenly alert, hands grabbing at shirt collars, spittle hanging in air. Tom thought he heard the metallic crunch of a pistol's magazine spring, hidden somewhere in the rising voices, chambering an anonymous bullet.

The priest waited through several more volleys before continuing. "I can appreciate the spirit that Michael and some of you others are expressing here, but I think it's clear that the time for entrepreneurship is past. We must remember that it is not this kingdom of Earth that we live for, but the Kingdom of Heaven. We knew that His Judgment was forthcoming, and thanks to His son, Daniel Fletcher, we are now privileged enough to know when."

Of course, the priest had made this connection, canonizing Fletcher and painting life on Earth as a worthless purgatory. To his right, Tom heard John Hupper cough once and anxiously shift his notable weight. The priest glanced in his direction, but at that moment a man behind Tom yelled out toward the pulpit.

"Father, all due respect, I'm more interested in feedin' myself than gettin' to Heaven right now."

"And what about heating our homes?" shouted a woman in the back. "Did you really bring us here just to fill our heads with God? What about medicine?"

Robinson seemed to be listening with one ear, his eyes on a memo pad tucked in his palm. Covertly recording.

The priest straightened, shutting his eyes and holding up a hand for pause. When it was quiet again, he said, "You must realize, and don't think that I'm not aware of these issues, but we here in our small village are living well, compared to the many. We should consider our blessings: our forests and our ocean. We must all come to understand that one day, soon, there will be nothing. Nothing but the Lord.

"That having been said," Gilbert went on. "I may be able to address your more physical concerns. I've been in radio contact with the diocese in Portland, and a plan for fuel consolidation is in place there, in Cumberland County. The bishop is happy to include us, but it will require everyone's full cooperation. I will be compiling a list today of those who wish to contribute what's in their possession, or who know where stores can be found. It is not only Christlike that we give in this way, but a matter of civic duty. The church is our refuge of civility in these final days. You can expect to see church officials arriving in the coming weeks, who will aid you in collecting the resources…"

A renewed explosion of hostility sent all congregants to their feet, and Robinson the cop felt compelled to put himself between the pews and the pulpit with his gun drawn. Those of the minority opinion—the nonbelievers or anyone fearful of being listed in the priest's catalog of gas hoarders—were lunging either toward Val Gilbert or toward the doors. No one made much headway in the throng, with furious bodies bottlenecking in the aisles and falling over seatbacks. Bradford used his size to keep the trampling and fistfights at arm's length, and through a split-second gap, Tom caught Lindy Bly's eyes on him, cool and strangely vindicated. An expression of overconfident taunting. Public opinion and the popular apocalypse be damned, this was all wrong.

"WAIT!" Tom shouted, and when the room, in fact, waited, he became instantly regretful. He looked at Bradford, who responded with a dubious frown of his own, and then at the priest. Val Gilbert's eyes narrowed with recognition and spite. He clearly didn't want to hear what Tom had to say. The priest tried to speak, but was cut off.

"I'll tell ya, Val…" John Hupper began, his voice big enough to silence the rest. The priest was well entrenched, but John commanded respect like a landform.

"You can address me as *Father*, John."

"And you can address me as *Mr. Hupper*, you fuckin' weasel." There were both gasps and whistles from the crowd, but Tom just let go a breath of relief. John was about to take this bullet for him, it seemed. Let them call John Hupper an anarchist, thought Tom.

"Now, I know what you think you're doin'," Hupper continued. "If you can light a god-fire under the ass of this town, then the people will keep comin', bringin' goods into the church, and you might be able to save your own pathetic hide. A priest's livelihood is his congregation, after all. His *flock*, as I'm sure you're arrogant enough to put it. With no government about, you've gotten too big for your britches, and now ya think you'll just fleece us for whatever we got. Take our food. Take our gas.

"What you need to see is this: the church is a function of society. Ain't no way for it to exist without that there *be* a society, Val. And here you are, tellin' us we can kiss this world goodbye, just don't forget to kiss the ring of the Holy fuckin' Roman Church on our way out the door, and please leave a tithe in the basket."

"…the Church has existed through many crises…" Father Gilbert interrupted, but he couldn't break John's stride.

"My wife died last year, Val. And it weren't due to violence or suicide. I still got bite marks in my palm from her seizures. In a coma for three days, then I watched her slip away from me. Couldn't help her. Woulda given my boats, my land, my own fuckin' life, but I couldn't help. Why? Insulin. Insulin is a function of society too, Val." John parted the crowd with a raised hand, making to leave, his son Mike following his every move. "You might tell these people that you can offer them society, Val, but I'd call you a liar," he said, with his back turned to the priest. "And you can tell them that God has a plan, that they oughta sit on their thumbs and wait for Kingdom Come. That their own lives ain't theirs to control as they see fit…" John sprung open the heavy wooden doors with a shove and the room was suddenly furious with light. "…BUT I'D SAY YOU CAN GO TO HELL."

~~257~~ 249

Somebody was beating on the corrugated metal shop door. His clocks averaged five-forty-five a.m., and daylight had not yet amounted to more than a cold blue pallor in the sky.

Tom ran barefoot to the side entrance and peeled back a layer of cardboard to squint through the glass. The yard and the drive were empty, but slumped against a telephone pole were two white buckets that glowed in the not-yellow dawn light and the decrepit frame of a bicycle to which these were affixed. He pulled the door open and stood there with his toes hanging over the wooden threshold as the banging sounded once more from the east side of the shop.

"Two-Buckets! Goddamn you!"

A moment passed, with only the sound of marsh birds trilling. This somehow made him angrier. The banging had ceased.

"Two-Buckets!"

"Thhom?"

"Yes! Jesus fucking *Christ*, get over here and stop beating on my wall!"

Another long span and then the imbecile came loping, all stained sweatpants and stubble, toward his door. He carried a plastic mesh bag in his hand, a bushel bag for shellfish, but what this one contained Tom couldn't tell. Either the bag or its bearer smelled like rot, and neither would have surprised Tom. As usual, Two-Buckets looked at anything but the person to whom he was speaking.

"Iss cold, Thom. Yup. Canna come in?"

Tom stood and blinked at him for a time, glancing down at his mud-caked running shoes. The thing about Two-Buckets and his bicycle was that he never actually rode the thing. He just walked it along, laden with his various goods like a pack animal.

Still wary of the bag he held, Tom stepped aside and showed the man in. Two-Buckets kind of leaned, or swayed, as he walked through the doorway and all but grazed his shoulders on the frame. He was actually quite a large man, Tom noticed when seeing him in the smallish doorway. Before entering the shop fully, Two-Buckets surveyed it like a buffet and then smiled, big and toothy. He sauntered into the open space. Tom shut the door and edged around his guest, barely clothed and unsure what to do with this situation. Two-Buckets just looked over the shop with his saucer eyes and caressed his protruding belly, as though the very sight of Tom's home had filled him with some rich sustenance. It seemed to Tom that he could have gone on that way for a while, ogling the rafters and roof like it were the Sistine Chapel.

Tom rolled and lit a cigarette, pulled on a sweater and pants and canvas deck shoes, and managed to calm down a bit from his scare.

"Well? Did you just stop in at six in the morning to say hello?"

"Um sorry 'bout ya chicken, Thom." He relaxed visibly, a grin slowly emerging like a meaty blossom in time-lapse. It was difficult for Tom to believe that he even remembered stealing the hen. It seemed that this visit had been solely for the purpose of the apology, until he shuffled to the drafting table, deposited the mesh bag and whatever it contained, and then made for the door. Tom stood to follow him, but Two-Buckets was outside by the time he'd caught up. Tom stood in the open doorway, baffled and amused, and called to him.

"Two-Buckets! What the hell's in that bag? Where are you going?"

"Brought choo tha chicken thief, Thom." He didn't look back. He made his way up the drive.

"What?"

"Yup. Killed tha chicken thief."

Tom had serious apprehensions about opening the bag. He sized it up as it lay there on the table, amorphous and grim. He resolved to put on his woodcutting gloves and pick it up. It must have weighed fifteen pounds. Taking it outside, Tom set it in the grass very gently and leaned over to peer inside, holding his breath. A thick, urine-heavy odor seeped out as Tom undid the drawstrings and a mass of wet brown hair was revealed.

He thought maybe it was a cat, but no, too large. Tom decided to just upend the bag, tugging at the black plastic corners, and what poured onto the ground with a disturbing lack of ceremony was a big dead fisher.

"Holy God."

Its stumpy weasel legs were pulled in close, its eyes wincing over a carnivore's death grimace. Heavy and stinking and embarrassingly *actual.* Tom knelt there by the matted, mangled form, dumbstruck. He couldn't begin to imagine how, or why, but old Two-Buckets had indeed slain the chicken thief.

It was past the noon mark when Tom next emerged into the now-hot sunlight. The water was a hard, perfect blue, and the morning's wind had fallen away completely, leaving in its wake a bank of wet, unmoving air.

The brown pelt had half dried and stuck up spiky from the carcass. It lay there with its eyes now glazed over, its lips curled away from the gums, alternating splotches of pink and black like a dog's. Tom had a four-foot gaff he'd taken from the shop, and he stuck the hook of it into the fisher's cheek, half expecting those jaws to snap quick onto the metal, then lifted the thing and took it to the shore. He carried it way out before him, like something laden with rabies or plague, as it may well have been. The botflies had already laid into it and buzzed excitedly around each open orifice.

At the water, Tom stopped and thought for a moment about weighting the body so it wouldn't wash back up, but realized this was just his neurosis, and after all, it wasn't like he'd killed someone. It was just an animal, a weasel. A thief. And he wanted nothing more to do with it, besides.

He carefully swung the gaff over his right shoulder, holding it like a fly rod, and in one long, deliberate motion, Tom cast the fisher out into the drink. It didn't quite carry as far as he'd hoped, being long and cumbersome and heavy. It splashed down about ten yards from where he stood, and having watched it flipping end-over-end and crashing ungracefully that way, Tom felt a lurch of disgust in his stomach for himself and the fisher alike. The both of them caught there by the daylight in an ugly pantomime of river life. He turned back from the water, hitch-stepped his way up the pebbled bank, and there was Buck.

Tom caught him with his bare hands, avoiding the open wound that festered where the cat's right eye should have been, and as Buck kicked at his wrists and hissed in protest, Tom sealed him inside a cardboard box. Several days had probably passed since the injury, days that Buck had likely spent holed up and waiting for death while infection set in. It had been at least two weeks since Tom had last seen him. The cat was still going wild in the box twenty minutes later, but eventually resigned himself to lying still and emitting a low and doleful moan whenever he heard Tom's footsteps approaching. For a long while, Tom sat and smoked cigarettes and looked down on the box, considering his options.

"What do you do with a broken cat?" he asked the ether.

He could take the box somewhere. North to Dublin, maybe, and set the cat free. Tom would feel guilty, but avoid having to watch the animal die. He could ferry it out to some island and strand the cat there. Just cut open the packing tape and walk away. He could load the box onto a skiff, launch it on an outgoing tide, and let fate dictate the rest. Tom briefly entertained the idea that if he threw the box directly into the harbor, only a few meters from his door, it would sink within minutes and no one involved would suffer for too long beyond that.

He considered the pistol where it still lay on the drafting table.

There was a tote bag, with a PBS logo painted on it, that Tom loaded with water and three cans of sardines. He slung this over his shoulder and picked up the box. Buck mewled and scraped, a tense fury waiting for the lid to be sprung. Tom hefted the box and walked out into the blistering sunlight with Buck scratching and hissing just an inch from his ear.

When first incorporated as a township of Massachusetts Colony, Near Haven was a sprawling piece with unclear borders—a sparsely populated island of European settlers in the heart of Penobscot Indian territory. Years of raids and sieges by the understandably off-put natives made it difficult for those wide-eyed millers and farmers to survive, even in this wildly fertile crotch of land on the St. George River, at least in the beginning. But as the colonies grew, so did the need for more hearty building materials, and entrepreneurial eyes began looking toward Near Haven and its untouched miles of stone deposits. White workers poured into the region by the shipload, bringing their rifles and horses and infrastructure along, pushing the Penobscot further from their ancestral fishing grounds and birthing the cut-granite boomtown of Limekiln. Much as Maine would soon break ties with its mother colony of

Massachusetts, so too would Limekiln cut its umbilical tether, taking the larger part of Near Haven's acreage with it. By the time of American Independence, Limekiln would secure itself as the most prosperous settlement for a hundred miles in any direction, laying the earth bare, while Near Haven would go on quietly whittling ship's masts and dreaming of the sea.

Tom checked the sun. At around seventy degrees to the horizon, he figured it must be roughly two p.m. He was approaching the Limekiln town line, the halfway point of a torturous schlep over the wide expanse of land known as the "Cement Flats" for the tons of limestone in that area. The stone ran in static underground rivers through the earth; layers of sediment, which had been simply mud once in pre-Cambrian epochs, had amassed and settled on the banks of a sea, a river, or a lake, maybe—Tom wasn't really sure. The continents weren't then what and where they were now.

He walked along the cracked asphalt of U.S. Route One, where on either side, spread haphazardly as the deposits had dictated, were enormous cavities blasted straight out of the rock. These were quarries, which men like Tom's father had been sent the task of excavating. The cement factory where Hank Beaumont spent the better part of forty year's labor sat half a mile from where Tom walked. It had, only a few years prior, been a humming campus of smoke stacks and cool, ubiquitous halogen lamps, but now sat silent, being gradually split apart as weeds digested the artifice.

Most of the quarries were abandoned long ago, before his father's time. The open wounds stood to remind that mining is a type of violence, in its way. Their edges livid with red brambles like a canker, and their white walls dropping precipitously into the ground, many, many yards. At the bottom of each was a pool of rainwater so vibrantly blue it looked manufactured. Minerals from the raw, cut stone leeched into this water and raised its acidity to a point that few algae or other plants could withstand. The only fish that lived in the quarries were shale-grey eels that thrived off of drowned insects and bird droppings. As teenagers, Tom and his small cohort would swim in the dead quarries at night, goaded by fear and sex, and sometimes feel the mucus-lined bodies of those eels sliding over their bare dangling legs.

Sweat was coursing in tiny rivulets along his neck and back, like ants marching in file down the length of him, while a constant pain in his shot leg radiated its own kind of worrisome heat. Tom hefted the box from one shoulder to the other. The cat had been silent for the past several miles but wasn't asleep. Tom could feel the curled body, tense and alert, in one corner of the box. He thought, Shit, it's probably hot as hell in there.

Tom couldn't do much for the cat at the moment. He had to keep marching until they'd crossed the treeless flats and could seek some shade on the other side, once they were actually in Limekiln. Still, Tom stopped and set the box on the roadside. With the gutting knife from his belt holster, Tom carefully bored some extra holes in the cardboard, avoiding the side against which the cat's shaking body was pressed. "I'm sorry,

Buck," he whispered as he worked the knife. "I just didn't like the options back home."

The truck rumbled and backfired before cresting the hill. Otherwise, they'd have caught Tom in the open, and God knows what kind of awkward interrogation might have followed, out there on the flats. Tom scaled the embankment without a backward glance, there being nothing here to hide him but the low-lying brush with its root balls walling the roadside ditch. His shoelaces snagged in their bare branches, and he crashed forward onto his belly and stayed down, praying he'd been quick enough. The engine noise grew, and Tom raised his head to watch them approach, a big flatbed Chevy throwing rectangular sunlight from its broad windshield, coming on at a cautious speed, baldish tires spinning dust-devil chains into the road-hot air. He held his breath as the truck closed in.

Are you slowing? Please don't slow.

Down on the graveled shoulder, Buck waited inside his box. This could be it, thought Tom. I could just walk away. Maybe someone would take him. More likely, the box would sit there perpetually, passed by like any other highway garbage. Tom felt a sudden and childish stab of sorrow at the thought of losing the cat. He watched in mute horror as the truck crept up to and past the box.

Two men rode in the battered green cab, its doors stenciled with the nautically themed crucifix-anchor emblem of the Maine Catholic Diocese. Neither appeared to notice him, but talked between themselves. Words reached Tom's ears, plucked out of context, from an open window. The wooden flatbed held a collection of mismatched canisters, cylinders, and pressure tanks—color coded for gasoline, kerosene, natural gas, propane, ethylene, acetylene, and hydrogen—all crammed up against the cab and bungee-corded or lashed together with rope, like the chambers of a junkyard pipe organ. A couple of young guys rode farmhand-style on the back of the truck. The one facing Tom rode with a boot on the rear fender and the other hanging slack in the blowing dust, leaning on a long-barreled Winchester, watching the land go by. These were the boys from Portland, come to round up their combustibles, easylike, don't want no trouble, and leave the coastal towns bankrupt and freezing. Like hell, thought Tom.

The kid with the Winchester just bumped along, a look of self-possessed boredom blanding his features, his eyes exactly level with Tom's as they passed. Tom was sure he'd been seen, and rather than duck, he froze still as a deer and held those eyes through the brambles and sun glare and distance and dust that lay between. Only the kid's brows reacted, a slight confusion at having maybe seen something, not sure enough to speak it, and soon the truck had passed, and Tom had not flinched, and the thing was forgotten, Tom supposed, as a spasm in the brain which conjures faces from the weed-choked nothing of a long sweltering road.

He lay there for a while breathing, giving the truck a good long lead. Tom eased himself down the embankment, picked up the box, and walked.

In the world post-Fletcher, Limekiln was a positive vision

of collapse. This minor city was bigger and more developed than Near Haven. It was the County Seat. The courthouse, Sheriff's Office, Department of Motor Vehicles and County Jail and all. It was the County Dump, also, immortalized by the saying, "Near Haven by the sea, Limekiln by the smell." It was the nearest supermarket. The pub crawl on a Saturday night. There were chain stores and restaurants that had names one might recognize. It was a prominent shipping port, and the "Street-Drug Capital of Maine." Limekiln boasted two lighthouses and both were lately museums, tourist traps. There were Black folks here, though admittedly few. Jews and Hispanics. There was a culture that suggested connectivity and even the inkling of a greater worldview. And yet, in a world quickly localized, Limekiln was appreciably more rundown, derelict, and frightening than outlying towns.

If Tom had been inclined to count the boarded windows, he could have spent years. It was hard to determine how many still lived here. He imagined them in basement corners with firearms clutched to their chests. You might never see them. There were lengths of razor wire encircling the oddest of things: dog houses and vintage cars and lawn tractors; above ground pools; an avocado green refrigerator standing monolithic in an unmown yard. What of that? The artifacts of burgeoning insanity. And here he was, unarmed. Tom was too hot-headed to be cautious when he'd left, but not too stupid to be nervous upon arrival.

"You the boat builder?" the driver shouted over the throaty

idling of the Chevy. They'd rounded a corner on Ocean Street, suddenly heading back wherever they'd come from, and the truck was packed tight with canisters, and the boys who'd sat leisurely on the flatbed now stood on the rear bumper holding tight to their gateposts and their guns. Tom hadn't heard in time, found nowhere to run, couldn't run if he'd tried. They bore down on him, and Tom stopped dead in the road with his box on his shoulder and the driver yelling from a high window, addressing him. "You from Near Haven?"

"I don't know who you…"

"What?"

"Who are you looking for?"

The driver rolled his eyes and worked his stick, and the gears crunched and the engine coughed out. No one moved.

"We're s'posed to pay a visit to somebody—some shop owner in Near Haven harbor, skinny guy, walks with a limp. Don't ask me why; I'm just told it's somethin' to do with methanol and a bunch of machine tools. And then we're comin' up around this bend, and I see you, and I think to myself: well, now, ain't that just the guy?" The driver said all this slowly, plainly, leaning half out the window and treating Tom like an old acquaintance. Nothin' personal. Just doin' what I'm told. Blameless as a rattlesnake.

Tom pulled a confused face, playing dumb. He looked down the road and squinted tight and pretended to think. He affected an accent that felt unconvincing: "What's the fella's name? I know some folks in Near Haven. I maybe could help ya." Tom was a bad liar, a poor judge of what was enough. "Sure do admire what the Church is doin' fer us here."

This earned him a knit brow and matching frown from the driver. "I don't know what the lady said… Tim? Was it Tim? Hey, Robbie!"

"Yeah?" answered the bored-faced kid from the rear bumper. He'd been staring at Tom since the truck was put in park, obviously wading through a nasty episode of *déjà vu.* "It was 'Tom.' Tom-somethin'-French. Hey, we can just swing by that boat shop tomorrow, Luke." The kid seemed hesitant.

"*That's* right," the driver made a big show of recalling, "a Frenchman. Real uppity, said the local broad. Talks real *urbane*, she says."

"What's 'urbane'?" Tom asked, smiling all dopey.

"Like a shomee," Luke explained, smiling right back. "Robbie, check what's in the Frenchman's box, would ya?"

"Now, hold on, bud…" Tom was thinking in tight circles, imagining what Bradford might do. Robbie hopped off the bumper and checked his Winchester rifle, pulling the lever to shunt a round into the chamber as Tom watched. The gun was a repeater, an old model. Luke lit a cigarette and pushed his whole torso out the window to watch. He didn't seem wary of Tom nor of sparking up so close to his volatile cargo.

"Put the box down, Tom," said Luke, a playful elasticity to his words. "Right in front of you. Now step back, and let Robbie see what you've got in there."

Tom did as instructed. "You fella's ever tasted she-crab soup?" he asked, suggestively nodding toward the box. The two in the truck cab stayed put, seemingly unarmed, and the second gunman on the bumper kept to his post. Only Robbie ventured out, the picture of caution, watching Tom's mouth as the put-on Maine accent devolved into something impossible and Southern and piss-taking. Tom knew the stakes. He hoped the cat did, too. "That there's some honest-to-god Creole fare."

Robbie set his gun in the road beside him and squatted over the box. He glanced up at Tom, questions swimming behind his eyes.

Tom held his arms at right angles, now really pushing the grin and curious as anyone else there. Well, go on, kid… Robbie hadn't gotten four inches of packing tape off the cardboard when the flaps blew open and Buck sprang—a shapeless, hissing, electrified burst of hair and hooks that scaled the kid's front side like he were made of carpet. The cat ran straight up him, digging a solid claw-hold in his forehead and launching itself into the air as Robbie toppled backward onto the road.

"Oh, *shit!*" Luke cried, laughing, from the cab of the truck. His arm went up in surprise and came back down without his half-burnt smoke.

Tom dove on the rifle.

"Robbie!" shouted the driver, now going for the door handle, jangled and alert.

Robbie scrambled on the pavement and managed to catch hold of Tom's ankle. The gun was in Tom's hands wrong-way-round but he drove the wooden stock into Robbie's teeth and got clear of him. The boy writhed and gurgled as his mouth filled with blood.

"Goddammit, Robbie!" Luke was hollering with one hand

on the open door while the other seemed to be fishing blindly for his own weapon. Tom turned the Winchester on the driver, watching his passenger trying to flee the truck, watching the second gun holder climbing over fuel cylinders, stretching toward something on the truck's roof that he couldn't seem to reach.

Luke realized, at the same moment Tom did, that his lit cigarette teetered there atop the cab. A wispy smoke trail curling in and around the cylinders. His face went long and pale. He said, "You son of a bitch…"

Tom put the gunstock to his shoulder and exhaled. With one eye shut, he trained the long barrel on a bright red valve handle. The tall propane tank was strapped tight to the truck cab, cigarette ember smoldering inches from its valve. He pulled and felt the rifle kick and watched motionless as the valve cap was plucked clean, zinging metallically off into space, and a six-foot jet of blue flame shot up from the mouth of the tank.

"Luke?" cried the kid in the road, wet-sounding and desperate.

Tom levered another round into the chamber and buried this one deep into the mass of tanks, needing only to rupture one or two. He heard the bullet pinging around the canisters, heard a rush of air as the reaction began. He dropped the rifle, said, "I'm sorry," to the kid who gaped at him, terror stricken, from the pavement, and fled the road as quickly as his legs would move him.

"Get in the bag. I mean it."

The cat stared at him, one-eyed, from ten yards away. Tom would take two steps forward, and Buck would prance and circle and end up six feet further off than he'd been before. When Tom pulled the duffel bag from an apartment up the street, he didn't notice the stenciled *Everlast* logo or the fist-sized tear in its seam. He threw the bag on the ground and muttered to himself. The cardboard box was just ashes on a limb-scattered stretch of pavement, now.

Tom cracked open a tin and tossed a sardine to tempt the cat, while he ate the other two himself. He sat down in the dirt and waited. Buck minced up to the offered fish, sniffed it, and walked away.

He could have shot the kid, Robbie. That would have been the right thing. Better than leaving him to bleed out, a couple of charred stumps. The kid's friends had all gone quick. But more important to let it look like a stupid accident. If anyone asked, Tom was never there.

"No, go ahead, idiot. Take your fucking time. I'll wait. Eventually, you're getting in this bag."

The animal clinic was a squat brick-and-mortar affair with, surprisingly, no razor wire or other defenses built around it. Tom had finally reached it at dusk, and as the building sat on a hillside just off Ocean Street, it looked almost operational. This couldn't possibly be the case, but the windows here shone through with the sunset, clear of dust and spider webbing, and Tom thought it was the most inviting building he'd seen since entering Limekiln. There was such an aura of life about the place that he wasn't sure he should try to enter it. Buck mewled quietly from the bag at his shoulder, having not made a sound for several hours, his head poking out the sizable hole. Tom didn't know what to make of that, either.

The building's front entrance was double-doored and built to open by push-button like an Emergency Room entrance. It looked unused, dark, and as if it might only function with electricity. Tom pushed through some overgrown cedar bushes and made his way toward the rear of the building, where a plain white door hid among piles of weather-beaten pet carriers and spent nitrous oxide tanks. The handle had no keyhole on the outside, but the bolt had been secured in the open position with duct tape, and so the door opened freely.

He pushed his head inside, casting a quick look around and testing the air. He found a dark ceramic-tiled hallway with a decidedly fresh atmosphere. Someone had been coming and going, keeping this hall clear and this hidden entrance accessible, but there was neither a sound nor any candlelight within the clinic that said they were currently at home. So, Tom thought, it'll be a quick visit. Long enough to scour the pharmaceuticals and snatch a vial of tranquilizer, a suture kit, and hopefully an oral antibiotic. He set the bag down, as the door shut behind them, Buck scuffling and groaning inside his nylon straightjacket. Tom was resolute about exploring the facility without him.

The first rooms he came upon were lined with rows of cages in which former inmates must have stayed, either enduring or awaiting treatment. They were all empty. Tom had expected some odor of urine or decay, but there was none. He pushed through a set of swinging doors with reinforced-glass windows, and was struck by this new room's distinct feeling of life. It was warm and close and a little bit damp. Tom couldn't see his own hands as they groped the air before him. His boot struck something with a sudden thump, and a dog barked somewhere very near him in the darkness, and another dog, and it was then, it seemed, that he fell.

"Wake up."

He'd heard the voice from somewhere far-off and didn't respond. A woman's voice. Tom's first thought was of his mother. He could feel himself being unresponsive, nursing his reluctance like one hiding in bed, retreating from daylight to chase a dream. But he wasn't in bed; he could feel the solid, cool tiles of the floor beneath him, under his shoulder blades. He could feel the discomfort in his bony parts against that floor, and soon he felt the pounding in his head. He tried to brush it all away. He didn't want it. She said it again:

"Wake up, asshole."

Through just-cracked eyes he saw a cold white light. Artificial light. A head of long and unkempt black hair blocked it out some, leaning over him. There were snuffling and rustling sounds in the near background. It smelled like dog. Tom said, "Uh."

"Jesus..." said the woman, and Tom heard her stand and walk away. She was muttering something. When his eyes opened a bit more, Tom saw that he was still in the animal clinic. No idea how long. He was lying in a room full of kennels, half of which were occupied by dogs, who either turned in slow circles around themselves or else gazed at him with dull, helpless-looking eyes. Patchy dogs. Homeless, scavenging, fighting dogs. Big dogs. He sat up on his elbows and winced at the pain in his head.

"Where am I?"

"Really?" Her incredulous answer came from somewhere out of sight.

"No. Sorry. I mean: what happened to me?"

She appeared under the slowly strobing tubelights, and her feet moved silently, even on the tiled floor. She seemed to look him over before speaking, and her tone had lifted a little. She said, "I guess you bumped your head, didn't you? What were you doing breaking into an animal hospital? You wanted drugs?"

"Yeah…"

Tom heard her snort, and she turned to walk away.

"No." He passed a hand over his eyes. His vision was annoyingly swimmy. "I wanted drugs for my cat. There's something wrong… He's blind."

The woman returned after some minutes, holding a steaming cup between her hands. "Let's start again, okay?" The peppermint smell wafted, calm and foggy, to his nostrils. Of all the things he'd sought and stockpiled, tea was never on the list. "Sharon," she said.

"Sharon," Tom repeated.

"Yes. Sharon Grey. I'm the veterinary technician. Or I was."

"That's my aunt's name."

"Okay."

"She's a lesbian."

"And..."

"I was just saying... I'm Tom."

"Hello, Tom."

Tom didn't say anything more for a moment. He rubbed his eyes until an odd, furry light pulsed behind the lids. She'd given him an injection of something and the pain in his head was slowly ebbing. Tom thought it might have been just distilled water. It had no color to it.

"Where's my cat?"

"I put her in a single, back in the cat room. She's got about a month left."

Tom thought about that for a moment. Didn't make sense.

"No, Sharon, Miss Grey, you've got the wrong cat. Mine's a male tabby named Buck. I left him in a duffel bag in the back entrance. And he's not dying. I brought him here to prevent that."

"Buck."

"Yeah. Why?"

Sharon Grey looked him over quietly, pursing her pale narrow lips and blowing slight ripples over the surface of her tea. Her hands, clasped around the warm ceramic mug, were long and somewhat knobby, blocking a sharp chin and a neck that seemed fashioned from cables. In her avian build, she resembled Tom, and the two watched one another with deep-set eyes, skeptical as herons, in the flat neon light of the examination room.

"The wound is superficial. I flushed it, gave her a topical antibiotic. The swelling will go away, in time."

"Her?" Tom said.

"Buck is not a male tabby; she is actually a large and healthy female barn cat. She may look like an overgrown domestic, but her bloodline is, at least partially, feral. It never seemed odd to you that your 'male tabby' had no testicles?" Sharon handed him the mug, having never sipped from it. "How long have you had this cat?"

Tom accepted the tea and gamely swallowed a few ounces of the clean, hot liquid. He felt it travel the length of him, pooling in the hollow of his gut and radiating a tangible clarity through his nerves. How long had the cat been living with him at the boat shop? He really couldn't remember. Buck had been just another entity that passed into Tom's life, relatively unnoticed until disturbing his comfort. He considered then what he had been doing for the past six months, the past year. Walking in circles. Avoiding reality. He hadn't noticed it happening, not in all that time. So many days.

"Tom?"

"Yeah, I don't know." He stood up carefully, stretched, and began to shuffle about the room, gazing into the faces of caged dogs as they studied his ambling. He had to brace himself against the doors of their kennels, and their tongues sought his fingers through the bars. Such a direct attention. It astounded him. "A year, I guess. I've barely touched him. Her. Buck just started hanging around my shop. I never meant to own a cat."

"You're about to own several. Buck's pregnant."

"Pregnant," he repeated.

"What is it that you do, Tom?"

His laugh clearly sounded odd to her, the veterinarian crimping her brow with worry, but Tom was only laughing privately. Laughing at himself. He'd gotten so attuned to decay, expecting only endings, and here, suddenly, a green sapling poked through the ash.

Tom handed back the empty mug and told her, "I'm a boat builder."

~~249~~ 239

Inspiration was not a thing he'd ever been much good at hunting. He didn't know what its tracks looked like or what terrain it favored. Maybe he was lazy, he thought, or broken. He wouldn't know how to find inspiration, though every now and again, it seemed to find him. The wind carried it to him, and he snuffed it up like pollen floating by, or else he'd walk directly into its path as it hung there like a spider web.

There was a framed black-and-white photograph of Abel, taken many years before. Dark hair and dark brows, a younger man than Tom had known, looking upright and proud with his building crew of that year. Early 1970s. Baseball tees, moustaches, shag-in-the-eyes. A gel-coat-finished hull in the background. The other guys in the photo all grinned into the lens, graduate students seeking experiences and stoners gathering clout, smiling for pride and a long-deserved day off, while Abel directed his gaze elsewhere. He seemed to be looking out to sea. Happy, but knowing also that happiness comes in the constant doing. He'd build many boats, and he'd whip a few kids into craftsmen, but it was the ocean that best represented his work.

Tom wiped the dust from the small plate of glass and rehung the photograph above his drafting table. Below it waited a dozen potential hulls.

August had passed and taken the worst of summer's humidity with it. The air was thin enough to breathe again, and his rheumatic knee didn't squeak or throb so much on these pink mornings. Tom was compelled to be out of doors. He could feel the feral tingle of freedom in his testicles. Some years seemed to have been stripped away, along with the heat.

He found a teenager's discarded—maybe orphaned—bicycle on the side of a back street in Limekiln, stuck headlong through a thorn bush as though it had been ridden into the thicket and abandoned just as it lay. He took a look around, trying to shake the guilt of appropriating the thing before he boosted it. The bike was too small for him in the frame, but the big, knobby tires were in good condition and he raised the seat and stem so his knees didn't knock the handlebars. It was, he had to admit, a damn sight better than walking. Eventually he fixed a couple of milk crates to the back, an *homage* to Two-Buckets, as makeshift panniers. He rode around gimply, collecting little items of food or hardware. The marina in Limekiln was a virtually unpicked nautical supply of cleats and tackle and hinges and rigging. Someday, he'd come back with a boat and haul away some real tremendous finds. Someday.

Though the scavenging trips were productive, Tom couldn't

lie to himself. He was pedaling all those miles, now with a pistol and now on the back roads, to pay Sharon Grey the "unplanned" visits that quickly became custom.

He'd arrive at the clinic in the late afternoon, his T-shirt hanging damp and heavy, panting, and he'd sneak the bike around back, double-checking that no one had seen him. That the clinic remained a safe place was paramount. Only after a thorough look, sensing no other presence, did Tom stash his bicycle in the overgrowth and approach the door.

Sharon Grey would meet his knocking at the rear entrance after four or five successively louder attempts. In the wait, Tom would doubt her wanting to see him, and tell himself that he shouldn't have come, knowing that Sharon was simply busy at something or other and needed to see that thing right before pulling away. He hadn't once found her idle.

He'd hear the lock crunching in its case, and she'd shunt the door just a loud-scraping crack in his direction to peer around its edge. A hang of thick, wavy hair would appear, a pale forehead, a hazel-green eye. At first, he saw only plain recognition, maybe a bit of surprise or puzzlement. The boat builder, again. But in time, the creases parenthesizing that eye grew deeper. In time, she smiled. The feeling of this, seeing it, with his heart already pounding after a twelve-mile ride, it made an addict of him.

Their relationship was simple and undiscussed for weeks. Neither pushed nor insinuated anything further: he was helping with the clinic duties, and she was accepting the help. Tom cleaned kennels and bottle-fed puppies, feeling Sharon's presence moving around the space like a live electrical source. They spoke little, and Tom wondered what sorts of traumas had come to her in the past eight months, reflecting simultaneously on his own. He realized how hardened he'd become against loss, and what lengths he might go to in avoidance of any more. He imagined that she must feel the same. And he worried what she might suspect lay in his past. The violence he ascribed, in memory, to someone else completely.

At night, Tom slept on the floor with the dog smell and darkness. Sharon kept a bed somewhere within the building, hidden. He'd wake in the mornings to cooking smells, the clang of cookware. After breakfast he'd thank her, ask if he could come again, and ride all those miles to the boat shop and the world-as-usual. He'd be back in five days. Three days. One.

"I jus' don't see it, Tommy," said Bradford as he threw a long cast. His tackle flew out high, and Tom lost it in the morning glare, looking in the wrong direction, and finally saw it splash down somewhere else, somewhere he hadn't expected. Bradford fished with the matter-of-factness of a baseball player smacking a pitch out of the air. Some admirable intersection of nonchalance and power. "What's there ta gain in fakin' it?"

Just as it was with his fishing, Bradford's phraseology left Tom looking stupid and inept—clobbering his delicate theories with ham-fisted country sensibility. And it *was* silly. It was ridiculous for a blue-collar nobody to question the institutions that had protected him, had upheld the value of his money and his right to live in peace. Tom had no credentials here, no education to speak of. He knew less of economics than he did astronomy, and yet now his thoughts endlessly conflated the two, certain that the Fletcher Report was not an observation of God's actions, but a projection of some human want.

Tom pushed an oily chunk of mackerel flesh over his own hook and cast it out as far from the pier as he could muster, still short of Bradford's. "I read a book once by a psychiatrist named Frankl. He was a survivor of the Nazi concentration camps, and he compared the mental states of survivors to those who died. He saw that the survivors generally had either careers or families or something on the outside that they intended to get back to. Even if their wives and kids had actually been killed in another camp, they hung on as long as they still *thought* their loved ones were out there."

"An' the rest died a heartbreak."

"No, they were tortured to death. Or worked to death. Or just shot arbitrarily. But the point is that the ones who managed to hang on until the war ended had this thing in common: they were all looking forward."

"But this ain't World War Two, Tom. It ain't Auschwitz."

"What Frankl learned at Auschwitz, or Dachau maybe, is that our sense of life as being meaningful is what keeps us from falling apart. But what if you *wanted* people to fall apart? Make them easier to divide and to rob. You'd find a way to erase their meaning, to keep them from looking forward." Both men reeled in, checked their bait, and recast. Tom nervously turned twice to scan the shore, but so far it seemed that the two of them were safely alone. "It's the same thing Christianity's been doing for ages, but with a scientific flavor—a little more government clout."

Bradford shook his head slowly, looking out over the churning river mouth. "It's jus' that kinda shit that keeps ya from makin' friends."

Suddenly Bradford's rod bounced twice and then doubled over on itself as something big struck the bait. "Ho! Eee, shit!" he exclaimed, the line snapping straight as a laser beam and throwing little glistening droplets of seawater in all directions. The reel sang out high and whiney, as he let the fish run for a time. "Swim, ya big fuckah," he said. "Swim 'til ya fuckin' heart explodes." When the fish had sufficiently worn itself out, he brought it in slowly, methodically, but eager to see his prize. It was a huge striper, and Bradford scooped it into his landing net, savagely clubbed it twice with a bat, and tossed it into the bucket. Just like that.

"That's part of it, too," Tom went on, maybe just to dampen the excitement of Bradford's catch. He reeled in a couple feet of line, gave his rod a little play. There was a whole school out there, somewhere. "Whoever put the term 'shomee' into common use really knew what they were doing," he said. "Everybody's so busy wondering who disagrees with them, they never stop to question their own beliefs."

"Oughta explain that little paradox ta Lindy," offered Bradford, slicing into the sun-spoiled mackerel for a fresh portion of bait.

"You saw Lindy?"

"Lovely Lindy Bly says yer a shomee bastard an' she's gonna

turn you in to the fuel collection stiffs. Ya know, she probably jus' wanted some company, Tom. Lord knows ya could use it, too."

"I'm free to think and say what I want. Especially in my own home." Tom hadn't told Bradford about his encounter on the road. Nor had he mentioned Sharon Grey.

"Well," said Bradford, grinning, "whatevah you did or didn't say, Lindy's got 'nough sand in 'er clit ta make a friggin' pearl. And if she sends Val Gilbert's boys 'round to Stearns... ya bettah hope she was jus' talkin'."

"Let 'em come."

And then it happened. The fish hit so hard he nearly lost the pole, and as the tension built up, Tom kept the reel locked, fighting it directly. He felt the fish out there, making a hard run to the right but finding no slack and thrashing its way back into the shoal.

"Tommy, ease up on 'im, guy. Ya gonna lose 'im."

"Fuck no. This one's twice as big as yours, Nev."

The fish had nowhere to go but up. The line went slack for a breathless moment, and they watched the bass jump five feet out of the water, twisting and throwing its weight. Solid black stripes shining like polished metal in the morning sun, up and over and down again, swallowed up in a plume of white froth. This fish was a beast. An alpha fish. A Titan among its race. How many hooks had it thrown to grow so mighty?

"Tom! *Now*, guy. Let 'im run."

Tom didn't let the fish run. He foolishly took up any slack it gave, his rod bent like a horseshoe and its fifty-pound test line about to fail. It snapped with the daintiest sound—*tink!*—and

Tom fell backward onto the pier.

Bradford laughed so hard Tom thought he'd shit himself. "I told ya, son! Ya shoulda let 'im wear down on his own. Tell a fish it's caught, it's gonna fight ya."

Laid out on the spongy planking, Tom saw clouds skating by in small clusters, moved by winds too high for him to feel at sea level. He watched them pass, considering how—if not for a modern understanding of weather—they seemed like animate, willful beings. A perspective matter: a narrow interpretation of given evidence. The hook in one's cheek—to a fish—was more apparent than the line held by the fisherman. Tom imagined Fletcher's rock out there, distant and deific, tethered to some angler in this human mob.

They're letting us run, he thought. Eighteen months to fight each other, wear ourselves out. We took the bait.

"Y'alright, Tom?"

"Come follow me," Tom said, more to the clouds than Bradford, "and I will make you fishers of men."

Bradford only glanced sideways, threading another chunk onto his barb. "Ya bump yer head or somethin'?"

Tom swept up the dust and kindling splinters and petrified cat shit and bent nails and all, looking over the clean, bare space he had created. A full hundred feet of open floor, from the big hangar doors at the front of the shop to the rear loading dock. A thin veil of dust still hung in that sun-shafted air, looking like the cloudy beginnings of a universe in all the potential of space—a giant fallow womb. Tom could see the hull that he would build there. The thirty-foot plug—a wooden form upon which to shape this hull—which he would hammer together from framing lumber and laminate board. The thick hide of fiberglass he'd lay over the plug like bandages. He could smell the sawdust and epoxy fumes. He could imagine the seed of an idea somehow filling all that space, becoming a real object with structure and purpose.

Tom had never been a framer; in truth, he'd been a glasser. He would receive a finished frame, a plug, or a master mold, and he'd hand laminate or spray the fiberglass over this. He'd lay one coat, let it dry, sand it down, and lay another. So on and so on until he had the basis of a seaworthy hull. He was never a boat builder. He was a grunt who completed one toxic, laborious stage of the fabrication process for actual boat builders.

He'd rendered his many sketches into a set of blueprints, but without Abel around, Tom had only his gut to judge their soundness. He pulled a box of long framing nails from a shelf. He found his old kneepads and claw hammer and started banging together the very beginnings of a frame.

Time passed with the gradual, rhythmic shuffling of tiny pebbles along the shore. Out and back in, twice a day. His thoughts were colored by gull calls and gull returns. His own breathing. Conversations he'd meant to have, but didn't. He punctuated his sentences with the three strikes each nail took to drive it. With several thoughts in cadence, he quickly composed work songs, each sliding into the next on the cusp of being forgotten. Nail heads tasted a little like blood when he held them in his teeth. The hammer grew warm with friction. Tom slid back into the rhythm of manual labor and felt grateful.

After fifteen or twenty nails he'd stand and stretch his stiffened shoulders and neck, and he'd see that the sunlight which had fallen on one wall now fell on another. Tom wondered how anyone could have ever doubted that time itself was a thing of substance that shares our universe as appreciably as comets and planets and the great glowing swaths where stars are made.

Time or whim or circumstance, maybe all and more in concert, served to pull Bradford through the door at dusk. Tom heard the door shut, as he'd been busy pounding when it opened, and spat out three nails that tinkled like jacks on the concrete floor. Bradford rounded the corner and for a moment he just stood at one window, looking out on the water and the early stars above it. He'd spent his afternoon hunting trades for their morning catch, returning now with a jug of home brew and two pounds of some species of meat, bleeding through the brown paper package in his hand.

"Hey, Nev," Tom greeted him.

"Ya workin' in tha dark, bud." Bradford stored his acquisitions in the Coleman box. He lit the nearest oil lantern and began making his way around the shop counterclockwise, lighting each one in turn with a wooden stove match. Like a deacon visiting his stations of the cross, quietly guarding the flame with a cupped hand. He then replaced the various Tyvek sheets and old blankets, curtaining the windows, keeping in the light. "This way," he said, "we don't go blind."

Tom set down his hammer and stood to fetch his friend a

glass. They talked and smoked while the night outside darkened. They talked, for the first time in a while, about shipbuilding.

~~239~~ 234

The framing took five days in total, Tom being able to power only a handheld circular saw with his small generator, and only willing to run either of those by day. Working the two-by-six beams with hand tools was one thing, but cutting polygons out of wall-sized plywood sheeting, sharp-cornered to lay flush on the plug, required power. After each set of cuts, he'd stand for a time in the silence, waiting for the rumble of a truck engine or the crack of somebody forcing a door lock. When an intruder finally did challenge Tom's half-assed security measures, she found the main entrance unlocked, and the shop owner deafened by the screaming saw blade in his hands.

Sharon stood by the wood stove patiently, until he turned and noticed. He couldn't see her face for the afternoon light that streamed in white behind her, casting her in dark silhouette. She stepped lightly over bent nails and sawdust piles. Not incongruous here, in the shop, just unprecedented. As if he'd invited this light into his world, not knowing it would carry her in with it. She walked directly up to Tom, before either of them had spoken.

He held the saw by his right leg, putting its weight and his own on his left. He pulled the plastic goggles off his face and rested them in the dust-yellowed nest of his hair.

"Hi, Tom," she said.

"Hello."

"So, this is your boat shop."

Tom looked around, as if to assess for himself whether or not the place was, in fact, a boat shop. He raised his eyebrows, but said nothing. He shrugged.

Sharon smiled. Tom got the sense that he'd done something correctly. She seemed to be very happy with him in that moment, and he could tell that the reason was completely out of his control. He wanted to show it to her perpetually, always letting it be the side she saw, but he didn't know what it was or how to reproduce it. What could he do? He accepted. He was blessed. He thanked the world for aligning its kaleidoscope thus.

"Summer's nearly over," Sharon said, appraising the gleaming ends of cut lumber, the ribs of Tom's plug stretched out on scaffolds like the skeleton of some archaic fish. "If you're not too busy, I was wondering if you'd like to go swimming."

"Why vet?" he asked. Sharon's head rested on his stomach and he wove his fingers through her hair. Beyond the marsh grass where they lay, the river snaked languorously through clam flats and past the rotting stumps of mooring posts. She shut her eyes and smiled as Tom traced her profile with his fingertip. Over her smooth, aristocratic forehead, her fine brow, along that entirely singular architecture of her nose, long and swanlike. He thought, Why isn't there a better word for something swanlike? Tom searched his memory—signet, cygnet, Cygnus—but couldn't think past the root.

"Because I love animals," she said, laughing at her own intentional banality. "No, I can tell you: When I was little, my dad used to take me to a horse track in Syracuse. That was actually how I spent most of my dad-days. He was a gambler, and he'd woo me with soda and ice cream, so he could hang out at the track all day and still fulfill his fatherly duties, or whatever."

"Classy."

"Yeah. Not that I was aware of it. His subterfuge, I mean. Or his addiction, for that matter. Are your parents still together?"

Tom wasn't sure how to meet the question. It seemed that he and Sharon maybe didn't share the full retinue of experience, where this was concerned. "I guess some people would say so."

Sharon took a few seconds to absorb this deflection. "They're dead."

"Yes, they're dead."

"Was it… recent?"

"Yeah."

"I'm so sorry, Tom…"

"It's not your fault."

She didn't say a word.

"Horses…"

"Right. So, there was a bad fall during a race one day. A jockey broke his collarbone, and his horse broke a leg," she explained. Her hands made corresponding shapes against the clouds, angles that abruptly formed and shattered. "They carried the guy off on a stretcher. He must have been concussed."

"Blood sport," Tom offered.

"Of course," she agreed, "and the horse just lay there on the dirt, making these awful sounds, with a compound fracture of the radius."

"You really knew your horse anatomy as a kid."

"Fuck off," Sharon told him, like a reflex. "You could see it, really. I never forgot it..." She laughed and then said, "It's not funny. So. The track hands or whoever brought out this big folding screen with the track logo on it to hide the injured horse from the people in the stands. I guess it happened often enough for them to keep something like that on hand. But Dad and I were up in the top row because we'd been late from the betting office, and we could see the whole thing. Right over the screen."

Sharon's face darkened a bit. She was quiet for a moment.

"I remember the announcer; I guess he was probably having to fill time while all this happened. He announced the fall and said it was because of debris in the track. And he said the jockey's name, said he was okay, he was being checked on. And he went on to talk about where this left the other horses, how the race would be called, that kind of thing. But it seemed like he was deliberately avoiding any talk about the horse that fell. I mean, we're sitting there, watching them do away with the poor thing, but he just avoided the subject entirely. They shot that horse in the forehead with a pistol, covered it with a tarp, and a maintenance truck came out and took it off the track. I was completely horrified. We had to go home. My dad told jokes about it for years, but I never stopped being horrified."

"So, you became a vet."

"Yeah, I guess. I mean, if you asked me for the defining moment of life which led me to the career, I suppose that would be it."

"But, this isn't really a horse region. You don't seem to work with horses."

"No."

"Why is that?"

Sharon rolled her eyes. "Well, because nearly every time they suffer a leg injury, you have to shoot them. Dogs are more like people: they know when they're injured. But you can't tell a horse to lie down for three months while its leg heals."

"While its *radius* heals."

"Yes."

"That seems so… final."

"That's exactly what got to me. Here was this enormous, beautiful moving animal. And then just one rock in all that length of track… The horse fell, and minutes later, it was dead. I watched it turn to dog food, right before my eyes. They loaded it onto a flatbed and hauled it off because it was just *in the way.* I couldn't understand the reason in it. So I studied veterinary med. So I could fix things, save them from the pistol."

Tom smiled, but he didn't let Sharon see.

"Well?" she said. "How did you come to be a boat builder,

Thomas Beaumont?" As she asked the question, she inspected the matching scars above his knee. Sharon didn't ask him about these or offer any type of comment, just scrutinized them with sober, professional focus.

Tom hesitated. What was it that made these questions so difficult? "I went to school for English, initially. That was part of it. I thought I wanted to be a writer."

"You didn't want to be a writer?"

"I did. I was such a timid kid, and reading just… helped me enter the world. Reality was so big, so complicated and scary. Stories had this way of reducing the world to something I could understand, on my own terms. I could enter and exit whenever I wanted, and it taught me things, and for most of my childhood, I preferred books to actual experience."

"And then you grew up," she said, "and wanted to give back."

"Exactly. But you know, the ability stories have to make the world digestible, it goes two ways. You can reduce the world to essential truths, to teach something, or you can sort of construct new truths, in a sense, to push an agenda. I started to notice that literature does this all the time. Religions are obviously built on stories, but then so is money. The fact that a dollar, which has no inherent value, is worth one candy bar or whatever is just a story that we repeatedly tell ourselves. The idea that America was founded on democracy and personal freedom is just the mythos we use to justify a rogue capitalist state that was actually built on slave labor. Science, too. In the West, we lived by the geocentric narrative for ages, until Copernicus and Galileo, and then after a bit of argument, we adopted heliocentrism. In the nineteenth century, it was a scientific fact that whales were fish and that the shape of a person's skull determined if they'd become a criminal."

Sharon put her thumb in the divot of an exit wound, puckered and hairless, below his right patella. "I mean, some of that is our own evolution. The Earth does orbit the Sun, right?"

"Okay, sure. But none of these stories—not the value of the dollar, the history of the United States, or the origin of the Universe—are objectively true. They might be approaching truth, but their only authority comes from consensus. We all wake up each day and tacitly agree to assign value to the dollar. We ratify these explanations of reality by living in accordance with them. On the one hand you have actual reality, whatever that is. And on the other, you have this very different, subjective, human story of reality."

"So, do you call yourself a skeptic or just a wet blanket?"

"Yeah, yeah," Tom said, pushing himself up on his elbows and constructing a cigarette. He lit up, watching Sharon pull a disgusted face as the smoke crept by her nose.

"I still don't understand," she said, "how this relates to you dropping out of college."

Tom moved downwind of her, still smoking, watching a couple of tethered skiffs grind their hulls together on the incoming tide. He'd never had the opportunity to explain this decision without reprisal, and found himself unprepared. "I wanted to create something real," he said, letting that statement hang in the air, taking a long drag. "My instructors, to their credit, I guess, they all really believed in literature. They believed in the mechanics of it, the beauty of a well-articulated thought. They had lots of structural approaches to making a story believable. But I couldn't shake this suspicion that words were a flawed medium. I knew that I'd never be able to say anything that was universally, objectively true. The best I could do was express myself. Who gives a shit, right? Just another pessimist, bitching about the status quo and offering nothing to replace it." He pointed to the skiffs, still afloat despite the months they'd spent unminded out on the water. "So, yeah. Boats."

Sharon turned and looked into his eyes in her very specific, quizzical way. "Boats. You say that as though it somehow answers my question."

"Boats are an art form. They're almost always beautiful, in their way. Granted, the most beautiful ones are owned by the rich, unfortunately. Money twists everything..." Tom checked the riverbank. There wasn't another human soul, just a lone heron stalking the shallows. Probing with its dart-like skull, Jurassic eyes wary of two apes in the grass. "But if you build a boat and it sinks, then you've done it wrong. There was something false in your creative vision, some flaw in your assessment of the world. Boats demand objectivity."

Sharon's face went sober as she seemed to earnestly consider this platitude. "You're ridiculous."

"Anyway," Tom forged ahead, "boat building was just a place holder. I didn't think I'd found my answer, back then. I was just putting career on hold and earning my keep in the meantime. When I started here, at Stearns, I don't think anything mattered to me at all."

It was nearly high tide, and the warm afternoon water had pushed up under the spartina shoots all along the banks of the George. Sharon unwrapped her brown skirt and dropped it behind as she stepped carefully through the tall grass colony, feeling out each advance. The lines of her farmer's tan stark in the sunlight, black hair shining, and the rosy undercolor of her feet lifting and then settling back to damp, dark earth. Tom followed her toward the shore from several paces behind, watching her move, taking her in.

Out beyond the initial rocks and clamshell edges, there was a more sedimentary bottom to the river, where the water was not much higher than Tom's shoulders. He waded into it and swam, kicking and moving himself over the tops of oarweed that reached up on their float bladders toward the light. Tom put his head under and forced his eyelids open, despite the saline sting that came. In those shallows there were pink calcites and glinting shell forms, crabs that surveyed an empire on stalk eyes, waving claws, pipe fish who darted and nipped at the edible everything around them. He saw this, and he couldn't imagine it ending. It predated himself and Sharon and New England and everything he knew—this Earth that churned below the water line.

Her legs were long white shafts stuck through the green-shifted light of that place. Tom pulled toward her, pushing the water back and away. His body lurched forward, and the air in his lungs begged its way to the surface through pursed lips, one little pocket at a time. He touched her feet where the silt had crept over and settled in the depressions between *tarsals* or *metatarsals* or whatever they were, the skin there maybe the softest of all. He ran out of air and planted his heels and stood and burst into daylight and took a breath.

They lay down on a hillside above the river to let the salt water dry on their skin. Over the growing wind off the estuary, he heard her say, "Jesus, it's like little knives." She'd chosen a spot where the grass was sun-dried yellow and the stalk ends of straw were poking at her.

"It's better over here," Tom called out, his eyes shut. "It's alive."

Through the cherry glow of his eyelids, he saw her shadow fall over him. When Tom looked up, there were her long, bare legs straddling his waist. Her face, high up, was in shadow and her wet hair hung loose in the wind. Sharon put a bare foot on his stomach, cool with grass moisture. She dropped her things nearby, the brown skirt, a pistol that thumped on the ground, a grease-stained T-shirt with the words "Dublin, Maine" in worn-away blue. She had a grave look on her face and her nipples were puckered with the breeze. She said, "Do you think anyone's around?"

"No," said Tom, "I don't think anyone's around."

~~234~~ 222

Buck had her litter on the morning of September 22, 1987, the first day of fall.

Tom had only just opened his eyes, groping for the tobacco that was somewhere, somewhere, and heard the wet, fibrous sound of her lapping. The cat purred, inward, outward, with incessant rhythm, and every few seconds from behind this white noise, came a tiny bird-high yowl. Tom forgot about smoking and crept across the shop floor.

Buck had carved out a little four-square-foot grotto amid the cardboard and a few relics that had outlived their usefulness. The space was lined throughout with rags and even some of Tom's old shirts he'd given up searching for. A rhomboid patch of morning sun lit the scene like a nativity. The cat was carefully tonguing one of her new arrivals on its forehead. She stopped and looked up at Tom.

"Hi," he said.

Buck squeezed her eyelids narrow in feline approval and resumed her purring, returning to her work. Three rather large kittens, eyes temporarily stitched against the light, were busily sucking at her belly, which she offered in an awkward-looking state of repose. The two foremost were tabby in color, which Tom could see through the saliva that coated them. The leader, by Tom's guess, who sucked at the first of Buck's teats was especially robust and sported a telltale "M" on his forehead. A Maine Coon. The last, and apparent runt of the three-kitten litter, was a jet-black female who looked at odds with the rest, and whose coloring perhaps betrayed some hint of the litter's patrilineage. Buck licked and nipped at all three as they sucked with a very determined organization, her right foreleg raised like a featherless wing above the brood.

Tom was turning back toward the woodstove when he noticed a dark lonely thing lying just outside the birthing nest. It was barely more than a smudge on the concrete. He bent down over the stacked this-and-that and peered in, unaware that Buck had followed his eyes, that she'd seen him seeing it.

A fourth kitten lay there, beyond the warmth of the den. It was still wrapped tightly in the placenta, and Tom could tell by sight alone that it was cold and dead. Stillborn. Buck had done her best to clear away the translucent shroud that smothered the kitten, but while the ears lay flat and the eyes stayed shut, like its living siblings, the lips also remained closed, and this hadn't been remedied by any amount of careful licking and nuzzling on the mother's part. Tom reached a hand down to it and found himself touching boiled grape leaves left overnight, a cold, sticky residue on his fingertips.

He picked it up, testing the weight.

"One in four," he murmured.

Bradford came screaming into the harbor with another stolen vessel, this one apparently a Coast Guard cutter from the Limekiln station. Tom didn't want to ask how he'd come by it. The thing was enormous, white, and shiny with a whole array of strobe and spotlights adorning its wheelhouse and radio mast. *USCGC Fish Eagle*, it proclaimed across its bow. Too large a boat for the rickety and barnacled Stearns Fiberglass pier. Bradford bumped her up alongside the pier and neutraled the engines in a crash of coming wake, the stern rising five feet and settling again, commotion running riot along the scant spread of beach. Bradford stuck his bare arm out the cabin window and hailed Tom with a boyish wave. Tom was in shorts and a wifebeater when he'd heard the cutter coming up through the harbor mouth. He'd only had the chance to throw on some deck shoes before running outside.

"What the fuck, Nev? Shut that fucker down!"

"Whah?" Bradford shouted back, his voice small and only his hat visible past the gleam off the police boat's windows.

"Cut your engine!" Tom yelled, slashing a hand against his throat. The surf was still breaking crazily all over the shore. Bradford had overrun the buoys where Tom's crab pots lay, and they'd all disappeared. Even the wind seemed to have come up with him. Tom was shouting into a gale, his tiny noise thrown back in his face. He gave up yelling and ran for the pier, meeting Bradford just as he was hopping down to tie off. The big twin-prop diesel inboards had chugged to a halt. Tom nearly punched him.

"Mornin', Tommy!" he said, peachy as hell. "Well, don't jus' stand there an' glare at me, guy."

"Nev, who'd you kill for the keys to this thing? And where do you get off doing doughnuts in my goddamned marina?" Tom was irate, but couldn't stop himself from ogling the cutter's ninety-foot hull, its twin gun turrets.

"Ah, calm down, Tom. I come by this boat jus' as peaceful as any, and we're gonna need it. Marina? Shit…" Bradford hocked a good-sized phlegm to the water and, with the back of one hand, simultaneously wiped both the spittle and grin from his lips. Suddenly dour, as he could be. "John nevah come into Port Cloud yestahday."

"Who, John Hupper?"

"Yuh. Nobody's seem 'im."

Tom took a step back and crossed his arms, his face still flushed. "Well, maybe he just ran low on fuel. Came into Burnt Isle. Or Monhegan…"

"Coulda. Mikey's got a dif'rent theory, though."

"Like what?"

Bradford looked cross for a moment and began walking toward the shop. "Like John mighta been murdered."

Mike Hupper had never been a trustworthy kind of kid, and the whole county knew it. Everyone but his father considered Mike a bit of a dunce, and that sort of assumption is often easier to run with than to try and shake. Folks were alarmed when he started broadcasting his father's absence, for sure, but most just took it as more of Mike's talk. In fact, it was nearly impossible to imagine Mikey getting by at all without the benefit of his dad's cunning and connections.

The younger Hupper had spoken about gathering a search party to find the *Eleanor*, making a big noise down at the Harpoon Tavern, but not garnering much support. No one could picture Big John Hupper in trouble, it seemed, whereas Mikey's drunken hysterics were a regular encumbrance on the fishery's peace of mind. He'd told Bradford that he was taking his little lobster boat, the *Puffin*, and heading toward Monhegan Island to find his dad. John had always fished a deep stretch just north of Monhegan, water far off shore on the very outer reaches of Muscongus Bay.

Bradford had apparently thought it time to spring the Coast Guard's regional flagship, which had been impotently tugging at her moorings for the past several months. Just bobbing there, tanks full, all dressed up and nowhere to go.

Tom clothed himself and somewhat hesitantly climbed aboard. For a while, they trolled the big boat downriver and Bradford described to him the bloodshot craze in Mike Hupper's eyes that morning. "He may not be right, Tom, but his worryin' ain't fake." Passing Maplejuice Cove into wider spaces, he opened the throttle full. The bow rose, Tom grabbed hold of a post, and they tore over the surface with the boat, the wind, the gulls, and everything hollering in unison.

Tom stood at the bow telescope with the spray pasting his hair to his forehead, trying to maintain his equilibrium as the boat jumped and settled, and his scope-eye fought to keep focus on the horizon. He'd never been seasick nor motion sick in his life, but if he ever came close, it was straddle-legged on the bow of that cutter. The *Fish Eagle* was faster and more powerful than anything he'd been aboard, and in the foremost bow, one feels every little trough and breaker that comes his way. He scanned one-hundred-eighty degrees of mostly bare ocean for sign of *Eleanor*, ascertaining a certain swath to be clear and waving his right hand over his back to tell Bradford which heading to take. At times, he just swung the scope wildly, not seeing anything at all, his circle of vision a pinafore of light blue sky and dark blue sea with not a foreign dot between them to investigate.

Eventually, to their port side, Tom saw Hupper's Island as a dark hill in the distance, crouched behind the haze. They were in real open water now. After some time at high speed, penetrating that gulf, Tom thought he saw what could have been wreckage, and he signaled to slow down. Bradford barely eased back the lever, as though he'd seen a lack of assurance in Tom's gesture. What he'd thought a submerged and drifting boat was, in fact, a small pod of dolphin crossing the bay. Two dozen short-finned backs humped along the surface, their black oily skins gleaming, and soon, he could see the spouts as well. Tom was afraid that, at this speed, they might overtake the pod and catch the animals in the two spinning props. Tom thought about how to relate this to Bradford. Shouting would certainly do no good. Then, he worried that perhaps Bradford wouldn't share his concern for the creatures' wellbeing. Tom searched the telescope station and found the radio handset there, picked it up, and put it to his mouth, his thumb on the talk button. The

DC current was flowing, the red/green bow light faintly aglow.

"Nev?" he tried, unsure. "Hey, Nev?"

Some moments passed. Tom heard the sound of radio air, then a sharp clicking, followed by what he assumed was Bradford fumbling with his handset up in the wheelhouse. Eventually the noise cut and he heard a long, low breath through the speaker.

"...yuh."

"There's dolphin ahead, one o'clock."

Another pause. He could feel Bradford considering... "...'kay."

The boat swung ten degrees to port, and Bradford held that course for a time. They shot past the pod and Tom momentarily forgot his job at the telescope, watching them swim. Canny little whales, short-beaked and yellow-sided. A harem of gulls followed. Tom turned his eye back to the horizon.

"How much fuel've we got?" he asked into the mouthpiece.

"'Bout five-eighths a tank. Don't ask me how much *that* is."

Tom decided not to ask the question which naturally came to mind. He wanted to follow the dolphins, watch them ride the bow wake and leap in the air, and investigate their wide, wide world. This, of course, could not be. He wished they could be doing anything other than speeding toward the vast nowhere from which John Hupper, sooner or later, would surely emerge.

"Hey, Nev?"

"Yuh?"

"This is kinda fun, isn't it? With the CB and all?"

He heard an odd rustle from Bradford's end, as if Bradford

were scratching himself using his radio-hand. Another long sigh.

"Maintain radio silence, Tommy."

An hour later, Tom saw her. The word "Eleanor" in black script across her stern, unmistakable even through the haze. Tom grabbed for his handset.

"I got him. Two miles to port."

They were making twenty or twenty-five knots in that big military tub and gained on *Eleanor* fast. So fast that the lump in Tom's throat grew large before he could quite name a reason. She seemed empty. With his brow and cheek clamped hard on the eyepiece of the telescope, Tom peered into the distance between himself and that boat, begging it to reveal a human figure. There was none.

"There's no one at helm. I think she's drifting." Tom blinked and looked again, thinking that maybe his mind was the culprit. It often was. He wanted so badly to be wrong, but for the life of him could see no one aboard the *Eleanor*. Just gulls trailing her. A dozen gulls. A score of them. He heard Bradford's voice calling him back, off the bow.

Tom teetered his way aft and climbed the corrugated metal stairs up to the wheelhouse. Bradford sat in the stiff-looking captain's chair, squinting down the horizon, internally plotting his approach to *Eleanor*. From twenty feet up, the seascape looked very different. The pitch and yaw of the cutter were eminently noticeable, as was the boat's actual speed. Bradford throttled down carefully and cut the engines, but still Tom could feel the massive boat hunching and lurching beneath his feet. When their wake caught up, it lifted the stern two meters, and Tom held to a center post while they settled. His stomach lifted and settled with it.

Bradford had decided to intercept *Eleanor* using one of the two Zodiac skiffs that were lashed inside the *Fish Eagle*'s stern. Both of their outboard motors still had a full complement of fuel in its red plastic tank. Bradford walked to the stern of the cutter and readied a skiff to launch.

This could have been a dream, as far as Tom was concerned. He kept glancing out, toward the spot where *Eleanor* sat dead in the water, maybe a hundred yards off their starboard bow, harried with seabirds. Their continuous squalling could be heard even at a distance. It had always seemed to Tom that birds in any great number could sound murderous as a lynch mob, their cries implying that a death was somehow owed them. And in a larger sense, he supposed that it was. Tom glanced once at Bradford, but when the other noticed, he turned and pulled his cap down by a degree. They unbound the skiff and lowered it carefully to the water. The winch gears gnashed and the free ends of chain sounded in that open space where no surface stood to throw back an echo.

"You're drivin'," said Bradford, as Tom watched him tuck a pistol behind his back. What for, he wondered? The sun was full-up and put a shine on the bald spot showing under Bradford's mesh cap. "You're gonna pull us up along'er stern, and I'm gonna go aboard and you're gonna stay in the skiff and hold it along tight." Apparently, Tom was now a child. "Tommy?"

"Yeah, Nev."

"Got it?"

"Yeah, Nev."

"Now, don't go changin' the fuckin' plan once we're out there," he said as he reached to unhook the forward winch chain, his hands shaking terribly. Those big red scar-tissued mitts of his, and he couldn't hold them still to save his life.

Tom sat face-forward on the stern seat of the Zodiac, his hand quickly going numb on the vibrating tiller and the outboard humming loudly behind him. A cigarette barely held in his lips against the wind. He watched Bradford on the seat before him, facing him, kneading his hands together and popping his knuckles. Bradford seemed to be quietly speaking to his shoes. Tom kept their speed down to a minimum and rode the waves as gently as possible, not allowing his friend to be jostled. Bradford, like a prickly, domineering husband, and Tom mothering him just the same. This solemn marriage stretched over three long speechless minutes crossing the wind-humped sea, until *Eleanor* was within spitting range and both had to break character to face whatever lay within her idle, bird-shat hull.

"On your right." Tom spat his cigarette to the water.

Bradford looked tentatively in that direction and then righted himself. Tried to look purposeful. "Okay. Pull 'er up slow, now. Cut that motor an' coast 'er up slow."

Tom ran the rubber pontoon of the skiff against *Eleanor*'s starboard side on momentum alone, the outboard having coughed itself out. They rebounded a bit, and Bradford grabbed at the drifting lobster boat. He pulled the pistol from his belt, reached it skyward, and squeezed off a couple of cursory shots. The cloud of gulls, otherwise having cared little about their presence, were startled off for the time being.

From where Tom still sat in the back of the skiff, *Eleanor* looked like any other fishing vessel in the local fleet. A skeg-built Beals Island hauler, pricey but not showy. Maybe a little larger than most. Its only remarkable aspect was ghostliness, or maybe placelessness, as it was odd to see such a boat free-floating in water so far from any port. He could see the empty wheelhouse, the wheel turning there, spectrally, as currents swept the rudder. The windows of the cabin rimed with salt and the encrusted white droppings of gulls. Bradford rose and put his hands on the boat.

"Ah, shit," he said after he'd looked over the edge. Bradford removed his mesh hat, pausing for several seconds with his forehead down on the gunnel, mouthing words, before vaulting himself onto *Eleanor*'s deck. "Christ, John," he groaned.

"Nev?"

Bradford stood there with an odd slackness to his shoulders. His eyelids pinched as though he were facing into a hard sun or taking a pain of some kind. He glanced at Tom, once. Tom thought there could have been sympathy or pity or something in the look, but it was undirected, completely without recognition. Bradford didn't really see him.

"Nev," Tom said his name, like trying to wake him. "Nev."

Bradford didn't look up again.

There was nothing out here to reassure a person, to calm a

terrestrial soul. The nearest islands appeared as little more than a vague discoloration of the far-off haze. The horizon a taffy stripe of gold and cream linking the infinite terminuses of the sky. The clearly concave sky. If the earliest philosophers had been sailors, they'd likely never have suffered a flat-earth theory. They'd have been leagues ahead. They'd have built religions on the understanding of relativism, scripting them in ways to thwart the terror of being infinitesimal.

On a boundless ocean, in all that length of afternoon, only the sun travels any appreciable distance. A man can be still, can live within the quiet of his own heart. He has time to make decisions. He is undisturbed as he weighs his values. He can decide that there is no value to be found in his further suffering.

It was almost enviable.

Tom was forgetting his job. He'd let go of *Eleanor*, as a sudden gust caught the skiff and pushed it back along her stern. Bradford didn't notice and said nothing as Tom scrambled to find the gaff and grab hold before he'd drifted out of reach. He hooked a tow cleat and pulled in gingerly, hand-over-hand along the gaff pole. "Eleanor" in script there, huge in his vision. The scupper hole on her starboard side slowly leeched red down to the water. A stain spread in the water and small fish darted through it. Their silvered bodies flashed within it like heat lightning in a cloud.

"Bradford, goddammit! Is that blood?"

Bradford looked toward the stern, looking as though he had just woken from something else—from one dream into the next, maybe. Tom could see Bradford's gaze follow his own. He passed a hand over his face.

"Yuh," he said finally, with a difficult patience in his voice. "Tie off, bud. Ya bettah come up an' see."

Tom tied a short line to the cleat he'd hooked and secured the skiff there as tightly as he could. The two boats squeaked and groaned against one another as they rode the coming swells. He stood, waiting for a moment of stillness, and then put one foot inside *Eleanor*'s stern. The sole of his shoe squelched and slid in what oozed there, viscous and lazily draining toward the scupper.

"Jesus. He's dead?" Tom wasn't expecting an answer. He looked at the leg nearest to him, the foot twisted as it was at an unnatural right angle to the rest. John Hupper was suited in his bright-orange oilskins, as though it were any other day of work. He lay facedown on the deck with his upper torso in the shade of the wheelhouse, and Tom couldn't see yet what that all looked like, the captain's chair blocking his view. Bradford was just outside the wheelhouse, unmoving, and Tom thought that maybe he shouldn't even approach him. The deck between them was a sheer slick of blood and gull shit.

"Yuh," Bradford did answer, quietly.

There was an old single-barreled pump-action shotgun lying by Bradford's foot. A gull swatter. Bradford stood with his hands pocketed, looking down at it. He didn't seem to have much to say about that, or about anything else.

Tom edged his way slowly toward the bow, holding on to whatever he could, slipping in those condensed and multiple plasms underfoot. With a hand on the cabin roof, he leaned in closer, seeing the grey pullover sweatshirt John wore patched with stains, and the palm of one hand turned upward, curled and bearing only a small clutch of flies. They paced and buzzed robotically in small repeating circles. Here, miles at sea. Where do the flies come from?

John's broad shoulders slumped beneath his chair in a pose of relaxation Tom had never seen them accorded in life. He could not have found words, no correct description, for what remained between those shoulders. It was only a disintegration, a shattered and muddled reversal of what it should have been. The mess of it lay spread and being buzzed about like spoiled produce. The gulls had gotten to that, too.

Bradford handed something to him, nudging Tom's shoulder first, and he turned and took the long rectangle of paper from his hand. It had been torn from a logbook and there were entries in blue pen:

Oct. '86—4 strings at 80 pots, 43° 47' 09" N x 69° 07' 28" W (So-so. Lot's a crabs.)

Dec. '86—3 strings at 60 pots, 43° 51' 19" N x 69° 14' 04" W (Good haul. Mike's scout.)

"Hey," said Bradford as Tom was looking this over, a slight grimace of confusion coloring his features. He made a little corkscrew motion in the air with his finger. Tom flipped the paper around and saw the letter:

El,

I've decided to end it here, babe. It's almost six months you've been gone, and it ain't getting any easier. I know what you'd say if you were here, but you're not. You know, I'm not a frivolous man. There's just no more reasons.

I don't know how to talk to you. I guess I never did learn to pray. If you're out there, then I hope you can read it. You always did bring out the superstitious part of me. I guess I'll find out soon, if you could maybe be out there.

I know I'm leaving Michael alone here, and you'd be angry about that, too. Honestly, Mike's been all but alone since you and Jennifer passed. I've just been a mean-tempered shadow in his life, I think. You need to understand that Mike's going to be okay when it all blows over. I believe that. He's young and he's better suited for this world. These stories, this thing that killed you and me, Mike's going to survive it.

Who knows—maybe that was the point. Maybe we were just in the way. I don't know.

I'm not a godly man, but I'll admit my wrongness for eternity if it means I can see you again.

John

He read it in full and then turned away from John Hupper's

body, unconsciously folding the letter in eighths and slipping it into a back pocket. He looked at Bradford. Their faces met for a brief exchange, a kind of *Well?* Both of them dumb.

The back of Tom's left hand itched, as if mosquito-bitten, so he scratched and brushed away the irritant there. It stuck to his right index finger, and upon examination, he found that it was a bristle of short, wiry human hair. The color of rock salt and affixed in a clump to a tiny pinkish mass of flesh. Tom gradually leaned forward, flicking the thing over the side of the boat and then vomited in a hard white gush that entirely saturated Bradford's boots.

~~222~~ 200

Tom could see, when he looked at his hands, that he was getting older. The skin was dry, and not only salt-dry, but actually losing the elasticity of youth. They're stronger, he told himself, stronger with age. But it was an illusion, the idea that time preserves us, hardens us like driftwood. It just wasn't true.

He washed away the remnants of crab bait, leaning over the side of the boat and splashing his hands in the dark water. The days were long, for the time being, but winter never fully lets go of these latitudes, and the harbor was still very cold. His fingers were numb from handling dead mackerel and wet ropes. No spot of tangible warmth in the gunmetal sky this morning. Not yet. Tom sat back on the plank seat of the aluminum skiff and wiped his hands on his jeans. He shoved them in his pockets and just sat, looking back at the shore, at the barnacled pylons of the wharf. The boat shop sat hunched and sullen. These man-made things had a tendency of looking unimpressive when viewed from the water.

Picking up one of the oars, Tom worked it a few rotations

until the boat was faced away from the shore. He looked out on the nearby land forms overlapping and losing shape as they slipped silent into the water, pine forest covering each limb like bristles on the back of some outlandish mammal. He looked at the rim of white stone following the shore. It seemed to follow every shore in the world, garlanding each piece of earth and connecting them all, a ribbon laid in a billion gullies and switchbacks that one could stretch out flat and tie to the moon.

Back ashore, he flung open the double doors of the shop and the air rushed in, a warmth that was just enough. Tom shed a layer of wool and his stocking cap. A weak sun hung just over the horizon and the sky had cleared. He could see the vessel he would build in his mind, imagine its finished form, fighting through interference like a radio station just out of range. Autumn was around the corner, and this was reason enough to get working. Boat-building season would soon be gone.

He pulled the tarpaulins from the wooden plug and folded them carefully like flags, set them in a dry corner, and inspected his work. He'd taken a full day just fairing and waxing the plug, coating every centimeter of its shell with enough goop to keep the epoxy from adhering. It cut a nice figure, this greased mock-up of what would be his boat. Something fashioned in crude wood and nails that approximated a dream he'd had. The clean, hard lines. The convexes he'd drawn again and again in his sleep. A dream of whales and birch leaves. A dumb sonnet he'd written to Abel.

Tom pulled out every bolt of glass reinforcement he could find in the shop. He had gone over the math half a dozen times and come to the square-footage figure needed for a twenty-eight foot hull. He would set the initial layers in cheap electrical-grade cloth and work his way up to a finish of tough airplane-quality S-glass. Abel's tendency of never throwing away remnant cloth left Tom in a position to build himself a very fine hull, one that would remain seaworthy for many lifetimes. This detail was important to the project.

He laid out several brushes and pried the lid from a can of epoxy with a flathead screwdriver. Tom set the lid back on the can to contain the fumes, a cloth draped over it like a waiting magic trick. He double-counted his stock of resin and fixer, the various supplies he'd gathered, the rags and kneepads and such, and decided to begin. With his resin-spattered tennis shoes, not worn in a year, and a dusty respirator, Tom knelt and started laying out the first material.

He took to the work like an old habit, letting his body absorb the fumes and the itch of glass fibers, giving himself over to tactile memory. The confidence Tom once enjoyed under Abel's guidance came back within an hour or so, the pride of watching his hands move almost autonomously over the hull. Tom laid the cloth strips short to keep them manageable, brushing on the thick clear resin and smoothing everything down with a squeegee to press out the air. Overlaying each new strip by a precise inch, creating an impermeable shell in measured quadrangles. The brilliant resin sheen only faded after hours of letting the strips dry in the open, moving air.

Tom spoke idle thoughts to himself as he worked, recounted stories, narrated his progress. His voice coming out flat and archaic-sounding as a radio address, muffled by the twin cones of the respirator. He sang old standards. Rolling Stones, Simon and Garfunkel, Moody Blues. As the labor grew automatic, his mind drew further away. Disembodied and free to visit other corners of his life.

So, this is your boat shop.

By the time half of the hull was laid, the sun had risen and come around to shine through the southward doors, and the day truly felt warm. Tom stepped out into the light and pulled off the respirator, pulled off his flannel shirt. He put himself down on the cool, moist grass. There were massive white clouds moving fast against the sun. Tom's vision went black for a few seconds, and he readjusted his pupils on the steaming field before him, squinting down until he could make out each and every stalk, and then slowly opened his eyes again to the acres of yellow grass. A red fox paused with its head high in the straw, not ten yards away. The fox took the air once, wet nostrils flared, and then disappeared from view, its colors vanishing into the rest.

"You little fucker," Tom murmured. He felt no inclination to shoot the fox. It was a beautiful day.

Mid-afternoon brought warm breezes that curled through the shop and carried away some of the fumes. He laid the first complete layer of glass on the hull, lancing and pressing the bubbles, and decided that he was finished. Back when Abel had run things and there were two or three commissions at a time, the glassers would run oscillating fans over the drying hulls. Hair dryers, sometimes, for the trickier angles or spots of thicker glass. All Tom had, to this end, was time. It would be a long chilly night in the shop with the windows wide open, but as Bradford was never slow to remind a body, it was "Better'n wakin' up dead."

Tom left the hangar doors wide and went off to haul his crab pots. He steamed a small catch of rock crabs in a steel pot along with some tough, briny seaweed. The collected crab shells would bait his pots again in the morning. Through the shop door, he looked at his hull as it dried, eggshell-thin but existing. Not on paper and not in dreams, but in the clean late-summer air that tightened it, made it more cohesive and real. Again, or maybe for the first time, Tom was building a boat.

Mike Hupper had caught up to Bradford and Tom soon after they'd boarded *Eleanor*. Bradford finally responded to his calls on John's short wave, by this time mechanical in their insistence—*"Eleanor, this is Puffin, come in… Eleanor, this is Puffin… Eleanor, this is Mikey… Dad, this is Mikey…"*—and given him coordinates for their growing flotilla. Within the hour, they heard his little alcohol-fueled hauler coughing its way across the bay.

Mikey was short with them both, huffy, caught up in his own panic and indulging it visibly. He had run his boat up just short of where they drifted and cut his motor fast, almost ramming *Eleanor* as they stood and watched with incredulity. Mike jumped into the substantial chop and swam to his father's boat, his sternman Buddy dazed and blinking and readying to throw a preserver. But Mikey swam strong and, with only marginal clumsiness, pulled himself spitting and hollering from the waves, planting his still-shod feet at last on the deck in a slick of his father's blood.

They saw him see the body, and they heard him mutter things to himself, or perhaps to his dad, incoherent and breathy, and his chest heaved with the swimming and the stress and, Tom assumed, with emotional behaviors he'd maybe even practiced over the course of his frantic day. They stood back and gave him what space they could, Tom still green with sickness and Bradford silent. Mikey's deck shoes slid in the bird shit. Grieving can never be accomplished with grace, Tom thought. One really should never try it. Mikey swore aloud several times and wrung his hands limply, like a child. He sat on the starboard gunnel and put his pinched face up to the sky. For what seemed quite a while they bobbed there, unspeaking, under a vicious sun while ocean sounds seeped in, filling the quiet.

Bradford said they should set the whole fucker aflame, like Norsemen would do, an idea that struck him as fair and reasoned. "Besides," he added, "I doubt John wanted for anybody ta see 'im like this."

Mikey stared, open-mouthed, looking like he might just murder Bradford then and there. "We're gonna tow 'er back ta Port Cloud," he said with quiet resolve. The boat was, after all, everything that remained of Mike's family. "An' I'm gonna bury my dad."

Bradford persisted, only looking at the practicality of their situation. "You're jus' bein' sentimental, and anyway, there's no point to it, son."

"Nev..." Tom tried to caution. He glanced at Buddy, still posted in the stern of the *Puffin* and pretending to have other items on his mind.

People seemed to have a way of letting Bradford condescend to them, but Mikey was full of fight. "This ain't yer fuckin' concern, Neville. It's fishermen's business. Why don't you boys head in, get back ta varnishin' yachts or whatever ya do..."

"Mikey, don't even take that tone with me," Bradford answered, steadying his feet on the mired deck.

"Buddy!" Mike shouted, ignoring him. "Let's get a couple a lines ready. We're gonna haul 'er in."

"John's already arranged the burial, Mike," Tom said, trying not to salt the wound. "We're standing on the casket right now." He swept a two-armed gesture over the boat. "All we need to do is say goodbye and go home."

They all knew it was true. John had arranged this suicide, had considered his every last action. Even the boat's heading spoke it, pointed north as it was into the Gulf Stream current that would bear it up like a floating leaf and carry it to the Maritimes, the Grand Banks, hallowed fisheries of the North Atlantic. North to the cold waters, to be frozen in ice floes. To be dashed to bits by the sea. A damn sight better than six feet deep in the dank clay of Maine. There is ceremony for the departed and ceremony for those left behind. Tom sometimes wondered how often these overlap.

They pulled the *USCGC Fish Eagle* into port at Tea Harbor, with *Puffin* just a few minutes behind. The cutter was out of fuel, for the most, and they suspected it would stay tied off at this too-small mooring until forces out of anyone's hands freed it. Tom could plainly see that Bradford was reluctant to let it go so soon.

Mike tied off also and rowed in to the wharf, as Buddy rubbed his hands together rhythmically at the dinghy's stern. Buddy hadn't spoken the entire day, and everyone wondered if he'd entertained a single thought on its events. It seemed that some condition of the womb had scrambled poor Buddy just a touch.

Once ashore, Mike said resolutely: "I'm hittin' the 'Poon."

The Harpoon was one of the only still-functioning taverns in Fox County, a staple for those who still attempted to fish and live and get on with life. Its ownership had been a subject of dispute since the rock, but the gears of the tavern were greased by its patrons, who made sure that if beer weren't available through purchase or salvage, then whiskey would be poured, or else someone's moonshine would be tested and trusted on the willing throats of the fishery. A retired longshoreman by the name of Perch had been overseeing things at the 'Poon as of late, and a passably stand-up job he was making of it. Perch kept a ledger of each patron's consumption as well as their contributions to the tavern. Anything useful was considered fair currency, but booze was honored above all. If one hadn't paid in, and wasn't extended a favor, he could expect to go thirsty. Through shrewd management of this little cooperative, using the fishermen's own vices to prevent their hoarding resources, Perch had kept many mouths fed and many men working over the last year. If only the drunks knew what kind of quiet saint was filling their glasses.

On a good night, one had a choice between two different beers—both room temperature—and maybe three liquors. The John Hupper funeral party burst into the dark, cool staleness of the Harpoon Tavern just as evening fell. The smells of evaporating sweat and rotting bait permeated all, but at least a dozen townspeople had gathered under the kerosene lamps, unbothered by this funk. A trio of kids played tag, slapping their worn shoe treads over the stained hardwood planks and shrieking. Their faces were dirty under lank mops of hair, but Tom saw a fierce vivacity in these children's eyes. As his companions settled in to their drinking, Tom found himself drawn to this energy, heedlessly buzzing around him.

Mikey Hupper started off in what appeared to be good spirits. He signed off on a round for the four of them who'd just landed: a pitcher of warm lager and a serving tray of amber-colored shots, which they were to assume was some kind of whiskey. He thanked them, each in turn, for their actions that day. He told jokes about his father as they drank down the home-brewed lager, anecdotes about John's early days of fatherhood, "big fish" tales about the preeminent lobsterman in his heyday. They all felt alright. They all felt as though they'd borne witness to something of note, a landmark event in the county's history. Mike even lauded Tom's suggestion to leave the *Eleanor* adrift, which at long last they had collectively decided to do. He said he appreciated Tom's "knowin' what Dad was really tryin' a tell me, brothah." But the good times never last.

On his sixth shot of the thin brown fluid, Mike stood up quavering, his seat knocked away beneath him, and yelled,

"Fuck you, Tom Beaumont!"

"Shit, Mike. What the hell?" said Tom, after half swallowing his last draw of the same.

"You're a fuckin' fake, Tommy!" He stumbled a bit and righted himself. Tom could see that there were tears in his eyes, again. "You're just a tourist, Tom. A fuckin' shomee tourist! For all I know, you killed 'im!"

"Mike, that's insane," Tom said, pulling something from his rear pocket as he backed away from the table. "Look, take it."

Mike threw himself forward with the halting, rickety attitude of an animate scarecrow. He snatched the suicide note from Tom's fingers and held it, half crumpled, under the lantern. "The fuck is this?" he demanded. "The fuck is this supposed ta be, Tommy?"

"John's letter, Mike."

"Fake!" Mike hollered, balling the paper and discarding it without a glance.

Bradford stood up from his seat and put his hands in his pockets, watching.

"Fake? You honestly…" Tom couldn't decide if Mike was being serious.

"Got all the… fuckin' answers, Tom," Mike said, as he dragged his chin back and forth across his chest in a long, slow rhythm. Head lolling. Bereft, disconsolate, likely starved. He approached Tom gradually, but not without a certain menace. Mike's fists knotted up at his sides as he shuffled along. "So fuckin' smart. Ya fuckin' tourist…"

The first swing narrowly whiffed past Tom's nose, and he

staggered backward. Mike was also thrown off his balance from the effort, but regained himself and tried another punch. This one Tom caught with his left hand and tried to hold, tried to buy a moment of time to speak, to set things on a better tack.

"Mikey! Wait!"

Mike's eyes momentarily lit up with alarm. Tom thought that maybe he was experiencing some regret for his outburst. Maybe, in sudden lucidity, Mike had seen that Tom was not to blame here. That it was all some larger evil, bigger than both of them and growing stronger with each camaraderie it tore apart.

But no, it was Bradford who'd inspired Mike's repentance. His big gnarled red fist came down crushingly on the bridge of Mike's nose, sending the boy silent and slumbering to the tavern floor.

Perch shot a look at the quartet from his bar, put his rag away for the moment, and said, "Hey, now! C'mon boys… C'mon, now," in his thick and barnacled speech, not more than passingly concerned. Mike's sternman, Buddy, shifted his weight gingerly on the bench where he sat and, after some amount of grimacing, farted.

"You don't need to fight my battles for me. That boy was drunk. He was upset about his father, and he was blind drunk. Even if he weren't, I'd have held my own."

"I know, Tom."

"Ah, you're just placating me, now." Tom was putting extra muscle into his rowing, frustrated with their gradual creep over the channel and back toward Near Haven. Bradford stretched his legs in the stern of their borrowed skiff, eyes shut and slightly grinning. "I'm serious, Nev. I appreciate your help and all, but you don't need to come to my fucking rescue all the time."

"I know, Tom."

"I just can't understand him blaming me. With his father's handwriting there on paper. He refused to see it."

"It was either a whole planet's worth a bullshit beyond his powah," Bradford said, "or one skinny Frenchman with a bum leg. You were jus' easier, Tom."

~~200~~ 180

When the trade boat came into harbor, his first impression was that it looked worn. Tom had imagined them wearing a dozen bright flags, the crew and captain standing on deck with clothes that at least appeared clean, waving broad and slow to a whistling, shouting party ashore. They would be the very lifeblood of a brave new economy.

The kid clinging to the bowsprit of this ketch was scrawny and ragged, Tom saw through his binoculars, and he waved to no one; there was hardly anyone there. Tom walked around to the big tavern pier by himself and watched them lower a boat, and the two men who met him seemed unimpressed and unsurprised by his lack of company.

"What's ya name?" asked the stout dark man who rowed as Tom caught his rope and tied it off. The scrawny kid sat in the bow and eyed him with no recognizable intellect.

"Tom. Beaumont."

"It safe ta land here, Tom Beaumont? Fa them guys?" He nodded his head back toward the ketch where his crewmates were likely eager to get on land and stretch their legs. He spoke quickly and sounded Massachusetts, but not quite Boston. Maybe Lawrence, Tom thought. Tom looked around at the shore, thinking about the man's question. Nothing stirred. Not a damned thing.

"Yeah. I'd say so."

The Lawrence man squinted at him as though doubtful, but took a look around for himself and then pulled a flare pistol from under his seat and popped a round off behind him. Tom watched it arc up into the grey sky and then disintegrate in the wind. Like birds on a far branch, the crew skittered around the deck, lowering their slender bow and stern anchors.

"No friggin' welcome party, Tom Beaumont?" He and the kid climbed to the high deck of the pier, the one giving the other a hand-up. They stood with their feet squared and their arms hanging, and Tom could tell they were feeling out the solid planks beneath their heels. Tom thought they must not have come ashore for some time.

"You boys have been out for a while," he said. Maybe it should have been a question.

"Yah, well," began Lawrence. The kid didn't even shift his expression. "Most times, ya come inta port, nobody friggin' there. And then othah times, they's all hid in the rocks, waitin' ta get ya in rifle range. Lost the first Cap this way. 'At's why we put this friggin' canary on the bow these days. Fool me twice, an' all." He stuck his thumb at the kid on the word "canary." There was no humor in his tone, and the kid showed no emotional response to the insult. Tom figured the canary must be autistic or else deeply traumatized in some way. Even so, he was better company than Lawrence.

"They shoot rifles at you, down in New York?" Tom asked gamely.

"Fuck no! They shoot rockets at ya down in New York. I'm talkin' New Brunswick, son!"

"Jesus," said Tom.

"Ain't got nothin' ta do with it. Say, Frenchie, does this little pisspot of a town have anythin' ta trade, or 'my wastin' my time?"

Tom, laughing inwardly at all this *machismo*, didn't immediately reply. What did they have? He'd fallen out of communication with most of the fishery and most of the county. Jay-Cee'd been the one to talk to at the Harpoon. He'd get loose with his facts after a couple rounds, and it was easy to gather a sense of who had what. And Perch, of course, was keeping the most accurate ledgers. Not a word from him, of late. If there'd been a cod season to speak of or anything salted and stored for trade, then Tom wasn't the one to ask. And now with John dead... Tom said, "Well."

Lawrence gave an impatient look over his shoulder. Two boats had lowered from his ship—Tom had half-guessed at Lawrence's captainhood, but then, why had he risked coming ashore?—and there were two men in each. Six, in total. Tom had misgivings about this crew. They were a skinny, mean-looking lot who shortly gathered on the pier, and all felt out the land as Lawrence and the canary before. But then, Tom wasn't too fat or happy himself. Difficult to judge a person, those days. He thought of the man that Bradford had shot in a doorway, months before. Bleeding out through the neck and onto the porch boards. Their two sets of clothes just alike.

Tom, automatic in his maritime etiquette, had met the aluminum johnboats on their approach and lashed them in file along the pier. "Tell me, Frenchie," he heard Lawrence start in again, but then pause. He turned back and their eyes met and Tom could see that Lawrence had been studying his limp. He felt the ship captain's observation the way a fish might feel dolphin sonar pulsing through its bones. Lawrence's eyes betrayed no judgment, one way or another, but Tom understood that his handicap had been assessed and filed.

"What's that, boss?" he said. He approached the other man, letting his lopsided gait amplify into a kind of swagger and keeping his chin just a couple of degrees above deference. This pisspot town was still *his*, goddamnit. Tom spat on the planking between his feet and the captain's, knowing he'd regret the choice of punctuation.

"There any women left in Near Haven, son? Like you says, we been out a long, long time..." Lawrence's voice was light and free of animus, implying he'd dealt with much bigger fish than Tom. Some of the other men went quiet, but at least one of them briefly laughed.

"No," Tom said, looking past them at the anchored ketch. "But let me go and round up whoever is." He made his way up the length of the pier, keeping a patient dignity in his step. Having nearly reached Water Street, climbing the loose gravel of the tavern drive, he heard Lawrence shouting: "Don't go hurryin' on my account, Tom Beaumont! Ain't as though the friggin' world's about ta end!"

"Well," said Bradford, scratching at his lank hair, grown long over the summer, "what all have they got aboard?"

"Maybe a pair of scissors. You're shaggy, bud."

"Wicked, ain't it?" He smiled and restored his ballcap to customary.

"Honestly, I can't say what they might be carrying. I didn't even ask. Those boys are hungry, and I'm not sure we want to try and feed them, you know? They look desperate. Bunch of mongrels."

"You oughta turn 'em over ta yer vet," Bradford said, happy with his wit.

"She's the last person I want them to meet."

Bradford gave him a grave look and then seemed to turn inward, considering. "A'right," he said, "in that case, let's jus' squeeze 'em for whatevah whiskey an' smokes an' whatnot, then turn 'em loose. We could get square with Perch, get rid a them sailors, and stock up fa winter."

"Wonderful. But what in hell do we trade?"

"Don't worry, Tommy. Got a few tricks up my sleeve, yet."

Tom came to find that these "tricks" were actually a small fortune in firearms that Bradford had been stockpiling for six months, he supposed just for this purpose. Bradford wasn't fixing to outfit his own army, but he knew that, as things got more desperate, there would be a dearth of arms for those with certain agendas. Not to say that he was actively encouraging violence. Bradford had simply cornered a market, in a time when dried corn could determine life and death as easily as any mortar or machine gun. It was all business. Should there be any future to speak of, the man kept a nest egg sure to appreciate in value.

There was plenty of ammunition for the majority of Bradford's wares, even the more exotic semi- and fully-automatic models that he'd pilfered from the gun cabinets of the recently dead. Tom figured this was why he hadn't seen the collection, Bradford not letting on that he'd looted the homes of so many suicides. A number of these had been veterans, and another portion earnest gun collectors. And then there were the paranoid, old-guard rednecks who kept modified M16 saws in their broom closets. A measure to protect their daughters from leftist faggots like Tom. Bradford didn't discriminate and wasn't picky. He'd gathered them all and kept them clean, oiled, and labeled for sale.

When he caught Tom gawking at the handtruck load he'd put together for trade, Bradford said, "Aw, don't look so friggin' worried. 'At's only a quarter of it."

"You never even mentioned this stuff."

"Yuh. Well, I love ya, Tommy. But ya get a little talky when yer drunk. Here," he handed Tom his well-worn shotgun, "take this."

"Ah, Christ," Tom said. "I've only got the one good leg left."

A small crowd had amassed by the tavern pier, most of

them having seen the ketch's flag flying over the harbor. They were like a throng of rag dolls, a Dickensian glut of peasantry all pushing against one another to beg the sailors for yet-unseen provisions. Enough to make Tom ill, having met those sailors. The poor begging of the poor. Tom figured it would come to this; he just hadn't wanted to see it in his own home.

Bradford had his guns all bundled under a blue tarpaulin, and while it looked to Tom like a botched KGB maneuver, no one else had even a scent of what they'd brought. The crowd's offerings, by comparison, were tiny and worthless. Lawrence was milling through them by the ramp of the pier, laughing and shaking his head at them each in turn. The Near Haven men were carrying all manner of household items, antiques, silverware sets and candlesticks and jewelry boxes full of god-knows-what. These items had no value to speak of. Just heirlooms and anything that had been spared the indignity, on past encounters, of being put up in trade. The lucky ones had brought gold or diamonds; in exchange for a grandfather's pocket watch or a late spouse's engagement ring, they were handed sacks of rice and rancid wheat flour. The trade crew was taking a gamble on the future worth of even these trinkets, maybe just born of instinct.

No one had arrived with edible goods, and no livestock. But they'd come with demands. Men shouted at the captain for antibiotics, painkillers, dressings, and ointments. It was little use.

What wasn't asked for was treatment for the chronic illnesses. Tom could remember John Hupper, only a few months ago, offering both of his boats in trade to anyone within radio range who had insulin. There was none to be had, of course. And now, there was no one to need it.

The two made their way through the already dispersing crowd, Bradford tugging the handtruck with one hand and cradling the butt of an AR-10 in the other. Tom hung back and tried to look casual about the shotgun he rested over his shoulder. He made quiet greetings to some of the men he knew who shuffled past, but no one returned them. "Mr. Pottle," Tom said in a familiar tone as the druggist passed him. Pottle's eyes never met Tom's, but stayed fixed on his gun as he hurried by. Few of the men bothered to take their trade items home, but rather left them in the empty parking lot, so that the space looked like a knickknacks shop whose walls and roof and floors had simply evaporated and left its contents lying in all dispositions under the low pale sky. Tom put his boot in the center of someone's portrait, but lifted it immediately when he realized. The muddy print stayed on the face, done with such minute detail in oils. It was the portrait of a woman.

"Hey, skippah!" yelled Bradford. Lawrence looked around in annoyance, his fun imposed upon. He was busy haggling loudly with an old woman who'd brought a stack of blankets for trade. It seemed she came looking for kerosene, and the captain was trying to send her off with less than her asking price. Her angry gestures made her dissatisfaction plain enough, though Tom couldn't hear her smallish voice for the distance. Lawrence put up a dismissive palm to her face and then came sauntering over, leaving the canary standing mute, his face obscured by the pile of bedding in his arms.

"Ya lied ta me, Frenchie," he said, wagging a thumb toward the old woman. "There's a fine filly if evah I seen one." Lawrence cackled through his distinctly faultless teeth. Turning toward Bradford, he first examined the shouldered assault rifle and then craned his neck to look this giant in the face. "You hometown heroes don't fuck around much, do ya?"

Seeing that Bradford wasn't about to respond, Tom cleared his throat on his companion's behalf.

"Okay, big fellah. Whadaya got fa me?"

"You take them, I s'pose?" said Bradford, as he pulled a corner of the tarp away and revealed a dozen gunstocks.

"Jeez Christ..." Lawrence was clearly astounded. The privateer had eyes like silver dollars. "You s'pose correct, friend," he said in a saccharine version of his former self. "What can I do for ya?" He shot a look at Tom that was both vitriol and regret.

"All ya booze, all ya tobacco, all ya dry goods," said Bradford.

"And whatever you won't sell to her," Tom added, indicating Lawrence's last customer.

"Ha!" cried the captain. "You boys got me against a rock, here. Ain't got no tobacco. Nobody has, not 'til next summer, if that ever comes. I got five cases a Canuck whiskey, an' that's yours. I got fifty pound's a corn meal, only half a which is wet. Also yours. I got a piglet, swear ta Christ. Healthy as a little pink ox. I'll give it all fa ten automatic rifles an' ammo. Don't mattah what make."

"That's all you've got left?" asked Tom, rightfully dubious.

Lawrence raised an oathful hand. "On my mothah's life,

Tom Beaumont. 'Less, of course, yer interested in pots and pans. I got a mountain a bullshit back there." He rambled and nodded toward his ship, nervous dealer's chatter. "I got so much gold, I just throw it below for ballast. Scrap copper. Scrap iron. Ain't worth its weight in salt, 'tween you an me."

"A'right," said Bradford, sounding disenthralled, "how much kerosene?"

"Eight gallons. Less tha one I'm givin' her," answered the captain.

Bradford thought for a moment. "'Kay. We give ya *six* guns, all full-auto, an' six cases shells. We take the whiskey, corn meal, an' ya last seven gallons'a kero. Good?"

Lawrence nodded his head, frowning. "Ya don't want the pig?"

"Whatta we gonna feed a pig?" said Bradford.

"Well, you *eat* the fuckin' pig."

"*You* eat the fuckin' pig."

"Right," said the captain, deflated. "Okay, guess we got a friggin' deal."

Lawrence had two of his boys row back to the ketch and load the goods. Bradford separated four M16s, his AR-10, and one old Thompson gun, keeping the European models for himself. Five cases of matching shells. The Tommy gun was a belt-loader and he had two belts to go with that. He piled up the guns and the ammunition as neatly as possible for the men to load onto their johnboat, but not before throwing a loaded Kalashnikov over his shoulder.

The captain carried on a sort of one-sided small talk as the exchange was made, explaining how his boat, the *Nunavut*, had last stopped in Bar Harbor, a ghost port. It would be making the treacherous run south as far as New York City and then—hopefully—returning north "with all the riches of that singularly *cosmopolitan* warzone."

Lawrence said he'd be stopping again in this region to check in, then bound for Prince Edward Island where he had a line on some large quantity of liquid morphine "to assist with the suicide, naturally." He'd find ample barter for the remainder of Bradford's guns, rest assured. The boat would stay in port here for a further three days in case anyone brought goods from inland. If Tom and Bradford could get their hands on any livestock in that time, then let him know.

"Christ, boys. I wish there was more I coulda done fa ya. Sure would love one a them AKs fa myself..." he nearly purred as they made to leave.

"Yuh," said Bradford, with a wave behind his back. "Guess ya know where ta find us."

"In case I can swing a bettah deal, just hypothetical now—how many small arms could you boys gather up? Just an estimate..."

"Plenty," said Bradford.

"Just gimme a number. Twenty? Fifty? Two hundred?"

"Sure."

"*Sure*," the captain repeated. "*Sure*, he tells me."

"I don't like this, Nev. We're arming pirates, here."

Bradford pulled a little joint from his coat pocket and

sparked it. The handtruck behind him scraped along the gravel. "Don't worry ya self, Tom. Them boys couldn't tell their assholes from their elbows. They'll fuck up some ways."

"They'll murder us in our sleep."

"They'll make a *mistake*, Tom." Bradford handed off the joint instinctually, realized he was handing it to Tom, and put it back to his own lips. He puffed and then pinched the cherry between his fingers. "An' I'll get my friggin' guns back."

"Well, I appreciate your confidence. Wish I shared it." Tom scanned the tavern lot, searching the figures listlessly climbing the hill. "There she is. Be right back." He unloaded a portion of their kerosene and hurried away.

"Hey!" Tom called out. The old woman wasn't moving quite quickly enough to warrant a "Wait!" He limped toward her, two metal canisters hanging at his sides, as she labored before a wooden cart. She'd nearly made it up the hill to Water Street, and Tom was amazed at her vitality. The cart held her remaining woolen trade items, perhaps hand stitched, and the lonely gallon of kerosene that Lawrence had begrudgingly allowed her.

She glanced back at him briefly, saying, "Let me be, you damned militant." Her breath came as a thin white vapor through her scarf and mingled with her white hair, giving the impression of smoke peeling away from the woman's skull. The shotgun was still hung from Tom by a strap, and without the use of his hands, he tried to shrug it away.

"Ma'am, excuse me. I just wanted to share my kerosene with you." He lifted the cans in evidence. "It seemed like you were cheated."

The woman stopped and regarded Tom more closely. Her eyes moved over his stooped frame, pinched with judgment. He put the two cans in her cart, worried about the added weight, but feeling entirely earnest.

"S'pose I should *thank* you then?" she said.

"Well, no, it's just…"

"Here." She handed Tom a blanket. It was dark brown in color, very clean, and surprisingly heavy. "That's not thanks, boy. That's just fair."

"I didn't mean to presume anything, ma'am. Can I help you home?"

"Help me! No, you've done enough, I dare say. Young men and your wretched guns. Your wretched god and your wretched country. Your idiotic little fears. You've killed us."

"Ma'am, I'm sorry, but…"

"Don't be sorry, son; just be ready. Won't be long before this whole goddamned place is yours."

~~180~~ 178

“Nev? The hell are you doing?”

Bradford was on hands and knees, his torso swallowed up in shadow beneath the table, where Tom’s ship-to-shore and a few other gadgets were collecting dust. The halo pattern of a dying flashlight looped parabolically up the shop wall. At the sound of Tom’s voice, Bradford thumped the back of his head and grunted, slowly extracting himself from under the table. “Wirin’ for sound,” he said matter-of-factly.

“I’m sorry?” Tom closed the door and removed his heavy pea coat.

“We gonna need some music if we’re fixin’ ta throw a party.”

“Tell me you’re kidding.”

“We got our hands on enough whiskey ta choke a friggin’ whale, Tom. I’m tired a sneakin’ around and rationing every goddamn thing.” Bradford walked over to a soot-stained pile of plastic and artificial wood paneling and broken knobs that rested uneasily by the framing lumber, waving his hand over the musty lot as though it were a game show prize. “We gonna get loud and shit-faced tonight, boy. Like we used ta."

"Was that a stereo?"

"Still is a fuckin' stereo, dickhead. An' we've got just enough powah for it."

Tom frowned at the three deep-cycle marine batteries, wired in series and fed by a solar trickle charger, which provided the DC current for his ship-to-shore. "This is a bad idea," he concluded.

"Whattaya talkin' about?"

"You're gonna drain my batteries, for one."

"Oh, like you ever use 'em…"

"What about those assholes on the trade boat? This shop is supposed to look abandoned, like the rest of the waterfront."

"Maybe they wanna come, too. Doesn't bother me." Bradford went about his work, arranging the moldy speakers just so, fumbling with the corroded inputs and outputs with a childlike determination.

"Is that meant to be funny?" Tom, nay-saying the whole process, still hoped quietly that the venture paid off. The possibility of listening to music was so appealing it nearly frightened him. He worried he might fall to the floor in convulsions like a Pentecostal. "Anyway, we've got no records."

Bradford fished through his duffel bag for a moment, a self-satisfied smirk on his face. "Tha Rollin' Stones," he said, presenting the water-damaged album cover with a flourish. "*Exile on Main Street*. I know it's ya favorite."

"No shit?" Tom snatched the record and examined it by the fading light of a window. It was the real deal, a heavy double-LP in its original jacket. He admired its cover for the first time in years, a black-and-white photo mosaic of human oddities. He couldn't hold back his grin. "My gods…" he said. "Okay, what else?"

"Uh." Bradford fumbled with the album jacket, wiping away some soot. "Lynyrd Skynyrd," he pronounced, "*Second Helping.*"

"Well," said Tom, still beaming at the beloved artifact in his hands, this indelible piece of himself returned. "At least we've got the Stones."

Bradford looked down at the blackened cardboard square he held, a slight hurt weighing at the corners of his smile.

"Okay, I found him," Tom announced as he entered the shop later that evening, a large and ragged figure shuffling in the door behind him. The fire roared and *Shake Your Hips* played quietly through a single functional speaker. Tom's effortful afternoon of duct-taping windows insured that the *Nunavut*'s crew would neither see nor hear any activity from their distant mooring.

"Wendell?" Sharon cried with happy surprise.

"Tha fuck's 'Wendell'?" asked Bradford.

"Hi! Hi, Miss Grey!" said Two-Buckets.

"You've met?" Tom asked, not exactly shocked.

"Would you get him over here?" Sharon said, waving them both toward the woodstove. "His teeth are clacking, for Christ's sake."

"Oh, Two-Buckets don't feel no cold. Give 'im a drink," said Bradford.

"Give *me* a drink," said Tom. "I'm freezing."

Bradford locked the deadbolt and fiddled with the volume knob on his stereo, while Tom discreetly poured liquor into his guts to stave off a growing discomfort, the thumping strains of *Casino Boogie* helping him swallow it back. His qualm was not only with the indiscretion of their little gathering, but also Sharon's presence. She and Bradford knew him more thoroughly than any two people alive, and having them suddenly together left Tom vulnerable to more than just piracy. "Don't turn that up any louder," he said.

"You jus' drink an' let me do tha worryin' for a bit. Don't get too greedy though, Tommy." Bradford warned, "Four a them cases are goin' ta Perch."

"Who's Perch?" asked Sharon.

"He runs a bar down in Tea Harbor," explained Tom. "I guess you'd have to be a fisherman… Anyhow, he's a good man, and he'll put this whiskey to better use than Bradford and I, that's for sure."

"He's one a them socialists, ya might say."

"Not waiting for the wealth to trickle down," Tom added.

"A bartender?"

"Ya'd be surprised," said Bradford. "Perch is a man of ambitions. He's on ta somethin' the rest a this country missed."

The four of them watched the fire for a while. Tom got up to refill his glass and fetch another. Walking back to his seat, he glanced down at Sharon's cup. "What is that, tea?"

"Yeah," she said. "I'm… not much of a whiskey drinker."

"Makes one of us," said Tom. "Here." He handed the second mug to Two-Buckets. "Warm yourself, bud. We're celebrating."

"Okay, Thom, okay…" Two-Buckets lifted the mug, just letting its contents wash against his pursed lips. He made a face like he'd eaten a hornet and set the mug on the floor between himself and the stove.

"Can I ask what we're celebrating?" said Sharon, nursing her own mug.

Tom said, "It's open-ended."

"A whole pile a whiskey," Bradford asserted.

"Six pirates in the harbor and not a shot fired," said Tom, rapping his knuckles on a wooden table leg.

"How about you, Wendell?" Sharon asked. "What do you want to celebrate?"

The vagrant was so struck by this inclusion that Sharon might as well have slapped his face. He scanned the room slowly, as if considering the merit of everything in view. He first scowled at the whiskey cup before him and then smiled at Sharon, at Tom, and even at Bradford, who was impatiently raising an eyebrow and waiting for Two-Buckets to speak. At last he sighed, gazing into the fire, and said, "Iss stove."

Sharon closed her eyes, attempting to iron a deep grin from her lips. "To the stove," she agreed, raising her chipped ceramic mug.

"To the stove," said the men, raising and drinking, smoking liberally under the lantern light. The hi-fi rolled out a lo-fi *Sweet Virginia*, and they granted themselves, for a little while, the illusion of better days.

"You got quiet," Sharon said, nudging Tom with her toe. "What's on your mind?"

"Mmm. I got drunk," he replied. "I was thinking about making a phone call."

"Ha!" Bradford mocked.

"First," said Sharon, "you need a time machine. Then, you need a telephone. Who exactly is it that you'd like to call?"

"I'd like to call Washington."

"Ya reckon they need yer advice, Tommy?"

"Fuck off. I want to call, just to see who picks up."

"My guess is nobody," Sharon said.

Tom bit halfway through a thumbnail and tore the rest away with a jerk. "So, what if you dialed the White House or the Pentagon and somebody answered. What would you ask them?"

"Ya know," Bradford interjected, "I've heard 'bout such things as *red phones*. S'posedly there's these bright red telephones hidden around, an' they stay workin' in the case of a national emergency."

"Where could I find one?" Tom asked.

"They don't exist," Sharon offered.

"Nah, prob'ly not," said Bradford. "But tha way I heard it, it'd be in a basement somewheres, in a fire station or a public bomb shelter or courthouse or somethin'." He shot Tom a dubious look. "What a you goin' on 'bout, Tommy?"

Tom returned the look, considering how to proceed. He

took a long drink. "You remember Dar's plan?"

Bradford set his drink down and rubbed his eyes. This topic seemed to be in violation of the evening's intended mood. "'Course I do, Tom," he said quietly.

"Well, it's like throwing a stick of dynamite in the water and watching all the fish float to the top. Except, sometimes you get a shark, and *I* got a shark." Tom went to a high cabinet and retrieved some small item he'd discretely taped under a shelf. He returned with an off-white card, well worn in the months it had ridden around in Lieutenant Adam Murphy's wallet, and handed it to Sharon. "What do you think of that?"

She examined the card. She looked at the front and then the back. She raised her eyebrows in a way that indicated she didn't think much. "Did you make this, Tom?"

"I found it."

"Lemme see that, fuckah," said Bradford. Looking it over in much the same fashion, he said, "Did ya make this, Tom?"

"No!"

"Well, I don't know many folks who believe there's gonna be a 'May 2'. 'Cept for Dar Bly, of course. Where's this phone number s'posed ta be?"

"Washington, D.C."

"'Course it is. What about 1-1-2-3?" He'd read the four digits printed on a separate line beneath the telephone number, as though they were part of the number itself.

This gave Tom a bit of pause. "I guess... I just figured it was a phone extension. Like in an office. I mean, government offices, phone trees."

"Or some kinda code, maybe."

"What, like Fibonacci sequence?"

"Come again?" Bradford asked.

"Nothing. What kind of code?"

Sharon was looking at one of them and then the other, concerned at the sudden discomfort in the air. "Who's Dar Bly?" she asked, shaking her head. "Tom, what are you talking about?"

Bradford handed Tom the card, smiled at Sharon, and said, "Fishin'. Which reminds me of a story." Tom let out an audible breath of displeasure and got up to fill his glass, but Bradford continued, determined to turn the conversation. "Did you evah meet old Jason Moss out a Tea Harbor, dear?"

"No, I don't think so, Neville," she replied, still visibly confused.

"Well, he's dead now. Two-Bucket's knew 'im." He gestured at the old tinker who now slept in a nondescript lump of clothing by the stove. "Wendell, I mean. Anyways, me an' Jason was fishin' fa bluefish up near Maplejuice Cove in his little fourdeen-foot skiff when..."

The knock on the door made even Bradford jump; three solid knucklebone strikes that punched through the stereo noise and roused Two-Buckets from his fathomless dreaming.

"Tommy, get the door..." said Bradford as he pulled the .30-30 from beneath his seat.

"Fuck," Tom breathed. "What now?" He placed himself behind the door, and when Bradford nodded in readiness, shotgun leveled at the entrance, Tom swung it wide and braced himself for the coming blast.

The narrow figure in the doorframe cried out, short and shrill, his hands held flat before him as though to catch the scattershot.

Bradford handed off his gun to Sharon, who bird-dogged the intruder with its twin barrels as he was taken by the neck, tossed hard onto the concrete floor, and the door was locked behind him. Tom squinted his drunken eyes and leaned in—just to be sure—what with the kid curled fetal on the concrete and his hands over his face. Tom said, "That's the canary."

"Tha what?" asked Bradford.

"The trade captain's boy. I don't think he speaks."

"Edwin," said the boy, muffled under a threadbare canvas field jacket.

"Eee speaks!" said Two-Buckets.

"I think he said his name's Edwin," Sharon told them, still pressing Bradford's .30-30 against the boy's head.

"He meant the captain," Tom concluded. "The *captain's* name is Edwin."

"Um, *Wendell,*" said Two-Buckets, proudly.

Tom spat at the floor. "Sharon, let him up, would you?"

She backed and the kid pushed himself off the floor, rubbing at his elbows. The kid's eyes were too dull to imagine them afraid. Altogether, he gave off the general air of someone mildly put out, but not necessarily by the four who held him at gunpoint and waited for him to speak again. "Edwin ain't the captain; he's just a washed-up Marine. James Cadwgan was *my* cap."

"Happened ta Cadwgan?" asked Bradford.

"Got his throat cut. By Edwin's boys."

"Why did you show up here?" Tom asked him.

"Ta tell ya Edwin's comin'. He's gonna knock this place over for the rest a them guns."

Sharon said, "What are you, the scout?"

"Guess so."

"So why tell us? Ain't Cap'n Edwin gonna skin ya?" said Bradford.

"He sure would, but I'm cuttin' out. Soon as they get here. Anyway, Edwin don't know I can talk."

"That's a good bluff," Tom admitted. "So what, you only told us so we could distract Edwin while you run off?"

The canary shrugged and pocketed his hands.

Bradford, smiling, sauntered woozily to the loft ladder. He climbed halfway, reached an arm up to retrieve his duffel bag, and descended the ladder with whatever the bag contained clacking plastically and swinging from his shoulder. "How many firearms did you-all keep on that boat before ya met us?" he asked the canary.

"Just two shotguns, a repeater rifle. Couple a flare guns. An' Edwin's pistol. That's alls I know about."

"So, if them boys are gonna sneak up here from the river, their pro'bly bringin' *my* guns."

The canary said, "Well," shrugging his scant shoulders again. "I was countin' on it." He pulled his balled fist from a pants pocket and poured the contents into Bradford's palm.

A look of perfect satisfaction washed over Bradford's face as he looked down into his hand. "Tom, turn them lanterns up high an' pull all that shit off the windows," he said.

Tom stood in his shoes, blinking at him.

"Now, Tommy." Bradford was pulling automatic rifles from his bag, arranging them on the floor, slapping a magazine into each with a metallic crunch. He said to the kid, "You bettah hightail it somethin' quick. Be best if tha Cap don't see ya."

"There's *five* of them, Nev," Tom hissed. "With enough ammo to take Fort Knox."

"Good thing we ain't relyin' on yer faith, Tom." Bradford handed a loaded rifle each to him and Sharon. The Russian guns were eerily lightweight and sturdy, like skeletons of some extinct raptor. "C'mon," said Bradford, "let's give Edwin a nice send-off."

The stars gleamed little pinwheels in the November sky. Tom looked instinctually for the rock, knowing that such a thing cannot be seen. An object as black as the void it traversed. His vision was off, and everything swum together in a mélange of Christmas lights. He gathered himself and hugged the Kalashnikov to his chest and glumly shuffled his way across the lamplit boatyard. He pulled out the bottle he'd stuffed in a coat pocket and swilled and swallowed and felt the burning lump slide down to his bowels with nothing there to slow it. Tom turned to see Sharon and Bradford standing in silhouette before the shop windows. "We're like a… fuckin' shooting gallery," he slurred.

"How many times I gotten you killed?" said Bradford.

"This'll be the first, I think."

"Jus' wait, Tommy. An' gimme that bottle."

Tom took another pull. "I'll trust you. I will. But I'm keeping the bottle."

Sharon was scanning the shore grasses, glowing pale in the outer perimeter of the shop lights. She held her gun disinterestedly and said, “Where’s Wendell? He doesn’t deserve to get caught in the middle of this bullshit.”

“Jus’ wait, dear,” Bradford told her, extending his massive arm but thinking better, drawing it back again and looking out toward the same shore. He squinted at the lanterns across the harbor, the beacons telling him where the *Nunavut* was currently straining at its mooring. “You jus’ worry about where Tom gets off to. He’s about drunk himself numb as Two-Buckets.”

“His name’s Wendell,” said Tom.

“Th-thass right. Thass right, Thom…” said Two-Buckets from the shadows.

“Shush, all ya.” Bradford walked to the edge of the yard, paused there for a moment, and hurried back into the light. “They’re comin’. Two johnboats on the water. Them fucks think they gonna surprise us…”

“And what, we let them?” said Tom.

“Well, not ‘xactly…”

“Fuck that.” Tom spat and put his rifle butt to his shoulder, aiming for an indistinct point near the water. “Edwin!” he shouted. “Show yourself, you fuckin’ coward!” His voice high and quavering with soused ambition.

“Tom! What the hell is wrong with you?” Sharon pulled him backward by the collar, and he nearly ass-ended in the gravel.

Tom got his feet under him without letting a round fly from the AK. He smiled at Sharon, a half-hitched, one-eyed grin, and yelled again. "Edwin!"

"Jesus, Tommy..." Bradford passed a hand over his brow.

"Who tha fuck's Edwin?" came a distant voice, carrying from beyond the shore grass.

"Where's the canary?" Tom asked anyone who might respond.

Bradford said, "Long gone."

Tom cupped his free hand around his mouth: "The captain. Captain Edwin. The thief of Lawrence, Mass. Or is it Lowell?"

"Name's Cadwgan, actually. From Manchester. You ain't very good at this game, Beaumont."

"Well, fuck," said Tom.

"I can see them," said Sharon.

The leaf-bare primroses shook and Bradford's traded gun barrels flashed as five shooters carried them within range of the boatyard. They couldn't come a step closer without being caught in the outer lamplight.

"They can see us, too," Sharon warned, crouching and looking over her gunsights.

"Jus' keep 'em in view," Bradford said, putting a bead on the roses. "This ain't gonna take long."

"So much for surprise!" cried the captain, almost conversationally close. The grenade came in sly, tossed underhand, landing innocent as a baseball on the packed earth. It made two thuds and lodged in a plover hole somewhere between the thrower and the shop, and only after a brief, labored consideration, did Tom realize what the hell it was.

"NEV!" he screamed as he bowled his friend over, the two of them hitting the gravel at a skid. Bradford's rifle sounded a tight *ka-ka-ka-ka-ka* and the bullets flew haphazard into the night sky. The hand grenade blew with appreciable menace, and a couple cubic meters of dirt rained over the figures pressed into the gravel outside Tom's chicken coop. Tom raised his head to find Two-Buckets and Sharon looking back at him, stunned but seemingly intact. When they'd collectively gotten to their feet, they were unsurprised to find four M16 rifles and an AR-10 all fixed on them from ten yards. Tom saw Two-Buckets curiously touching his own head, his hand coming away bloody from a shrapnel grazing.

"Well, didn't kill any friggin' birds with *that* stone," said the captain with patent flippancy, stepping in closer and aiming for Tom's chest. "Wasted my last grenade on you lot."

"Two-Buckets is bleeding, you fucker," Tom told him.

"Ain't sure what that means, Tom Beaumont. A'right, drop them guns and get on ya knees. All of ya."

"Nope," said Bradford, and raised his weapon.

The captain's eyes flashed with anger, his gun swinging on Bradford.

Click.

"Tha fuck..." whispered Captain Cadwgan or Edwin or whatever his name might be.

Click, click, click, click, as his men all pulled their disabled triggers in turn.

"These guns were *checked!* Twice, all of 'em!" The captain took his useless M16 by the muzzle, pitching it end-over-end in Tom's direction. Hysterical. "How tha *fuck* did you do it, Beaumont?"

"Tommy ain't done nothin'," Bradford corrected, reaching into a jeans pocket and throwing a handful of small objects at the captain. The man gaped, fish-white and speechless, at the assorted firing pins that landed at his feet. "But you oughta be nicer to the help..."

Sharon dropped her weapon to the dirt and wrapped an arm around Two-Buckets' head, pulling him down into a forced embrace. Tom watched, powerless and shut out, as Bradford put one eye to his gun sights. For what seemed like whole minutes the harbor absorbed it: the sound of rifle fire rattling off clapboard and sheet metal sidings, rolling across the water and back again from the far shore. What had begun in tentative celebration ended—foreheads pressed to the gravel, hands clapped around ears—with Bradford cutting down the *Nunavut*'s remaining company to the very last man.

~~178~~ 177

He'd fallen into his cot like a dead man, Sharon soberly staring at the rafters beside him, but his blackout sleep hadn't lasted. Within a few hours, still well before dawn, he'd awoken sweating and fever-hot. Tom's mind played him images: the spasmodic snap of a neck or wrist when the cinderblock was thrown, vacant eyes slipping below the water, seemingly fixed on his headlamp. He heard the sound of his own grunting and hawing over wet ropes, and recalled his fear that one of them might animate and speak before he'd tossed it from the skiff. As Tom waited for the sun to rise, these memories staggered up from the harbor to wait with him.

Sharon turned slightly in her sleep. He moved out of the cot and away from her, trying to prevent whatever followed him from being communicated.

Bradford lay curled around the woodstove in a duck-feather sleeping bag, his outstretched hand still vaguely clinging to his hat. Tom crept silently around him and arranged things before setting out. There was something in him that just had to be walked like a nervous dog, tired out, and finally put to bed. It was this therapy Tom planned for as Bradford woke. The figure curled by the stove let out a yell of waking, as though the stress of it was unbearable, stretched and hugged himself in again, and replaced the cap on his naked head.

"Uh..." he said, "Tommy."

"Hey. Morning."

"Whatcha doin'?" Bradford passed his hand over his face and audibly shivered.

"Putting my rucksack together. How you feeling?"

"You off somewheres?"

"I wish I had some coffee, but it ran out two weeks back..."

"Yuh. No worries. Tha fuck you off to?" Bradford was fully awake and tired of oblique pleasantries.

"I'm gonna go inland for a few days. Do some lake fishing." He couldn't bring himself to tell Bradford he was slipping away to seek imaginary telephones and be alone.

"Fishin'. Ya want some comp'ny, bud?" It was an earnest offer.

Tom would file this away in memory, the offer. If ever forced to eulogize, Tom could say that Neville Bradford had been the sort of guy who'd kill five men and still get up in the morning to fish. He could make a charming anecdote of dropping the bodies in the harbor. Tom's love for Bradford was a complicated thing. "I guess, I'm looking for the woods more than the fish."

"I get it, Tommy. Ever a man a tha people, you are." Bradford turned himself over and rested flat on the concrete. "Ya know, sometimes I look around this place an' see it jus' shuttin' down all ovah. An' I get lonesome lookin' at that an' havin' to sit in the quiet all the time. An' then I think ta myself: I bet this suits Tom Beaumont jus' fine."

"Yeah," said Tom. "I'm not proud of it, if that helps."

"Christ, I get it, guy. I'll keep the crittahs fed an' whatnot."

"Thanks."

"'Course. Ya goin' afoot?"

Tom looked around himself as if checking for another means.

"Ya wanna take my shotgun? Make me sleep bettah if ya took it."

"Too heavy. I'll bring a pistol if it's gonna keep you up nights."

"A'right. Gonna be cold out there."

"I'm human," Tom said. "I'll make fire. Hey," he pointed at the cot, "when Sharon wakes up, just tell her…"

"Ya went fishin'."

"Right. Thanks, Nev."

The sun wasn't high yet. It was likely six or so in the morning. Tom was wrapped in more layers than needed, but his pack was light, with just a few brown packages of smoked fish, some tackle, dry socks, a full canteen, and his 9mm. He took a short pole with a spinning reel, hefting it from one shoulder to the next as he walked, keeping it opposite his smoking hand. Tom walked west on Water Street until the green bridge, where he'd intended to turn north and make his way through Near Haven, then cross the river westward and go for the Hawksboro town line. He'd seek out the old schoolhouse, the town office—anything with a central location and a deep basement.

At the foot of the hill stood an old vine-cracked gas station, where Tom glanced in both directions and puffed his cigarette for a long interval. Without any real reason, he turned south and crossed the bridge. He would not go inland, but further down the peninsula, into the forgotten village of Olsens. Something pulled at him, as if the ocean wanted to keep him close.

The road, never well kept, was now so pockmarked and overgrown that Tom couldn't imagine an automobile navigating it at speed. A stretch he'd once shot across on Friday nights, cannonballing toward keggers and bonfires, rural-kid hedonism that could only be found in the dark woods. Tom remembered, or his body remembered, leaning into each turn as though the battered sedan would respond to a shift in weight like a motorbike. Snaking through that darkness with a slippery, demonic ease. The drag racing that inevitably followed meeting another young, cocksure motorist at the one stoplight in Olsens Center. That road no longer existed.

The path he now walked was only the remnant of something paved, grouted like a long mosaic with expanding grasses and moss. The blackberry vine that had once remained obediently outside the ditches now closed in so far as to leave only a four-foot clearing, a fleck of yellow paint showing weakly along its spine. Tom moved over and past two hills with skeletons of deciduous trees looming above. A wall of pine with dark, forlorn under-cavities, intermittently a birch or maple, sometimes highlighted red as leftover foliage fluttered in the upper branches, sparsely, like a gathering of cardinals. Tom saw a fox standing in the path. It remained still for several seconds, triangulating his position with its cockleshell ears, and then shot westward in a copper flash.

The road opened and there were pastures on either side. The interior of the peninsula was broad and windy, with a spine of small hills, dunes, furred in yellow straw. There had been horses here, once. He passed a property where the birds were all balanced on dead electric wires, the wires running the perimeter of a horse pasture and remaining taut in their rubber insulators atop an otherwise collapsing wooden fence. There'd been a chestnut mare and a true black stallion. Kids would pick up apples in the neighboring lot, and the horses would clop to the fence and take the ground-fruit from their hands—snorting plumes of vapor on a cold morning.

Fifty years prior, the farmers had used electric fences, too, but the insulators were ceramic instead of rubber. As a little kid he'd pulled one out of the backyard, a white insulator, his first archeological treasure. Neither Tom's mother nor his father could say what the object was. A teacher at the elementary school had finally enlightened him. At that age, half a century was an impossibly long time. Tom kept the insulator in a tin safe with a combination lock, and he imagined it having been used, once, by real cowboys to contain their animals—cowboys who chewed tobacco leaves and saddle-broke wild mustangs and killed other men thoughtlessly for small reasons. That world, of course, had never existed here, but New England had its own gritty palette of earth tones. It knew, by older examples, about the beauty of heartbreak and the tiny flame of sadness that inhabits all who are quiet.

No one had hayed this season. No one would likely go to the trouble. Maybe the horses had been sold to some pushover when money still meant a damn. No one lived here, now. Given over to hysteria, and they abandoned their plots. The horses, he thought, were most likely eaten. Or just left behind to starve.

He made camp on the east side of the peninsula, burning drift logs in a windbreak among the boulders. A grey-shingled farmhouse leaned forty degrees over the hilltop behind him, catching the weather in its glassless western wall and sheltering this tiny cove in its lee. Tom left his things on the beach and inspected the house, the floorboards absorbing his footsteps like wet paper. He found nothing inside, just jackknife inscriptions climbing the walls and a possum who dispassionately listened for his exit. Tom returned to the beach, building up his fire and collecting a bucket of mussels, shearing them away in clusters from the rocks.

The moon had taken on that jaundiced, close-hanging surrealism that made Tom's heart race when he was a boy, made him sweat in spite of the outer chill. It was the season of static electricity. It smelled of wood-hard apples and wind-ruffled hair. The air moved quick and dry with a brown-yellow-red mosaic of curled leaves scraping their stiffened edges over the stones, acorns raining incessantly with a brittle patter.

Tom hunkered down in his layers and tried to invite some affection for the world. He felt the granite against his back, still sun warm from the day. He felt his own epidermal crust of oil, salt, blood, and excrement. The grout of dander and soil in the seams of his clothes. There was wood smoke in his lungs. In so many ways, the objective reality he'd always sought was here. Only now, could he really taste the weather in his food or appreciate the intoxicating power of his lover's pheromones. He could understand that driving cars had once shaped his attitude toward sex and that light bulbs affected the way he walked. Money had made sunsets undesirable, once. Refrigerators nullified the seasons. Books and televisions and washing machines were all just filters, ways he had kept the world at a distance.

But the world, ignorant of these barriers, was still there.

III.

Talk not to me of blasphemy,
man; I'd strike the sun if it
insulted me.

—Herman Melville

~~177~~ 128

Tom carefully unfolded the map, its creases worn to parallel gaps in the paper. A tourist map of Fox County landmarks, like one might find in the lobby at the Chamber of Commerce. Bordered and interrupted with advertisements for fish 'n chips joints, historic inns, marine services. Stearns Fiberglass was on there, just beside the compass rose. "Afloat since 1952." Tom drew an X over another of his circled targets. After two months of fruitless break-ins, days spent carrying a wrought-iron crowbar in one hand and a collection of vague hopes in the other, his Xs now covered Walden, Hawksboro, Olsens, and Tea Harbor. His search moving roughly northward through the coastal towns, turning up little but exhaustion and the nagging anxiety that they'd been right.

There were no red phones.

Limekiln waited, its government centers circled and untried. Tom had saved the county seat for last, preserving his hope like fuel. The only town on the map that remained unmarked, entirely, was Near Haven.

Sharon walked ahead of him, the dog tugging anxiously on the rope she held. It was the German shepherd called Moose, and it was Tom's favorite, an old dog, strong in the shepherd role and alert. The dog used its oversized paws to pick a route through the glass-strewn back streets of Limekiln, ears swiveling on the slightest whisper and tongue lolling absently between high yellow teeth. After several blocks, Sharon unhooked its lead and let the dog move freely. If Moose noticed her lagging by more than about ten yards, the dog doubled back and turned circles until she was again at its side.

The afternoon light was waning and hundreds of crows were using the last of it to pick the streets clean of animate life. They knew the real freeze would come any time now, and their world would be altered profoundly for months. Tom shuffled along behind the woman and her dog, admiring their easy symmetry.

"I guess I just don't understand what you're doing," Sharon said without looking at him. "Breaking into public schools, town halls. I know you think there's some kind of grand design here, but..."

"Listen..."

"The boat's one thing. You loved your boss, and you're building a boat for him. I get that. But the rest of it, how can this shit even matter? You act as though you're going to *win*, somehow. As if there were anything to win."

"I just want to know what's real."

Sharon distanced herself from Tom and pretended to

concern herself with the dog. "Those men that died in the boatyard," she said eventually. "The fact that they'd have killed us, if not for being a pack of traitors. That's real."

"I've been reading about astronomy," he said.

Sharon kept walking.

"Fletcher's rock is what's called a 'periodic comet.' It has a fixed orbit around the sun, which it passes every one hundred and thirty-three years."

"Tom..."

"It's passed Earth over and over throughout history. We've been dancing with this thing for centuries, glimpsing it here and there when our orbits cross. The Chinese saw it in A.D. 122. And this guy Clarke in 1855. I've been reading an astronomer named Mint. He says the comet was rediscovered in '85 by a Japanese scientist named Tsuruhiko Koto. That's over a year before Fletcher."

"This shomee thing was sweet," Sharon said without warmth, "for a while. And if you want to believe it, if that helps you..."

"Mint did the math, Sharon, same as Fletcher claims. And the rock passes us again, in the spring. *Just passes by.* I mean, if you really knew when the end would be, don't you think you'd also have the wisdom not to tell? Hasn't that ever bothered you, the angle and timing of the report? Doesn't it all feel a little too intentional?"

"Of course, it bothers me, Tom! Fletcher's a prophet! Fletcher's a liar! Don't you see, though? Can't you just look around and realize that it *doesn't fucking matter anymore...*"

The shot struck her just above the elbow and buried itself in the crumbling stucco of an apartment complex behind them. Tom grabbed Sharon by the shoulders and threw her to the roadside, slipping in the wet refuse underfoot and coming down hard on his bad knee. They had to find some cover, but there was little. A rusty shopping cart and a telephone pole wouldn't do any good. Tom hadn't seen the shooter, and the dog was missing.

He saw a narrow alley between buildings that could have been a throughway or a total dead end. Either, Tom decided, was better than the open street. After a breath, he got to his feet and hauled Sharon up by her bleeding arm by mistake, thinking only of moving her.

"Tom!" she yelled, as another shot sounded and the slug glanced off his left shoulder blade.

"Fuck!" Tom managed to drag Sharon into the alley, despite his panicked stumbling, and pulled the .38 from her belt. She hooked her fingers into his sleeve and cried "No, goddammit!" trying to keep him planted in the alley. Tom tore loose and ran back out to the street.

Dusk had settled and his vision was poor in that world of grey tones and stained concrete. He scanned the street in both directions, squinting, seeing nothing. Tom began to question which direction the bullets had actually come from. He reached up and fired off a round, and the heavy Smith and Wesson pistol boomed menacingly between empty brick walkups. "Hey!" he screamed. Nothing. Almost nothing.

A distant growl, nearly too low to discern, drifted along the darkening street. "Moose!" Tom cupped his hands to amplify. *"Moose!"*

Three quick barks came in reply from the west, some three or four blocks away, and everything fell quiet, again. Tom followed the sound, looking back once, not knowing what to expect. Holding the gun at heart level, he wove his way through the rubble. His eyes caught a brief motion to his right, and he shot, startled again by the blast's echo in that narrow space and hearing in its wake only the angry chatter of a raccoon. Jesus, he thought, what if that had been the fucking dog?

Coming to a corner, Tom glanced down the street adjacent and saw several large green dumpsters in a row. A tall sapling had sprung up ironically through the cracked lid of the furthest container, and in the dusk light, he could just make out the shepherd's tail hung low on the far side.

"Moose?" Tom almost whispered, approaching slowly, both hands sweating on the pistol's grip. He could hear the dog's throaty rumble slipping out between jaws that sounded full with something.

The rifle caught his eye first, a lever-action Winchester repeater. It was still within the boy's grasp, but his hand lay limp, and he was unmoving, flat on the pavement. He wore a wool cap of hunter green and a thick rubber slicker. Outstretched legs looking like tent poles inside too-big denim pants. Tom kicked the gun away and the hand curled back on itself, fleshless as a dead spider. Tom had to kick the dog away as well, and then he saw the torn-up throat, the larynx punctured and collapsed. A pool had gathered beneath the boy's shoulders, as thick and dark as molasses. The kid's jaw showed teeth missing, and those that remained were bare to the roots. A ropey topography of burn scars covered half his face. They'd have made the kid harder to recognize, had Tom not been the one who put them there.

Robbie.

"Okay, Moose," he told the dog. "It's okay, bud," and Tom put a hand on Moose's arched spine. The dog whimpered and backed off, looking cowed, panicky.

"Oh, Christ. *Tom…*" Sharon stood there, holding her bleeding arm and looking down at the body. She slumped over and grabbed a hold of the agitated shepherd. The dog didn't seem to know what to make of the matter either, and its whining grew more insistent. Sharon stared at her shooter for a full minute in absolute silence. Then she growled. An uncanny animal sound that burned through her and issued from her snarled mouth. Sharon held the dog tighter and began to sob in a way Tom could never have imagined her doing.

"Hey," Tom said stupidly, pleadingly. He considered all the ways he wouldn't be telling her that this was his fault. That he'd killed three men on the deserted road when he likely could just as well have run. That, in the end, he'd run anyway.

"Christ, Tom. I'm fucking *pregnant*," she spat more than said, clutching the dog's neck ever tightly. "I'm fucking pregnant…"

His eyes welled up, and he opened his mouth but nothing came. Tom looked down, trying not to betray the strange exuberance he felt, his sudden, rushing pulse, and found himself knelt in a widening circle of blood.

~~128~~ 127

"Tom, this has nothing to do with Fletcher or your comet. This isn't about 'maybes.' This is about the world we live in, now. It doesn't matter if you're right or wrong."

"I think it does. It changes things. How we should make decisions. Having a future makes us responsible for that future."

"It's not the future that bothers me."

"So, what are you going to do?"

"I'll deal with it."

"Don't say it."

"There's a doctor who runs a clinic in Boston. Or she used to. I'm going to find out."

"Boston? But you're a doctor. And I want you to stay."

"I'm not that kind of doctor. And you don't get to choose, Tom."

On the black expanse of the cement flats, the temperature dropped below zero for the first time that year. Tom felt it on his lips, in the brittle foliage of his lungs. The air pressure, too, fell noticeably, and he wondered if he'd see snow tonight. There was little else to see. Somewhere high above him, a thick batting of clouds kept the night starless, and he navigated the road by sound, following his own metronomic crunch along the gravel. This darkness was his only protector as he slowly stitched a path across the flats, aching for the familiar womb of the boat shop and the unbiased company of a bottle. Tom kept half wary of vehicle lights coming out of the north, but they never did, and Sharon's words, instead, matched him step-for-step, crossing the Near Haven line and winding on toward the harbor.

There was blood streaked in long arcs across his bedding, muting the other older stains; he stared perplexed, until his memories aligned. Unable to bandage his shoulder, Tom had opted to put back six shots of liquor and simply lie down in his own ooze. The glass lay overturned on the concrete, vibrating with every pound at the door.

Tom crossed the cold floor with only a few steps and had the door flung open before his vision was clear. He meant to strike whoever he found on the other side. Two-Buckets stood there with a gaping look of fear and the grey hairs around his ears flew in the wind.

"T-t-thom!"

"What the *fuck* are you…"

"Tha…" he stuck an arm out and pointed at something behind him.

Tom realized that he'd answered the door stark naked. "Well, fuckin' spit it out, Wendell!" He stood upright and tried to look composed. Tom may have been embarrassed, but Two-Buckets was genuinely terrified. The mind behind those recalcitrant features frantically sought a way to communicate. The tinker simply couldn't speak it.

Tom looked past him to see the sky in the near distance lit up fire orange, haloing Two-Buckets' form like a painting of a saint. Great black smoke clots swam up to cover the morning stars.

"Oh, Christ. Come on, get in, get in…"

Tom dressed quickly, his multiple sweaters hanging limp over thin shoulders. He stood with his arms wrapped around them, watching the fire grow on the hill above. "We've gotta get up there, bud." Tom pulled on his work boots and cinched them tight around his ankles. "There's some shovels and things in that corner, in the back. I don't know what else to take…"

Two-Buckets sat exactly where he'd been left, trying to avoid eye contact and muttering half-statements to the air. "In tha pit, yuh… kept'ah in tha pit. Win done ah! Was tha win done ah, Thom…"

"What? What do you mean, 'the wind did it'?"

Two-Buckets looked to the rafters, chewed his teeth a bit. He pulled a sort of pout, a puffed-cheek, bottom-lip-thrust look that he affected to signify he was no longer speaking. It was enough to make Tom spit.

Main Street, where the fire began, looked like a newsreel

of someone else's tragedy—Dresden in Technicolor. What had already burnt out lay black and smoldering in right-angled skulls of brick. Further south, the blaze was still alive and moving quickly along the street. If anyone was trapped within those buildings, Tom would never find them soon enough.

He wrapped Two-Buckets' threadbare scarf around the tinker's face, as many turns as he could stretch it, to keep him from inhaling the ubiquitous smoke. He warned his friend to keep low, but all that could be heard was the wind and the odd, empty roar of consumption by fire.

Tom peered into the blackness that lay north of them and tried to understand how the fire had evolved. At the intersection of Beechwood Street and Main was an office block, the darkest and coldest looking of all the remains. He assumed it began there, maybe hours before. Behind that block was a parking lot, and beside the lot, Two-Buckets had kept himself a squat since autumn began, back where the wind didn't bite so much and close to the road. His makeshift home occupied a ground-level office, behind an old wheelchair ramp that used to lead to the bank. And tucked inside that dilapidated limb of woodwork and rusting screws, Two-Buckets kept his fire pit. The wind had done her, alright. The wind carried Two-Buckets' cooking fire against these standing relics, and they gave in to it like a mile of kindling in the parched winter air.

Tom thought of Bradford, who's most recent home was a big forgotten two-bedroom above the pharmacy. Now just a scorched hole in the brickwork.

"Bradford!" he called in the empty street. Tom picked up

his shovel and paced through the ashes, shouting, "Bradford! *Bradford!*" The pharmacy had collapsed into itself, beam work lying aslant and barricading the door. "Goddammit, Neville! Where are you?"

Bradford wasn't dead. Absolutely not consumed by smoke in his sleep and incinerated where he lay. He was kicking around somewhere, cursing this night, looking for a tender throat to maim in retribution. But he certainly wasn't dead. Tom could feel him. There were tangible waves coming off his hulk as he cursed and spat in the cold, windy street. Bradford had a way of sinking into things. The sidewalk he'd trodden seemed to retain memories of his heavy feet, as though it were made of sponge. He effortlessly existed where others struggled. He was immune to destruction. Timid like a cannonball. *"NEV!"*

Tom tightened the handkerchief over his mouth and took off at a run, ignoring his stiff knee and the thinning air, south toward the prison as the fire itself had moved. Ahead of him, the darkness was rent by limbs of flame blowing eastward against the buildings on the far side of the street. Fist-sized embers roved in schools through the blackened rusty skeletons of automobiles. Embers flew before his eyes and dazzled him, etching neon trails over his vision.

He scanned each building for inner movement as he ran the width of it. When he came to an intact windowpane he smashed it immediately with the shovel blade and yelled Bradford's name, the sound inevitably torn from his lips by the infernal vacuum. The further he went, the less he could see, and soon the fire was consuming too much air for him to breathe at all. Tom beat his shovel against the pavement, a tiny sound like glasses clinking in a hurricane, sobbing with fury, and then turned back.

Two-Buckets was half-heartedly scraping at coals and beating them out on the pavement when Tom reached him. The fire would burn until the wind died or the whole town was consumed. "Thom?" he said.

"Yeah."

"Canna go home?"

Tom just stared past him. He couldn't meet the vagrant's eyes, didn't trust himself to be as big a person as the situation demanded. He pulled the rag off his mouth and took a few breaths, smoke and all.

Two-Buckets glanced about himself at the smoking remains of buildings, his face struck through with a kind of wonder, as though he didn't know where he was. It was possible that he didn't. It was possible, also, that he didn't understand his own culpability in all of this.

Tom fleetingly imagined himself smashing in Two-Buckets' skull with his shovel.

"Yeah, bud," Tom said. "We can go home."

Two-Buckets stood so close to the shop door that Tom thought the old tinker was fixing to leave. But he didn't move, just hovered there and tried not to make eye contact. Tom approached him very slowly and put a hand on his back. "Hey, bud."

The man didn't take a step. He stood in place, facing the door and shifting his considerable weight from one foot to the next. A part of Tom had always been nervous about what might happen when this enormous child lost his temper in a time of stress. Tom felt a lump in his throat now, not knowing what might come. If Two-Buckets had gotten it in his mind to do so, he could have knocked Tom senseless.

"Wendell," he said. "You need to stay here, at least for tonight. It's freezing out there." Tom motioned toward a space on the floor by the stove, indicating that he'd make him a bed there. Two-Buckets followed his extended hand with his eyes and then finally looked at Tom directly. There was a red smear of moisture rimming each of those wide white orbs, and his lip was trembling. Two-Buckets felt an unbearable guilt, and Tom thought: what do you call the moment of noticing another's awareness? He wondered how many times he'd undervalued this person's intellect.

With his arms limp at his sides, Two-Buckets shuffled to the spot Tom had shown him and lay down on the bare concrete. Tom sighed and went to fetch some bedding, and rolled Two-Buckets over as he lay in an odd open-eyed catatonia.

Tom restoked the fire and fell to the cot where he would be asleep within minutes.

The accumulated smoke and ash on their clothes, the two of them, put a stink of sulfur through the air of the shop. Neither of them noticed until the white dawn came, a twenty-inch snowfall barricading them within, and this scent hung around as a cold acrid reminder.

~~127~~ 100

1988 fell on Near Haven like a white curtain, its first snow arriving as a two-day blizzard that entombed all evidence of the fire, and carried on in periodic squalls for the duration of that month. If anything more damnable than famine or despair had dared the snowdrifts and fallen trees along U.S. Route One, then it had quit before stumbling over town limits. The harbor froze completely in early January, and the pack ice wouldn't break up or roll out to sea until April. No more trade boats came calling, no traffic of any kind from the outer world. Those sloops or yachts still moored in the static river lay crazy-angled, time-stopped, their masts like absurd cocktail swords pinning them to the ice.

It seemed that the skin of his cheeks was chafing closely against his teeth. Tom lifted his shirt reluctantly, if ever, and there was a scant bit of muscle to be found. He was wintering without canned goods. Without any livestock, save for the chickens, and they wouldn't begin laying again for months. He would not eat the chickens.

The hunger would ramp up in the morning and gnaw for several hours, eventually subsiding around noon and giving way to a profound, aching emptiness. He would spend the remaining daylight working on his boat, hand brushing a gel coat over the finished glasswork or planing lumber for the build-out in spring. By evening, though, it had become hunger once more. Some nights he fell asleep just letting it be hunger. It took hours to fall asleep this way.

The thermometer outside had a round face, like a pound scale in a fish market. Its black needle lay dead to the left-hand side as though broken, even below the hash mark labeled "0." The instrument's maker had evidently felt as Tom did: those degrees below zero were useless figures. None were offered; the needle merely gestured toward an infinity of null space.

Even before stepping outside, he could hear the tree trunks moaning, threatening to snap. The sap in their veins might as well have been glass. Toward the shore, the grasses were wind-flattened, and pockets of snow crusted over the low parts. Tom crunched through to check his crab pots. The lines that tied them were cemented to the ground and buried, tunneling out into the water where a chunky band of rime separated the shore from the pack. He wondered how far the ice stretched.

He remembered Limekiln harbor freezing over in the past. One could walk across it, clear to Osprey Head, though it probably hadn't happened in decades. There were photographs from bygone ages, black-and-whites on Eastman film, of men driving Ford pickups right out over the water. The trucks, with their bowed steel mantles, all appeared to be matte black and identical, but could have been green or maroon or navy. The pictures left that much up to the viewer. Used to be, earlier still, that families relocating their homes would put entire houses on skis and drag them from one peninsula to the next with draft horses and men tugging at ropes. Whole enterprises predicated on the stability of ice.

He could tell by the calm and the cold that there would be precipitation again. He could smell it on the air. Tom reeled two pots in to shore and found nothing in them but the bait he'd placed there yesterday. He thought to change it for fresh, but decided it didn't matter. The rock crabs had long ago moved out to warmer water, and it seemed he was only wasting fish by baiting these pots in winter. He pulled in the other three pots, threw their bait sacks to the gulls, and coiled each rope in turn. As Tom walked back to the shop with the dripping crab gear slung over his shoulder, a thin and grainy snow began to fall.

Hunting around in vain, looking for stashed nonperishables in the far end of the shop, he came across a mesh dipnet hanging on a nail. Somebody had bought it years before for catching smelt or alewives, but he doubted it had ever seen use. The sticker left behind where a pricing gun once licked its handle said, "$2.99." Tom held the thing up in the light, wondering if he was desperate enough to give it a try.

Abel's old neoprene waders slid on stiffly. Two sweat shirts and a Grundens jacket. A wool hunting cap and lobstering gloves. He stuck the net in a clean, white bucket and made his way to the river mouth.

The cloud layer had broken when noon came, and there was little breeze. A distilled, sterile, motionless winter day. Tom walked slowly in the bulky waders, like a rookie astronaut in some humiliating training exercise. His boots crunched in the top crust of last week's snowfall, and the net handle bumped flatly inside its bucket. Tom removed one glove to smoke a cigarette, and soon his knuckles were blue and cracking. The hairs in his nostrils froze together into an itchy, distracting bristle.

The river was a mosaic of floating bergs with slushy edges. They bumped against one another and rose and fell and occasionally made a hollow groaning sound like wood. Tom followed a narrow and snowed-over footpath under the bridge and to the water's edge. He waded out until the water lapped at his torso, having to pole the floating ice out of the way with his net handle. Pressure sucked the neoprene waders tightly against his body, the temperature of the water instantly apparent, but he seemed to be staying dry. After a few minutes, he could tell, strangely, that the water was slightly warmer than the air. Tom felt an unexpected coziness—a contentment that stayed him in his place for an unrecalled amount of time, eyes closed and slowly breathing.

The current slid around him, and he felt it must be carrying something with it, but the first passes with the net yielded nothing. Ice chunks and dead winter flotsam, brown and sopping. He passed the net again, very slowly, letting the water fill it and billow it out, and came up with a living glimmer of hope:

a single fish stuck slantwise in the meshing. Tom pulled it up, dripping, and set the net on a nearby floe, carefully spreading the material. There was his fish, tiny and silvered and big-eyed. A shad or a minnow or a smelt, but no more than two inches long. Lively as hell. It flipped itself around the ice like a chrome jumping bean, until Tom firmly seized its hard wriggling body with two bare fingers and returned it to the water.

Tom dipped the net again and again. Slowly, like waving a flag in a thick, resistant dream. With the current, then against it, then crosswise. Everything about him, even his thoughts, torpid with the cold weight of the river. He brought up fish, larger fish, in twos and threes. None of them more than a hand's length, but all quick and shimmering and alive. He collected them in his bucket, giving them a gallon or two of the water from which they'd been pulled.

Hours went by, and not once did the hint of a melody or a cross thought or a happy one enter Tom's mind. Only the sounds of the river, most of them small, and others simply spread so thin as to seem it. He breathed in and out. He stopped once or twice to smoke, his gear bobbing around on separate ice floes as if hanging in zero gravity, not moving and not still, Tom with his elbow in his hand and looking out on the whole scenario. Alone for now, but perhaps not forever.

He'd never asked for fatherhood, but the notion settled squarely within him. He thought of Sharon's qualities and his own, mixed in a person who could be better than either of them, who would outlast them both. Tom didn't need to conceptualize or abstract Sharon's pregnancy to give it meaning; he felt the weight of it in his actions, heard its implication between the clauses of his own thoughts.

Maybe Sharon would hear it, too.

The sun fell quickly behind Main Street's redbrick row, days being at their shortest, the solstice had just passed. The afternoon had more dusk than daylight, and few colors could hold up to this kind of lighting. The bricks, to Tom's eyes, looked convincing, but the flaking blue paint of a doorframe or the dumpster-green in the periphery of his vision all shrank behind themselves and forfeited to the grey tones. A world like a black-and-white film that some distractible colorist had set herself to briefly, but abandoned.

He leaned his weight into the sled rope, picking through soot-coated remains of buildings and searching mostly for firewood. Pounds of framing beams and table legs and chair rungs and whatnot all piled above the sled's metal runners, pulling stubbornly through the top crust. There were very few footprints here after the last snowfall. When Tom did notice traces of humanity in the alleys or parking lots, it was like finding a gum wrapper on the moon. He paused to stare at a boot print for so long that his eyes crossed. Tom left one next to it, in reply, and went on.

What had been Jameson's Grocery when he was a kid, then Near Haven Grocery, was now just a snowy dark wind tunnel with no doors and a collapsed ceiling that lay in sections over the deli case and soda coolers. The place looked like it had been shelled. Tom threaded himself carefully through the doorway, over brick fragments and toothy glass edges. A crow exploded from somewhere within. The wind had pushed snow drifts through the Main Street entrance and clear to the back door, the snow moving in snaky ripples, cross-hatched with the asterisk tracks of birds. The shelves were bare but for frost, droppings, and ash. A sandwich list lay on the floor in a broken laminate board, hand painted by a child, maybe a teenage girl. A human leg with a tennis shoe fastened to it stuck out from under this.

He lifted the plywood sign, or the half of it that broke away, and threw it into a corner. Everything eeked as he pulled at the solid, frozen mass. The leg, already visible in stained blue coveralls, was joined by a curled hand, lilac in color. Tom had known that he was looking at a dead man for several minutes, but he suddenly let out a small childish noise—a whimper of recognition and no one to hear it.

Not even Two-Buckets.

Tom pulled up the other half of the signboard and looked down at him for a while. Several hot tears fell and perforated the snow at his feet before Tom noticed that he was crying. Two-Buckets was asleep. That is, he was in the position of a sleeping person, as if he'd crawled under the refuse and curled himself up against the cold, but it got him anyway, and there he'd died—sleeping.

Tom wondered if it even occurred to Wendell that he was dying, if he'd maybe dreamt of death, or if the process of dying had woken him. His mouth was open and pale, and his nose was blue, and his eyes were pinched tight and crusted with frost. The hood of his sweatshirt pulled up over his ears and his right hand held close to the face, like an infant. He looked *perfect.* Just Two-Buckets, infantile, lying there frozen. As if, with a warming god-hand, Tom could have simply woken him.

He rested the sign where it had lain and weighted it with bricks, a measure to keep the birds off until he could return. Tom sat for a while in the entrance, letting his own extremities go numb and watching the last light drain from the sky. He eventually gathered himself, wrenched the sled runners out from their frozen ruts, and angled his salvage back toward Stearns.

The metal runners made a jilting racket on the dry concrete floor, and blackened ends of kindling toppled as Tom hauled the sled across his threshold. Two lamps were already burning, the windows fogged with warmth. A snow-crusted army duffel lay conspicuously by the woodstove, sizzling as it dried.

"Jeez Christ, bud. Got a wicked haul there, ain't cha?" Bradford said, emerging from the back of the shop. His face was ruddy with whatever he'd been doing. His sleeves were rolled, his hands blackened. Bradford inspected the heap of firewood, poking around in the table legs and wainscoting. "I'll be damned if that ain't my fuckin' breakfast nook..."

"You son of a bitch..." Tom whispered. He hooked a wiry arm around the bigger man's neck and locked him in a chokehold embrace. "You stupid son of a bitch..."

"A'right, Tommy," Bradford said quietly. "I'm a'right." He held Tom at arms length and tried to shake a grin out of him. "This prob'ly don't need sayin', but you ain't lookin' quite healthy."

"Fuck," said Tom, wishing there was a way to skip past the truth. Just for the night. "Two-Buckets is dead."

"Dead! Oh, he ain't eithah, the old mongrel."

"He holed up inside Jameson's market and froze. I found him this afternoon. He's dead."

"Jesus, Tom."

Bradford put his hands in his pockets, moving toward the woodstove as though he might stoke the fire, but walked back in the same moment and sat down. Tom uncapped the last bottle of whiskey and poured equal measures of it into unwashed coffee mugs. He took a sip and then plucked a spider carcass from his cup. Bradford had a length of dowel in his hands and was busy cutting inchoate runes into the thing with a utility knife. For a while, they just let this be. Any observer would understand that the two men were keeping a sort of vigil.

Tom held the bottle out over Bradford's cup and noticed his blackened hands. "What have you been at all afternoon?" His voice felt rude in the quiet.

Bradford passed a hand over his face and grumbled, as though he didn't want to say. It left a greasy black mark on his brow and cheek. His jeans, also, were caked with grease and wood dust. "Well…" he began. He gestured vaguely toward the back of the shop. "I been workin' on ya boat, Tommy."

Tom smacked shut the latrine door and ran back to the shop, a worn pair of leather moccasins between his skin and the slick crust of ice that had consumed the boatyard many weeks before. He stood on the doormat and said, "Fucking *Christ*," through his teeth as he rubbed his palms and shivered. Bradford leaned over their bathing tub, about to test the water with his index finger and already all but disrobed. Tom considered how strange it was to see Bradford's ribs showing in the pale morning light. He could only imagine what he must look like through Bradford's eyes.

"Eee, shit. She's screamin' hot, guy. Y'll wanna wait a minute."

The only bathing option was heating a metal tub full of snow or ice atop the cast-iron stove, and sponging it over themselves. They decided to forgo modesty and share the hot water, after the effort of producing it. Tom felt ready to strip down and just drown himself in the simmering brown pot. A thought crossed his mind that a warm death is preferable to a cold one.

He'd gone a sleepless night on the production floor weighing dead-end thoughts like this one.

Bradford opened a brown paper package the size of a baseball and revealed the amorphous yellow lump within. It was soap, unperfumed and handmade using whatever rendered fat was on hand. An old crone living far down the St. George Peninsula made the stuff, and took most any kind of food in exchange for it. A strange thing to wash oneself with, frightening as it was to contemplate its origins. Tom pictured a kindling bin of assorted frozen mammal parts. Some of them primate.

Tom peeled off his grimy layers, leaving them in a pile to deal with later, and felt cool air bite into his shoulder. Robbie's bullet had left a nasty red scorch mark, but hadn't let much blood in the end. Bradford gave a raised eyebrow and made to ask about the wound, but Tom waved off the question. "It's nothing," he mumbled.

"Y'okay?"

"Yeah."

Tom's stiff fingers loosened in the heat rising from their bathwater. He loaded a sponge and wrung it out several times over his knotted hair, feeling the grease and blood and parasites swept away from his scalp. He soaped the sponge and dug the frothy mass of it into his eye sockets, behind his ears. The sinew of his neck unclenched after weeks of strain. Dirty water splashed the concrete floor and rose steaming within the halo of the woodstove's radiance.

"'Cause ya don't seem okay."

Tom held his eyes closed and turned slowly in place, keeping the water coursing over him. The heat on his skin only illustrated the narrowness of the body within it. He didn't care how small he might look to Bradford. He briefly wished that Bradford would hit him, standing there pale and naked, just for something tangible to address. "Sharon's pregnant. Has been for a while."

Bradford threw his sponge into the aluminum basin and said, "Fa real?"

"That's what she says. She'd know." Tom scraped at his navel, down to the mat of his pubic hair. He opened his eyes, looked down at his feet.

"How is she?"

"I mean, there's no future in her mind. It terrifies her. It's one thing to accept that you're going to die, but…"

"You ain't given'er ya whole shomee song an' dance?"

This wasn't put nicely. "Yeah, we've been over and over it. In Sharon's opinion, I'm just being naïve. That's as far as I can get with her. I've told her everything I know. I don't have anything else to say, to convince her."

They stood there, soap spatters falling intermittently from their elbows and testicles, smacking the concrete. Neither spoke for a time. Bradford plucked his sponge out of the water, wrung it out, and just held it. "Whatta ya think she'll do?"

"I'm trying not to think."

"Whatta *you* wanna do?"

Tom reached out and jerked his stringy towel down from its nail. It was a changed world. Sharon was right about that.

It wasn't as though they could just pick up where they'd left off. He could barely feed himself. With every long winter night came the very real danger of freezing. Tom stood there, toweling at the channels between his ribs. His hope had never felt more ridiculous than it did in that moment. Yet there it was; a pathetic little light within him flickered toward the future. And Sharon was in it; she was part of that future. Tom was sure it existed. "I want to keep it," he said finally. "I want to keep everything."

"Ya sure he's still in there?"

"Yeah, Nev. Pretty sure." They stood outside the market in the high-noon sun.

"Well, guess I'll jus' go an' check…"

Bradford was gone for maybe three minutes. Tom heard some uncomfortable coughing sounds from within the building. He stood there with his shovel, looking out over the empty street, hoping to see even a dog. Bradford returned in a hurry, squinting down the light and dabbing his nostrils on a coat sleeve.

"'Kay. Let's dig."

They couldn't actually dig into the ground, as the ground was frozen solid. But there was a small lot next to the market where Two-Buckets had often camped in summer, just a postage-stamp yard of wildflower that nobody seemed to own or care much about. They would excavate a patch in the snow here and inter the tinker under a mound of gathered bricks. It would have to do.

Bradford took off his coat and rolled up his sleeves, while Tom shed his stocking cap, his still-damp shag of black hair steaming as the temperature rose above freezing. The snow pack threw sun warmth back at their faces, but insulated everything beneath, and their shovelheads rebounded from the soil in jilting, ringing retorts.

Tom stopped, lodging his shovel in a bank and wiping at his eyes. "It's the glare," he explained when Bradford glanced up.

"Yuh, I know." Bradford kept digging.

Together they brought the sled into the market, and together they laid the body on it. Tom lined the hole they'd dug with a thick woolen blanket, the same he'd been given for a gallon of lamp fuel in the fall. They bore the body up in silence and transferred it to this unlikely spot of amenity within the snow. The men were unable and unwilling to try and pull Two-Buckets out of his fetal curl, and so they would bury him in this child's pose, swaddled in clean, dry wool. They closed the fabric over him, leaving only a flap of gumless sneaker-sole exposed to the daylight and their own considerations of its significance.

Tom smoked, listening to the tap of Bradford's pick against the masonry of a brick façade. Bradford thought it useful and fitting to demolish a portion of the grocery store, freeing its material for this more relevant purpose. Some time passed, a few muffled curses, and then the charge blew. Tom heard a brief cascade of clinking ceramic and then walked into the dust cloud to help Bradford gather the bricks. The men took turns hauling and stacking, building a rough and rust-colored cairn over the grave. More and more bricks came, as though they didn't know how to stop, and soon the tomb they'd built looked like a giant slept within it. They built as if this thing of sheer mass could somehow balance the loss. They had to be certain, in their own secular way, that whatever magic was to be had in a burial, held fast to the burial in their charge.

Tom leaned on the shovel, looking over the finished mound. "We oughta mark it, somehow."

Bradford thought about this for a time, considering the materials on hand. "A'right," he said, "gimme a minute."

He disappeared behind the market for a while, and Tom busied himself with collecting odd fragments of brick to reinforce their work. Bradford returned, carrying the handlebars of Two-Buckets' flat-tired ten-speed. He selected a spot and stabbed the fork down into the frozen earth, driving it firm with the back of a shovel. Bradford stepped back and glanced at Tom for a ruling.

"Hold on," Tom told him. He walked away and came back with a cigarette pinched between his lips and a white plastic bucket in each hand. He hung these, one and then the other, from the recurved horns of the grave marker.

These open vessels, now posted on a high flat place above Main Street, seemed to be asking for alms. Tom and Bradford turned their coat pockets inside out, finding small tokens to leave. A matchbook and a fishing license. A periwinkle shell. A pocketknife. A Bicentennial quarter. Should the man who lay resting here somehow wake, arriving at some implausible new reality beyond death, he'd at least have this small collection to remind him where he'd been.

Having barely spoken through the hours they'd worked, Bradford now put a hand on Tom's shoulder and said, "A'right?"

"Yeah," Tom replied. "Okay."

~~99~~ 95

He first heard one blast, sounding off somewhere very near the shop, and then a second. Tom ignored these, working his hand-plane repeatedly over an oak burl, grinding at the hard brown anomaly like a nutmeg clove. He'd begun filing down lumber even before the sun started its shallow arc over the river, working in lieu of breakfast, working alone. Shavings piled thick on the floor as another blast rang out, and then shortly, the door opened and in walked Bradford. With one hand he held the shotgun, while in the other hung the dripping and mangled remains of a gull.

"Ah, Christ, Nev…"

"Well?" Bradford said uncharitably. "We'd 'bout starve on your convictions," and he went about cleaning and dressing the bird.

"We'd be fools to eat the hens. They'll lay again, come spring."

"Come spring!" Bradford swung the kindling hatchet repeatedly, his third pass dropping the big yellow-billed head to the concrete. "Come fuckin' spring, he says..."

When a rubbery pan-fried leg eventually came his way, its webbed foot still attached, Tom couldn't get up the nerve. He just scowled, recalling a mental image of Coleridge's albatross, and cut up his portion for the cats.

Bradford hadn't spoken more than a handful of words since the burial, even as a new storm front battered the coast and drove the two of them into close quarters. He grew particularly volatile on the subjects of food and drink, complaining of an ambiguous hurt in his guts and pacing the boat shop like a circus tiger, dull-eyed but quick to strike.

Even stoned as a scarecrow, Bradford's eyes had always been bright. They were half the reason why anyone had ever trusted or befriended him in this life. And constantly, sometimes bafflingly, he laughed. It had driven Tom halfway to violence, often, trying to reason or communicate with this creature of seemingly inexhaustible laughter.

All this seemed more and more just a memory, as Tom realized he'd been watching Bradford age, from very little distance, and failed to note the change. He'd been gazing inward, only concerned with his own resilience, as tragedies piled high and Fletcher's date drew closer. Bradford had been such a regular champion, had been holding him upright for so long that Tom seldom looked back at his brother to see that he, too, was trapped in this same god-awful hamster's wheel of sunrises.

In the afternoon, palms blistered from working the brass handle of the plane all morning, Tom walked several miles along the north shore to get away from those four walls and the smell of raw wood. He spent some daylight jacking open car hoods with a crowbar, looking for any batteries that still held a charge. Eventually his digital multimeter died, its own batteries having given out. He imagined a hollow, sardonic laughter as the numbers faded from its waterlogged screen.

Tom crossed under the train trestle while the incoming tide crept up through the ice sheet and covered the flats. Two-Buckets' old hen-cooking pit mutely greeted him, the circle of stones holding a few inches of fresh, white snow.

As he left the shadow of the trestle, Tom found the shore ahead littered with gulls. A dozen or more of them scattered at random, the blood matting their white feathers, showing garishly in the cold light. He walked carefully through the massacred flock, grimly noting each bird. A herring gull, its breast loaded with shot, lying in a tidal pool with a wing raised in odd salute. A couple of ringbills, their speckled bodies ripped open and leaking guts. A great blackback, crumpled and undignified as a swatted fly. Very soon, the ocean would take each of these in its chill grip and carry them off with the rest of the day's leavings. Bradford had maybe thought his mess would be tidied in this way, before anyone stumbled across it.

Tom came at last to a tiny mottled grey thing, a yearling or whatever the term. The bird had tumbled out of the sky after a cloud of buckshot tore past and vaporized its left wing. To his horror, it lifted its head and fixed a pair of unblinking yellow eyes on Tom as he approached. It had bled heavily and was left with no energy to kick its way across the smooth wet stones of the beach.

Tom kneeled over the gull, reaching out a finger to stroke its bill, to test the soft grey filaments that insulated its throat. The gull breathed rapidly, but made no effort to avoid his touch.

"God damn you, Neville," he said quietly, as he reached behind and put his fingers on a round lump of quartzite granite. "You can't just come apart on me like this…"

In one quick motion, Tom smashed the bird's skull.

He pushed the door tight within its frame and stood there for a moment, feeling his frozen skin burning against the glow of the woodstove, and kicked the packed snow from his boots. The tools in his rucksack clanged together as he dropped his things on the floor. Tom pulled off his gloves and poured a mug of the pine tea that simmered on the stove.

"Hey, Nev."

There was no response.

Tom rolled a cigarette and wondered how many of these he might actually have left. Could be eighty-something, could be twenty-something. He tried not to worry about it and opened the stove door, lit the papery end of his cig in the leaping flame. "Nev?" he said, still not having looked up to check that Bradford was actually in the room.

Bradford sat under a lantern with a book in his hands. He held the thing so closely beneath his nose that Tom, who'd never caught him reading, thought he might be going far-sighted in his early-middle years. "Neville."

Bradford finally laid the book open on his knees and adjusted the little red ribbon that hung from its binding. Tom noticed the delicacy that Bradford effected to do this. "Ho, Tommy."

"So," Tom began, eyeing the book. "I think I got a line on fifty pounds of chicken feed today. Harlan says it's still good, kept it in dry storage."

"Yuh?" said Bradford, distractedly. "Well, 'at's good, then."

"Also, Harlan's alive."

"Yuh."

"No batteries, though."

"No. S'pose not."

"I was thinking. You know, there's a lot of good soil on this bank, between here and the trestle. Maybe we should keep our eyes out for some vegetable seed. I don't know much about planting, but you grew all that dope out past Sawyersville that one year."

Bradford sighed, rubbing at the bridge of his nose.

"Saw you've been doing a little sport shooting down there."

He looked at Tom for a moment and then simply said, "Yuh."

"You got anything to say about that?"

He didn't.

Tom nodded at the book in Bradford's lap. "There's no answers in there. Not to any relevant question, anyway."

"Yuh? Why's it here, Tom?"

"Know thy enemy?" Tom put his hands against the hot cast-iron stove. "I'm really not sure."

"*And the Lord saw that the wickedness of man was great in the earth,*" Bradford quoted, "*and that every imagination of the thoughts of his heart was only evil continually.* Sound's 'bout spot on, don't it?" Bradford kept his eyes on the page and Tom noticed the heaviness of their lids, the reluctant tears glimmering in lamplight. "Ain't we been wicked, Tom? I get it—you don't believe in no god, but ya can't tell me we ain't wicked. God knows I got blood on my hands..."

"You can't blame yourself for that. That's what makes a priest's job so easy—we're always ready to blame ourselves for what we can't control. You mean Cadwgan? You mean those fucking savages that killed my parents? Did they give us a better choice?"

"It ain't always about choice. Oh, but look who I'm talkin' to. Tom Beaumont, master of 'is own private universe. Ya think ya can choose a world without God. Ya can choose ta outlive the rock. Everythin's up ta *you*, because *you know*. Well, I don't see what makes yer opinion so much bettah than this," and Bradford shook the Bible at him, moisture now carving through the dirt and stubble that masked his features. A man willing to give in, finally, to the temptation of drowning.

"But I don't!" Tom's voice boomed in the cavernous shop. They didn't have to agree. He simply needed to believe that his real, living bond with Bradford was stronger than the story. "That's the whole point—*I don't know*. I embrace my not-knowing. And yes, I'll cast fucking aspersion on anyone who speaks for God, because the man who claims to know the mind of God has an agenda." He backed away from the stove, suddenly blistering with his own heat. "Who would you rather believe? Val Gilbert? Fucking Daniel Fletcher? I'm not saying I'm right, Neville. I'm just saying that *they're not right either*, and there's a *motive* behind their words."

Tom spat on the floor and took a drag, as though he'd said his piece, but he was still burning through it. The endless, unconsummated rage of fighting faith with reason. "Even if some god decided to recall all Creation three months from now, what's the point of knowing it? Why live your life any differently? We're all gonna die someday, Nev." Tom looked at his friend, and found the flat resignation of his own youth in Bradford's eyes. "Please, don't let some ideologue tell you you're already dead."

Bradford set the book down on the concrete, same as the kindling and spent bottles and cigarette ash. He put those big red hands over his face and just let a few breaths pass. Hands that had built and destroyed and rebuilt but could never make things right. "I ain't sure I want 'em ta be wrong anymore, Tommy," he said, hardly louder than the wind outside the brittle windows. "Sometimes it feels like tha best thing this world can do is end."

~~95~~ 94

Where morning led them, the world might as well have ended already.

The feeling of suspension—of banishment to a blank, white purgatory—closed in on each man, not long after stepping onto the ice. A brume of storm clouds had moved in and settled windlessly over Near Haven that morning, snow falling steadily from the featureless sky and reducing visibility to a stone's throw. Surveying in a broad circle, Tom failed to locate the shore, though he knew it to be less than a hundred yards from where he now tugged an empty sled over the frozen expanse of the harbor.

"We could die out here," Tom said, his voice dissipating into the cottony space between them. "I lost Stearns already."

"We could die at Stearns," Bradford answered.

"They'd never find us. The ice would go out in spring, and we'd go with it."

Tom followed Bradford's boot prints, wondering how quickly these were being erased behind them as the storm bore down. Beneath the snow, a layer of sea ice—four inches thick at most—kept them from plunging into the lightless fathoms. Even unladen, the wooden sled pulled along reluctantly, its runners bogged in slush. Tom leaned his weight into the effort.

"She's probably been ransacked already."

Bradford had been quiet all morning and remained so, feeling out a path to the *Nunavut* by dead reckoning. Whatever was left onboard the trade ship, they could only hope it would be enough to see them through these snowbound weeks. Bradford responded to Tom's comment only by pointing toward something ahead.

Tom squinted after the gesture, trying to pierce the semi-solid atmosphere and his own breath hanging opaque before him. After another dozen paces, a queer bright orb started to materialize: the *Nunavut*'s orange mooring ball, floating high enough to have been frozen above the flat plane of the harbor. Bradford's gait quickened once this beacon was clear, and Tom found himself struggling behind, cursing the sled, terrified at how swiftly his companion's silhouette faded into the white.

"Watch the ice!" Tom yelled, trying to do the same. He pushed harder against the pain flaring in his knee and withered muscles of his back.

"I see 'er, Tom..." Bradford's voice carried back, as though from much greater a distance. "She's layin' on 'er beams, but she's dry..."

"Slow-up a little, Bradford."

Bradford didn't slow, but rather hastened his approach

to the ice-locked ketch, its main- and mizzen-masts stuck at a precarious thirty degrees to the horizon—her exposed hull as imposing on the terrain as a dead whale. Bradford turned, making for her port side, running along the *Nunavut*'s buried gunnel to where her companionway opened like a window in the midship deck, but didn't get that far. Suddenly, like a trick of the eye, he was gone.

"Bradford?" Tom stopped only long enough to realize what had happened, and then broke into a flat run.

"NEV!"

The air swallowed his cries. It seemed this environment would simply consume whatever deigned to cross it.

"FUCK! NEVILLE!"

The breach in the ice was small, maybe ten feet wide, and within it floated a pack of rime and fresh snow which had rendered the hole invisible. Bradford grabbed at this flotsam instinctually, clawing at the edges of the hole but finding no purchase on its wet rim. His parka and boots were clearly soaked, hanging like sandbags from his limbs, and as he thrashed, Tom watched the black water open around him, easing his way down into the void.

"Tom!" he gasped once and then submerged.

Tom stopped himself from moving toward the hole, instead turning away to find something, anything, to serve for an anchor. The orange mooring ball glowed from under its snowcap, three or four yards from where he stood. There was a very slight rise in the ice, where the mooring line lay embedded, tethering the ball to the ship itself. Tom dove on it, hacking at the ice with his gutting knife, slicing through the rope and tearing the shipward end free. He bound it with a square knot to the sled rope and kicked the sled backward. It shot over the trampled snow, drawing the ship's line taut and stopping with its runners hung just inches over the hole.

"NEV!"

Bradford was tiring fast, barely keeping his nostrils above the debris-strewn surface of the breach. He turned, red-eyed, toward the sound of Tom's shouting and then swam heavily for the sled. Grunting hoarsely through the pain and exhaustion, Bradford laced his cold-stiffened fingers through the metal rungs and held them.

Tom grabbed the rope, tight as a piano wire, and dug his heels. He pulled with every tendon and muscle of his emaciated body. He pulled with every fiber of him that still buzzed, spitefully, with the spark of life.

The *Nunavut*'s cramped galley filled first with wood smoke and then a soft-yellow radiance as Tom got a fire built. Mounted on gimbals, the galley stove hung perpendicular to the earth, unlike the bulwark where Bradford slumped to shuck off his waterlogged clothing or the floor planks rising crazily like a funhouse wall. Everything not lashed in place now rested in the trough of these inverted surfaces—mostly spent food canisters with ragged aluminum edges and petrified lumps of unclassifiable feces. In the emergency kit, Tom found a headlamp with a bit of juice in its batteries and a foil blanket that he handed to Bradford.

"Feel like a... fuckin' popcorn bag," Bradford managed to complain as he drew the blanket close, his body wracked with shivers. He curled himself under the gimbal stove, holding his hands flat against its steaming cast-iron box.

Tom restoked the fire, checked the pistol in his belt, and then went topside to inspect the holds. He had to lean against the deck and walk on her rails, ducking under hanging canvas and halyards that trailed weirdly down into the ice. A crust of frost sealed both hatches, and he chipped them open with his knife, scaling the slick deck and peering over into the gloom. His headlamp beam showed the first cargo hold to be little more than a dump, the garbage and artifacts interstrewn like a slovenly, jumbled tag sale. When the second hatch fell open, a noxious cocktail of odors bloomed from within, and Tom had to let it vent before hooking his elbows over the jamb and hoisting himself up for a look. In the fading electric light, he found makeshift stables of two-by-four and chicken wire, leashes swinging empty from stout posts in the underdeck. The floor was grouted smooth with an adobe of straw and dried slops, and down along the hull planks, he saw carcasses with peeled yellow skulls. Long desiccated, they could have been goats or sheep. The *Nunavut*'s bilge had also ruptured, Tom saw, her ballast spilling over into the hold. Chunks of masonry and pig-iron scraps had lodged in seams and mingled with the bones.

Tom shut this hatch and went forward to check the crew quarters. The forecastle companionway was already blown open, snow drifting over the ladder rungs. Inside, four bunks lay tossed and settling into a corner, their thin mattress pads overturned and moldy. Tom discovered a candy bar—sealed in its foil wrapper and frozen stiff—as well as a year-old issue of *Hustler* among the refuse. On the magazine's rumpled cover, a model pressed one eye to a hobbyist's telescope, her tits like gold-plated planets rising in the foreground.

"It's just trash." Tom moved crabwise across the galley, pausing to sit on his haunches and warm his hands by the stove. Bradford was still wrapped in Mylar, its crinkled edges throwing scatters of firelight. "Torn up feed sacks—cornmeal and what-not. But it's all been eaten. Something got to every last bag."

"Coulda been anythin'," Bradford said, staring at his own feet as he flexed them slowly, one and then the other. "They burn."

"That's good. You'd be in trouble if they didn't." Tom threw him the candy bar. "Here."

"No shit?" Bradford seized the thing and fumbled with it, his fingers torn and swollen. He ripped the foil lengthwise with his teeth and said, "We oughta split it."

"You keep it." Tom stood up, forcing himself not to watch Bradford eating. "I don't like peanuts." He rummaged through a toolkit, looking for something to pry apart the galley cabinets. Bradford's clothes hung from a nail, dripping across the warm planks below. Tom pointed at them with a claw hammer. "Guess we're here for the night."

"Mm," said Bradford, chewing.

Tom dismantled a wooden cupboard, checking first that it

was empty. He snapped the thin pine slats over his good knee and fed them to the stove. After building up a cache of wood, he sat, gazing wearily at his companion.

"What, Tom?"

"Thought I lost you."

"I ain't yours ta lose."

Bradford looked over and registered that Tom found no humor in this.

"I'm with ya, Tom," he said. "But in this world, ya go crazy try'na keep people. We're all headin' for the door at once."

Tom brooded on the image for a while, breathing in deep, slow cycles. "I gotta go to Limekiln tomorrow. I have to see Sharon."

"Be a couple days yet. This weathah won't do for travel."

"Well, I hope it keeps her there. She told me she'd leave for Boston soon."

"Boston? Tha fuck why?"

"There's a doctor."

"Gotta be some doctor closer by…"

"Not this kind. Sharon's going to abort the pregnancy."

Bradford was looking worriedly at the fire, probably searching for a meaningful way to respond, when Tom abruptly stood and reached for his gun.

"Did you hear that, Nev?"

"I don't…"

"I think there's somebody else on the boat."

The galley's back hatch led on to a storage area full of rigging and spare canvas, its portholes showing that night had fallen over the static harbor. Tom held the headlamp and pistol before him, picking his way through these musty coils and skeins, following the faint reverberation of knocking and scratching that carried over the *Nunavut*'s beams.

He pressed his ear to the next hatch, beyond which would lay the captain's and first mate's berths. The noise was unmistakable: someone rooted through the cabins ahead. Whether they'd come across the ice as he had or somehow hidden away during his earlier perusal of the ship, Tom couldn't begin to guess. The scratching carried on, as if they'd set to digging a way through the *Nunavut*'s planks with a garden trowel. Tom checked the safety on his 9mm, took a breath, and kicked open the hatch.

Swinging the headlamp beam, Tom first saw the mate's berth sloping toward him on the elevated starboard side of the boat, its contents overturned but otherwise unremarkable. To port, the captain's room was littered with fallen junk, and a figure moved clumsily across the gouged woodwork, skittering out of the light.

"Hey!"

Tom got no verbal response, but a bunk mattress suddenly flipped up on its zippered edge, blocking his view. A shotgun barrel clattered and rolled across the floor.

He fired two rounds into the mattress, blowing it flat against a far bulkhead and releasing a flurry of goose down. Tom dropped low and sent a third bullet whiffing over the floorboards.

A speckling of blood fell across the wall, and from the

adjoining cabin, Tom heard Bradford bellowing, "THA FUCK IS GOIN' ON?"

Tom held the lamp high, creeping around the captain's bunk. The body lay wedged between mattress and cabin wall, shallowly panting and already glassy in the eyes—a rosy, happy thing, fattened on months of cornmeal and leisure. Tom smiled and raised his pistol.

"It's alright."

"What is it?" Bradford called again, more curious now than alarmed.

"It's dinner," Tom told him, and shot Captain Cadwgan's yearling pig.

~~94~~ 87

They dismantled the *Nunavut* and its last remaining passenger in similar fashion, not wasting an edible scrap of the pig or a fathom of dry uncompromised rope. In several days, the weather turned, a warm current freeing the trade ship, which rolled back onto its centerline for a few proud hours before sinking finally to the bed of the George.

From the shore, Bradford and Tom watched her slip away, their larder by now reduced to bone marrow and offal. Bradford turned his sights on the next solid meal, while Tom prepared for the long walk to Limekiln.

Melt-water seeped into his cracked boots, dampening socks with no heel or toe left. Still February, and the sun could only climb so high, but when it hit the apex of noon, the melt was on in full. It might have been fifty degrees. It felt like seventy. Small rivers gurgled at the roadsides, chewing on their snowy banks. The road north was covered by a skin of translucent, sweating ice. If not for the machine screws driven into the soles of his boots, Tom couldn't have walked it without sliding and falling. They made a good deal of noise as they broke through the crust in his offbeat left-*right*-left, and he felt the fear of exposure creeping up the back of his neck. He was likely not the only desperate creature to have been coaxed out by the sun, but he couldn't afford to wait for the next break.

He came to the edge of town, with the cement flats ahead and his own watery tracks behind. To his left, the Old County Road branched off from Route One, dipping immediately into a world of overhanging branches and snow. Dead ahead, Route One lay wide and open, leading straight across the flats. Tom climbed a long icy hill and pulled out his binoculars to survey the latter path. He put the glasses to his eyes and winced at the sunlight that reflected off acres of glittering snow. He pushed the focus wheel with his index finger until the scene was fixed and clear.

The hulk of the cement factory sat cold and dead on its hill, and the road appeared not to have been traveled. He held the glasses up, searching for smaller things. Nothing moved over the fields, the snow only interrupted here and there by quarry mouths and low skeletal bushes. A dozen hawks turned in a slow funnel, rising on invisible thermals, scanning the ground below for hares. He watched a single hawk break into free fall, *down-down-down*, and then its wings burst open, inches from a crash, and it skimmed the white field looking bashful before returning to its brothers. The whole gang of these raptors, taut as bowstrings, hasty for a kill.

Despite the lonesomeness, Tom couldn't say that no one was watching. He pulled the 9mm from his belt and checked its clip, returned it. Broke open the stock of Bradford's shotgun and blew down the barrel. These were needless actions. He might as well have genuflected, crossed himself, and said "Amen." He elected to turn back and take the sheltered road north.

The Old County Road was a narrow winding rural street that snaked between century-old lime quarries, a relic from the time when roads weren't built for 18-wheelers. The most notable landmark along Old County was the Limekiln City Dump, which, though still a kingdom of over-large seagulls, had lost its human traffic altogether and lay shrouded under several generations of weeds. The houses on Old County were all dilapidated single-levels and mobile homes, far spaced and poorly tended now, as ever. This had all been the low-rent district of a low-rent city. Fletcher's rock had since made the housing market a much more level playing field.

The back road allowed Tom an easier gait and a shaded snow pack to dampen the sound of his footsteps. He made several miles in the early afternoon, listening to his own breathing and the muffled, uneven crunch under his boots.

Birdcalls and the plunk of water droplets bounced through Tom's head, where he dreamed of a cave system, vaults and tunnels. The echo brought him back to consciousness, back from what he'd only intended as a brief sit-down inside the tree line, to chew on snow and rest his feet. He'd let himself grow deaf to the protests of his guts, but his body was determined to override him. He wouldn't make it more than another mile or so without eating.

With the surrounding branches bare and the earth frozen, Tom would have to hunt. As he pushed further into the trees, his boots disrupted the many separate histories of predation recorded there in the snow. The shamrock stamps of coyote and frantic crosshatch of a turkey flock moving east. The barely perceptible architecture of vole tunnels terminating at the impact crater of a pouncing fox. Winter belonged to the predators.

Tom came to a clearing, where the oaks thinned out, and he could see what had been someone's backyard in the near distance. A pack of grey squirrels foraged among the remaining trees, searching for the caches they'd buried the year before. The squirrels were spaced wide, and he'd have to get them all together before he took his shot. He pulled a handmade shell from his coat pocket and fed it carefully into the shotgun. The cartridges were intended as buckshot, carrying far too much lead for these squirrels, but Tom was hungry and enervated and couldn't worry over it.

He stepped out of the shadows and said, "Hey!"

The nervous little animals, maybe eighteen in total, all flew up the nearest oak. Tom paced around the trunks, looking for the shot. A few yards above his head, the pack chattered and angrily shook their tails, raising an alarm. He stopped underneath a wide forking branch, where five of the things had huddled near one another, and raised his gun. Tom aimed straight into their midst, took a breath, and squeezed the trigger.

He heard the firing pin strike with a small *click*, but nothing more happened. He broke the stock and pulled out the dud, cursing it, and the squirrels resumed cursing him, but did not flee to a higher branch. Tom eyed them maliciously and loaded a new shell. It'd be a hell of a time picking them off with his handgun if Bradford's cartridges all proved duds. Without much consideration for aim, Tom raised, pulled, and blasted away one whole quadrant of the oak.

The nearest squirrel was more or less vaporized. A cloud of guts and splinters fell over him as Tom watched branches thrashing, survivors fleeing to adjoining trees. Still, he'd managed to knock a couple of fat ones from the tree intact. The little beasts lay belly-up on the snow, broken and panting. Tom leaned over each one in turn, saying, "Sorry, friend," and stove in its tiny skull with the butt of the shotgun.

Tom approached the nearby house cautiously, taking only a few steps at a time through the backyard, pausing repeatedly to listen. He walked the entire perimeter, checked the windows, checked the snow for footprints. Nothing. He pulled out the buckshot cartridge he'd just spent, slipped it into a pocket along with the dud, and reloaded the gun. Tom blew out the deadbolt enclosure of a rear entrance, as well as a good portion of the doorframe. The door flew back on its hinges and slammed loudly into a washing machine. Tom stepped through to the musty interior gloom.

Out of the sun and into a pit of shadows, cobwebs, and rat shit. The roof leaked; chunks of rotten plaster lay in piles wherever the ceilings had given out. Tom decided this place had been abandoned even before the rock. He walked into the kitchen and laid his shotgun on a Formica dining table. A stack of mail sat in the corner, many times rewetted and clinging together as one pulpy mass. Tom peeled away magazines, bills, a wedding invitation from someone named Charlie and someone else named Ruthanne. At the bottom was a thin edition of the *Bangor Daily News*, Sept. 7, 1985. This house had a story, and he knew it was all around him, if he felt inclined to look further. He didn't. Once again, Tom was chilled with the notion of being watched.

He dressed the squirrels with his gutting knife and left the entrails in a neat pile on the kitchen counter. Tom crossed into the living room and began smashing furniture, dismantling any wooden object he could find and piling up the spoils in the fireplace. The furniture pieces were damp, and he anxiously popped his knuckles as they sizzled and slowly caught flame.

A decent blaze going, he walked back to the kitchen with a wire coat hanger. He unwound the wire and ran it through one little squirrel carcass and then the other, from mouth to anus, leaving himself ten inches with a hook on the end to hold. Tom crouched before the hearth, holding his meal over the foul-smelling fire and charring off the fur in a slow, deliberate manner.

Tom was too famished to pay any mind to the blackened rodent as he chewed. Its fleshless skull snarling at him, little gnawing razors glinting white. The boiled-out holes of its eyes. He pulled strings of flesh from the tiny body with his fingers and teeth, swallowing, forcing himself to tear and swallow and keep going. He was about to rip into the second squirrel when his guts heaved and he nearly vomited, just managing to hold back the wet, acidic mass that had bubbled up to his throat. He swilled from his canteen and washed out his mouth, spat into the fire, and quit the meal.

Tom wrapped the leftover squirrel in a center page from *Better Homes and Gardens*, a photo spread of decorative waterfalls carrying the caption, "Bringing Nature Indoors." After fetching the shotgun and taking a last look around, Tom walked straight out the front door.

He approached Ocean Street from the north, having skirted every major thoroughfare and burned away all but the last available daylight. On his left, the tide was consuming Limekiln harbor like an ambivalent sea monster, rolling one great grey tentacle over another, slowly taking the beach. On his right, the suburban skyline was a jawbone of severe black tenements and sun-gilt ruins. Tom walked a narrow, in-between space, carrying with him a kind of full-body nausea. He passed familiar buildings that had recently fallen and houses that were only basements full of wet ash. Unseasonable warmth magnified the gamy smell of everyone and everything that had died in the winter.

So, this is your boat shop?

Maybe he'd misunderstood her, letting the few days they'd spent together grow monumental in his own thoughts. Maybe it had only been a diversion for her—an easy abatement to the fear and anger and boredom. Still, Tom was intent on trying to show her more. They could be one another's means of looking forward, truly, if she were willing to believe it.

In his pocket, he thumbed the velvety hide of a stuffed pink rabbit.

He crossed Main Street between smashed automobiles,

glancing briefly into a marine supply that had been thoroughly ransacked. A gang of extremely well-fed raccoons paraded out from an alleyway and started marching in his direction, their twelve sets of eyes collecting the scarce evening light and shooting it coldly back at him.

"Get!" Tom barked as they muscled in. He pulled his pistol and held it in front of him, vaguely trained on the leader, and wondered if he should stand his ground or simply run. Raccoons or not, Tom was outnumbered and outweighed.

The entire group, following the leader's cue, suddenly moved off as a single unit. He watched them hurry through the snow pack and waist-high thorns of Main Street, and then they were gone. Tom looked at his gun, still held there, and wondered what could have startled the brutes. He wondered what was behind him at that very moment.

It was already rushing for him, snarling, crashing through the top crust between Tom and the shadows it had burst from—a large, bounding, wolfish thing—a dark thing. Tom stood behind his pistol, shaking slightly, when suddenly the little 9mm went off in his hands.

The round kicked up a spray of ice chunks in the middle of the street, and the animal abruptly stopped its charge. For a moment they both looked at each other, jaws hung open, and then Tom recognized the German shepherd from Sharon's clinic.

"Moose!" he yelled, and tucked the gun away. "Moose!" He held his hands out flat and the dog cautiously pawed up and huffed at the air. Something like embarrassment slunk into its posture as it recognized Tom, and then the dog began jumping excitedly and barking in its big, throaty voice. Tom tried to pat the dog's muzzle, but Moose was leaping and turning aerial twists, shaking with stress and excitement and confusion. The shepherd was collarless, unattended, and dirty. Rusty stains on its muzzle suggested it had killed and eaten something.

"Moose," Tom said again, and got down on his knees. Eventually, the dog contented itself with standing heavily against Tom's chest, panting and looking, listening in all directions. "Why you all alone, buddy?"

The dog whined and shook, barking in a high painful plea. Tom stroked its head and neck with both hands. He could feel the heartbeat racing up inside Moose's wide maned throat.

"Here," he said, "hold on…" Tom dug in his rucksack for the glossy paper package that contained the charred squirrel. Moose paced incessantly around him, sniffing the evening breeze and attempting to watch in three-hundred-sixty degrees at once. Tom got the small blackened lump of meat unwrapped and extended it to the dog. The dog looked at him directly for a few seconds, snatched the offering very delicately with its fore-teeth, and then disappeared, without another noise, into the night.

From where he stood on Ocean Street, the clinic appeared to have sunken just slightly into the hill, as though some underground vault was preparing to swallow it. The windows were all dark and the building cut a low boxy silhouette against the stars, broken in places with cedar crowns.

Tom pushed his way through the bracken and pine boughs

and slush, feeling his throat tighten with every moment of silence. The kind of dread silence that hisses and rushes in, pouring through a crack in one's established sense of normalcy. Tom's pulse didn't quicken so much as pressurize—a pneumatic thump within his skull. He rounded the building, stumbled over a kerosene can, regained his balance and found the back entrance. The door was wide open, pinned against the concrete wall with a cinder block. The intense blackness of the inner corridor seemed to draw in any ambient light and snuff it.

Tom set his pack and shotgun against the wall and ripped a plastic tarpaulin away from the outdoor generator. He yanked on the pull-start twice with no success, spat, and took a breath to calm himself. In the dark, he patiently felt his way around the engine until he located the primer bulb. He gave the primer three squirts and tried the starter again. Tom put all one hundred and twenty-odd remaining pounds of himself into the pull.

The generator shuddered and chugged itself to life, suddenly filling the previous vacuum with sound. Tom cut down the choke until the engine hummed evenly, and he looked up to see two small emergency lights glowing within the building. The gas canister was light and sloshy when he shook it. He wouldn't have electric lights for very long. The dull orange glow of an exit sign tinted the rear corridor, and Tom drew the pistol from his belt, vaguely mouthing the word *"Please."* He snaked a hand inside the doorway to slap a flat panel-switch on the wall. After some seconds of flicker, the space was filled with institutional white light.

Empty kennels. Cage doors hung open at various angles,

speaking to a mass exodus, and even the smell of dog seemed absent. Worn towels and chewed rawhide scraps littered the floor. The following kennel room, the same. Someone had let them all go. She'd let them all go. And in a hurry. The dogs liberated in a haphazard rush, the door left wide to channel them out, their claws clattering over linoleum and spent syringes, vaccine bottles that would no longer protect them, and emptied cans of food which they'd never taste again. The dogs bursting excitedly, naively, out into the wild, rotting city.

He turned the corner, into a grooming area dominated by a stainless-steel basin. Long, tubular fluorescent bulbs shook themselves to life when he thumbed the switch. Everywhere, the sterile light landed at once. Everything suddenly jumped at him in unison. The gleaming metal, the white walls, the brown tile floor, bare and empty. Tom's heart began to beat percussively in his throat and ears. He moved on, through the "kitchen," but there was nothing there and he went still further, quickly, kicking doors wide to witness the appalling vacancy of the examination room, the surgery, bathrooms and hallways. Not a lasting note of her presence in the clinic, as though Tom had merely dreamt her.

Finally, in the storage space where Sharon had kept her twin mattress and minimal wardrobe, Tom found a single teacup, its cotton string stained and dangling a mint leaf tag. He plucked it from the floor by its dainty handle, pressing his palm against the bowl of the cup to test for any hint of warmth. Still half full, the cup gave off a faint odor of fermentation, its contents sealed within by a fragile lens of ice.

The cabinets yawned wide, showing the washed-out pigment of what few garments had been left. Boot marks on the linoleum suggested a last once-over, no time left even to scribble a goodbye, before a departure free of any backward glances. No sooner had he taken in this scene, fish-white like a Polaroid, than the generator cut, and the whole clinic was plunged back into darkness.

She didn't intend to come back. Whether she believed that Fletcher's date was the one true End or not, Sharon saw no future for herself in this clinic, in this town, or anywhere over the lime-heavy bedrock of Fox County. Tom considered that, maybe, they'd been staring at the same object all along, but calling it by different names. Where he saw possibility, she knew there would also be chaos, deprivation, and violence unmitigated. Sharon would not subject a child to Tom's "possibility." She would act, while a choice was still to be had.

He didn't blame her. He couldn't pretend that they walked identical paths—that the rules he'd established for his own life should also dictate hers.

Tom retrieved the kerosene can from the clinic's rear entrance. He hobbled back into the darkness, back to the empty cabinets and stripped mattress of Sharon's quarters. The frozen tea cup struck him, more than anything here, as an artifact of his heartbreak—inconsequential and abandoned. He emptied its slushy contents and filled it instead with kerosene. Tom poured a stream of kerosene through every room and hallway, splashing it over walls, leaving pools of the stuff on exam tables and counter tops. He held the can out before him with shaking hands, working his way backward, filling the entire structure with fuel and fumes. He kicked doors open after soaking their woodwork, leaving a slick of it along baseboards, sopping the carpets, until finally, he tripped over the back threshold and dropped the canister just inside the door.

Tom snapped a branch from the nearby thicket, dipped its fibrous end in kerosene and lit it, watching the flame quaver in the open doorway.

"It's just difficult," he said, speaking back to the dark corridor, "not knowing where to put the anger."

Tom threw the branch deep into the corridor and watched it land, watched the blue perimeter race outward and climb the walls, heard it gulp at the air around it. Appendages of flame shot across the linoleum, seeking the unlit fuel.

He turned away, climbing a muddy hill and dropping himself onto bare, wet earth. Stars showed, a swath of them widening through the fast-moving clouds as he sat there—brilliant over the sullen, empty architecture of Limekiln. Tom watched them for a while, long enough to see whole constellations move within their traces, gradually arcing past tree tops and church spires and the clinic windows glowing below.

~~87~~ 86

He moved through the boat shop like a sentient gale, knocking and spilling and throwing objects out of his path—sleepless eyes bloodshot and his mouth a grim, flat plane. Tom combed the shop, grunting impatient curses and stuffing a few artifacts into his open rucksack—a candle, a flint kit, and the spare off-white calling card—a small clutch of books.

He'd only returned from Limekiln at dawn, but burst out into the bracing cold of morning, and threw the shop door rattling back into its frame. He crossed the boat yard, making a straight line toward the woodshed, against which rested only the rotten leftovers of last year's cord. A wooden maul handle stood there, its heavy wedge buried in a waterlogged stump of pine. Tom twisted it loose, shouldering the maul like a rifle, and strode quick, silent, and murder-blind to the crest of the hill.

Neither his threadbare shirts nor the weak February sun did much to warm him, but Tom had no concern for the weather. As he closed the distance, that three-quarter mile of ghost town, his temperature and his violence grew. Every other step sent a jolt of pain crackling up his right leg and he grinned, beating the pavement ever harder, sucking the wet air and snorting it out, feeling his heart soar with malice. Like the wolf that gnaws itself free of the trap—loping, lustful, driven toward the unforgettable scent of its hunter.

Tom noticed the church's advanced state of decay. It might have made some impression, maybe softened him in some way, on a different morning. His parents had worshipped here, though he seldom accepted "worship" as the correct term. He couldn't allow that his family had been so very different from himself. He divorced their memory from the sight of this place, and any place like it. These cheap monuments to the god of imaginary endings. Tom would bluntly rechristen this place in the name of a more nuanced philosophy.

Not stopping or slowing, barely thinking in this state of inflamed gall, he came to the wooden doors, the same doors he'd witnessed John Hupper throwing open in righteous indignation—oh, that beautiful moment of violence and clarity—and put all his momentum into a solid running kick. Instantly, an electric pain ran along the length of his femur, suddenly brittle-feeling inside its narrow sleeve of flesh, and he nearly toppled over backward onto the granite steps, but the door itself didn't budge. Tom stood there, blinking in confusion while the shock subsided.

He pulled the straps off his shoulders and set his pack a safe distance away in the mud, took a step back and reexamined, holding his splitting maul in both hands. He looked at the doors, at their brass handles and the big, solid housing where the lock must be.

Tom brought the maul up and over his head. His hands were wide on its shaft and his feet were wide under his own body, and he raised the thing up like a spike driver, like a railroad folk hero, and when the steel blade was all the way behind, he swung it back down, his hands coming together, the head swinging quick like a pendulum and its blunt hammer-side crushing down on its mark.

The concussion shot straight up the ax handle and crackled through his arms. It rang his skull like a bell. He wasn't sure there'd been any effect on the lock, so he swung again.

Iron wedge against the brass. The maul left a chevron scar on the lock housing. A brilliant gouge through the dark patina. He swung again.

Tom thought his shoulder would dislocate. He thought he'd rattle the bone right out of its socket.

Again.

There was a bright noise of snapping metal and then a rude, hollow clangor as the lock housing slapped down onto the granite steps. A muffled banging from beyond the door told him that the push-bar on the inside had also fallen. Tom poked out the remains of the lock cylinder with one finger and pulled open the heavy door. Its frozen hinges groaned.

Tom's boots crunched in the skirt of frost that had blown under the door. The air inside was moving and ammonia-smelling, and he looked up to see a handful of broken windows lining the nave. The remaining stained glass gave an impression of sunshine, throwing spots of color around the room, trying to warm it. "Hello!" Tom yelled into the cavern. His voice rebounded off the walls, spooked the itinerant pigeons, and died in a whisper somewhere high above. There was no priest, no deacon, no parishioners. Not a soul.

He did his stations like any good Catholic. Tom stood before Jesus as He was condemned, and Tom condemned Him, too. Once again with the blunt face of the maul, he shattered the plaster effigy and its little wooden cross. The most thrilling wave of doubt and then excitement washed over him as he pulverized Christ with an ax. It's only a story; it's only a story. Tom felt he could go on smashing, layer after plaster layer giving way until he'd obliterated the root fable, the first catalyzing utterance of baseless, mystical fear. The cross hit the floor in pieces. Only Pilate remained, judging.

One by one, Tom destroyed eleven Stations of the Cross. The small plaster reliefs crumbled like sand castles. He stopped to regard each plot-point of the Passion before giving it the maul. Jesus accepts the cross. Jesus meets His mother. Veronica wipes His brow. Tom, feeling charitable, left three stations intact—Jesus falls a first time, Jesus falls a second time, Jesus falls a third—and moved on.

The altar came apart in large venous white bergs; bursts of stone dust and shards of holy marble that pinged off his eyelids, stuck in his hair. Its destruction had a smell. Calcium and sweat. The effort was exhausting, but Tom hammered away, hewing the precise marble platform into a nondescript boulder, surrounded by its own fragmented mass. Every crash of the maul against new, virgin stone sent another ugly rift through its white substance, another malevolent crack of sound through the empty church, another curling, fractal plume of quartz dust into the air that he breathed.

Tom thought of Fletcher's rock and the great cloud, thousands of miles wide, that was to erupt from the point at which it and Earth first touched. Faster than human perception, it would lift land and sky and ocean and every living thing in the hemisphere and expel them all to the void in a vast mushroom of organic vapor—the ghost of a world, rushing to escape its bludgeoned corpsc. Maybe.

When the altar was so scattered that the rubble climbed up his boot shafts—and the tabernacle was a crushed, golden butterfly bleeding unwatered sacristy wine from its secret heart—and the majority of colored glass had been freed from its leaden grout work—and the sunshine yellowing the wooden sills was real—and his veins bulged as if to tear loose from his limp, hanging arms in their bruised sockets, his cracked palms barely clutching the maul to drag it behind, through the stone and glass and saliva and blood—when it was all over with, Tom pushed outside into the light of midday and slumped himself down to the church steps.

He couldn't say if there was any relief in smashing up Val Gilbert's church. Maybe it would come in time. For all he knew, the priest was dead. Of his neighbors, friends, family, the great majority were dead. Tom spat on the ground.

Godspeed you, Father.

He looked up and noted the height of the sun, just a white nebula in the grey ceiling of clouds. There were still hours of daylight ahead, and he felt vaguely positive about this, as though his flat plane of numbness now had a light border rather than a dark one. He rolled up some tobacco dust in a paper square and lit it. He drew in the smoke, blew it out, and picked some grit from the tip of his tongue. At length, Tom rose from his seat and readied himself to move on, lifting the maul to his shoulder with a long groan.

The library's thick metal door was stuffed awkwardly into the basement stairwell, as though someone had built a temporary shelter down there, but couldn't make it sound. Tom briefly puzzled over the desperate illogic of the set-up. He decided to inspect the upper floor first and deal with this obstacle later.

The wooden steps leading up to the main floor had a season's worth of dry leaves and blown debris packed against their risers. Climbing hesitantly, Tom ducked as a blackbird shot through the hallway, over his head, and on to open sky.

Inside, the collection stood largely intact, the weight of the books keeping everything planted in its place. Nothing seemed to have been altered by a human hand in months, but other inhabitants were quickly changing the space through their own processes. Nests of all types—robin, mouse, spider—were crammed, chewed, or spun between volumes, or else bored straight through the plaster of the walls. Bats had invaded the vaulted cavern of the lobby, their shit painted over every surface like quicklime.

"Hello?" Tom tried, but the response was just another explosion of flapping wings. Another colony of pigeons crossing the space above him and exiting through the glassless gap of a window. His skin tightened with ghost fear as he stood motionless and waited for a more human reply.

Tom made a thorough search of the library, everywhere finding life, but never a hint of Miss Neary. Tom had once thought her indestructible, and perhaps this was true. Maybe she wasn't dead, but had rather returned to whatever plane and corporeal arrangement from which she'd once materialized. The banished angel, inviolate and free from the trappings of this Earth. Maybe Neary had passed on like any other woman, but her body had smelled of flowers like a saint's, and when she breathed last, it disintegrated to a mass of livid petals against the white sheet.

Or maybe, Tom had just missed her, and on occasion, she still stopped in to organize her index cards and feed the birds.

Tom set his three books on her desk, next to a block-lettered sign reading, "Margaret L. Neary, Head Librarian." Margaret, he thought. That's kind of pretty. He took a last long look around the room. Sunlight played off the dust motes and the lazy snow of bird feathers that spiraled to the floor.

The metal door in the basement stairs would not be moved. Whoever put it there had jackknifed the thing just so, its corners biting into the concrete walls, firmly stuck. Its angle was such that Tom could neither pound it down further with the maul nor wrench it up and out of its position. Still, the door's surface didn't take up the entire opening. It looked possible that he could squeeze his way past it. As if someone had merely intended the door to act as a kind of baffle.

He left his pack in the hallway, stood on the flat, horizontal surface of the door, and it took his weight. Tom held the maul out over a triangular two-foot opening behind the door, and let it go. The maul dropped maybe eight or nine feet and clanged on a concrete landing beneath. Checking that the candle and tinderbox were still in his pocket, Tom slid himself down into the hole.

He struck the flint once and caught a glimpse of his surroundings. The wet, grimy union of floor and wall. In two strikes, this expanded to include a dust-caked fire extinguisher, a puddle of yellow liquid, and a very large rat that skulked along the corridor, unconcerned with Tom's presence. Finally, he got the tinder to catch, lit his candle, and closed the box.

Crossing the landing, he descended two short steps to the main corridor. There were large halogen lamp bulbs in cages hung from the ceiling, and more rats, squatting and sniffing the air or crisscrossing the path before him, narrowly avoiding his boots. The air was pungent with rot, sweet and acidic. If there had been anything in his stomach, it would have been rat food by now. All around him were signs of inhabitance, but none of them recent. Only garbage, and the least edible components of it.

Tom came to a door on his right and lifted his candle to it: BOILER. If his idea of the floor plan overhead was correct, then these rooms stemming off the corridor to the north would all be smallish, probably utility oriented. Not what he was looking for. He passed two more doors of similar description: ELECTRICAL and STORAGE. He was running out of corridor, and still there were no doors along the south wall.

The concrete floor suddenly dropped away into total darkness, and the air became fouler still. An unadorned stairway led even deeper into the reek. Tom put a hand on the steel railing, but immediately pulled it away, wiping his palm on his jeans.

Counting twelve steps down and tapping his way along with the steel wedge of the maul. Three stories beneath the library and getting hard to breathe. The stairway ended and his steps echoed back from where the corridor came to a brick wall, quite close. Whatever the floor was made of squelched under his boots. Tom held the candle up.

"Oh, *Jesus!*"

He staggered backward and fell against the stairs. In the amber candlelight, a living, vibrating mass dominated the corridor. He regained footing and saw them dart under his boots, the sleek backsides of a couple hundred rats, all seething and fighting over two nondescript lumps that rose from the gelatinous floor. Holding the candle out above them, he caught a flash of orange fabric, a brass button.

Tom swung his maul through the center of the throng, slicing and slapping the vermin away, again, again, leaving many of them cleft, hind parts and fore parts squirming under the candlelight as if trying to reconnect. The majority just squealed and dove for the corners, waiting for the intrusion to pass.

What he found, when the rats cleared, were two human corpses. Just skeletons, really, with ropey clumps of hair trailing into the black ooze, and tatters of fabric stuck through the spaces between ribs. An empty glass bottle glinted in the dim light, poking at an angle through the disintegrated mounds, as did the barrel and drum of a small revolver.

Tom leaned in, holding the candle out and over the bodies, holding his shirt over his mouth and nose. Clean-picked teeth looked like they might snap at his hand. Bullet holes in the skulls—one in the right temple and the other, tellingly, between the eyes. This was nothing one could call a suicide pact *per se*, but nothing more surprising than that, either. The two were locked in a forever stare, jaws and orbits gaping, just tragic lovers, maybe, having reached their story's end. Melting into a human puddle on the wrong side of a security door in the south wall of that fetid, concrete tomb.

Christ, this is it.

Tom stood up and cleared some grime off the stainless-steel surface of the door with his sleeve. A yellow sign bore the words FOX COUNTY FALLOUT LOCATION C—CAPACITY: 100. The door was sealed by an arm-thick steel crossbar fixed to a handwheel with interlocking metal teeth, the wheel like one might imagine on a submarine's hatch. Tom held his candle between his teeth and tried the wheel, just once. The departed individuals lying at his feet had tried it ages ago, clearly, and it didn't budge. He ran his fingertip around the doorframe and found it as tight and hermetic as he'd hope a bomb shelter to be.

Hot wax stung his wrist, and he realized that his candle was getting short. His candle and his available air. The both of them, as a matter of fact, consuming one another while he fumbled and wasted time.

There had to be something more. Tom began scratching at the concrete wall outside the door, holding the candle high, searching for a lever or a knob or a panel, any change in the wet, porous surface, anything that might grant him access. Even just something to hack at with the maul. The door itself was too monolithic, too absolute.

Tom's fingers brushed over a smooth recessed metal square, about twelve inches to the right of the handwheel. An arrangement of nine push-buttons rose slightly from the metal plate, and when his index finger landed too heavily on one of these, Tom was shocked to hear an electronic *beep*. A bright red number 3 glowed, then, from the top of the panel.

"Oh, fuck..." he muttered.

Tom looked at the thing for a moment. He felt briefly embarrassed, as though he'd damaged someone's very expensive *something* through simple dunderheadedness. Fuck it. He stabbed at the keypad again. A red 7 lit up alongside the 3. Again: 3-7-4. After one more exploratory fingering, the numerical phrase 3-7-4-2 flashed twice in red, and then all four digits disappeared.

Okay.

He tried several four-digit combinations at random, each giving him the same result. His candle melted away, and he tossed the soft lump of wax across the corridor. Tom continued to fecklessly molest the keypad by feel. Nothing.

I'm just going to fucking smash you, he decided. Tom had the maul in both hands. Its blunt, inarticulate power hung dully somewhere out in the darkness. All he had to do was swing it once. One blow and this little nexus of confusion would be obliterated. Brute force versus the unknown.

There was no way that this system had been designed to admit desperate smashers of keypads. Catharsis it might gain him, briefly, but he'd never know what lay behind that door. Tom cursed and set down the maul.

Four digits. Of course, four digits.

Tom was scared to try it, scared to face the tremendous anticlimax of being summarily rejected by the keypad, scared of wasting his lucky charm on a dead-end prospect and climbing back to the daylight, demoralized and empty-handed. Nothing gained, and one of very few points of faith lost. Tom took a moment to stand quietly, to utter a little lottery-ticket prayer, and then he pushed the button.

"1" glowed red. Just two digital segments like neon rice kernels stacked on end.

"1-1" His scrotum tightened with apprehension.

"1-1-2" and Tom suddenly thought, What if somebody's in there?

1-1-2-3 flashed twice in green with a long electric *beep*. The wall itself seemed to vibrate, and a whirring sound filled the corridor. Tom stumbled back and heard the steel crossbar of the door shunt itself glacially to the left. All noises ceased, and he stood there in the dark, sucking short breaths of rat-piss ammonia and carbon dioxide.

Lightheaded and blind, Tom leaned into the door, putting all his weight against its eight-foot metal surface. It fell away slowly, yawning wide as he pushed through it. His boot caught on something slick and rigid—a wet protrusion of bone—and he felt himself falling. His palms slapped against clean, smooth concrete and his forehead bounced once, and Tom winced and rolled over, and suddenly the room filled with white light and the soft hiss of pure, compressed oxygen.

Incandescent-filament bulbs hung in long rows from the concrete ceiling. The concrete walls were smooth and mostly featureless. The concrete floor was broad and solid as lake ice under his prostrate body. Tom lay there motionless for several minutes and gulped like a landed fish, greedy for the air that flowed from some kind of mechanical filtration system above. He squinted and covered his face while the artificial light gradually became bearable. When the pain in his forehead began to register in full, he figured he was oxygenated enough to try standing up.

The shelter was sufficiently large for, Tom guessed, maybe three hundred. The place was probably installed decades before, at the height of the arms race, but he assumed the door mechanism and a few other accoutrements had been added since Fletcher. The workmen in the basement, Peg Neary had said.

It was all so ridiculous. The fortification was designed, or retrofit, to shield a small handful of citizens from the immediate fatal effects of a single gamma ray burst, the shockwave of a distant bomb blast. But what would become of them? Several weeks, maybe six months, in the bunker and those survivors would go stir-crazy and animalistic, clawing their way out into a poisonous, ashen world.

And as for the rock?

"At one hundred thirty-five thousand miles per hour, the comet's nucleus will enter the upper atmosphere like a colossal bullet." Fletcher's pronouncement already felt so much a part of history, as if components of its language had slid into extinction along with its broadcast medium and an untold quantity of listeners. "On May 1, 1988, some hours after dusk, a Manhattan-sized fireball will light the Western Hemisphere with the intensity of several noonday suns. Forty-five degrees to Earth's axis, it will barely slow in its descent toward the North Atlantic. Eight or ten miles above the open sea, at roughly fifty degrees north latitude, due to the low density of its nucleus and increasing friction and atmospheric pressure, the comet will explode."

Fletcher had assured those unable to visualize the explosive force of a comet.

"Thirty million megatons is not a magnitude which anyone will live to relativize. I could ask you to imagine the combined nuclear arsenals of both NATO and Soviet powers, heaped in a great bonfire and lit altogether, but even this would give no comparison."

Once the initial shockwave had redrawn the New England coastline, tearing up bedrock and throwing it miles inland, a three-hundred-foot tidal surge would wash the eastern provinces, obliterating any man-made structure between here and the Mississippi. Not only would this bomb shelter be atomized and blown away like dust, but so too for Near Haven, Boston, Halifax, Cape Breton, Reykjavik, Copenhagen, London. Fishing hamlets and seats of Western power alike, just anonymous compass points along the crater rim. According to the narrative, these allied nations would be the first losses in a rolling global Passover. A black cataract of ash would close on the Earth, and their featureless wastes would lie dark and cold beneath it.

Tom split open a wooden packing crate and found it full of MREs. He tore one open: chicken cordon bleu, a package of cheese crackers, and a bag of dried apple. He wolfed down the crackers and apple and repeated the process with a second MRE. There were crates of potable water, matches, Sterno fluid. A pallet stacked high with folding cots. There were lots of useful artifacts packed neatly inside the bunker, plenty to come back later, with Bradford, to haul away. But no sign of his red phone.

The north wall of the shelter was lined with metal lockers, like in a YMCA, each numbered in order from 001 to 100. Tom approached the wall and opened the nearest locker. It wasn't locked, and there was nothing inside. He tried several more and found the same. Each locker was about ten inches wide and three feet tall, and each had a slotted metal hasp designed for a combination lock. He opened another, found nothing, shut the door, opened it again, knocked his fist against the back wall. Solid.

He rifled through rows of steel cabinets, tossing aside gauze, iodine, antibiotic creams, and cases of tampons. He searched the poured concrete walls by sight and by feel, convinced there had to be a seam. He beat his palms bloody against a strange lead case full of wiring, but desisted when it turned out to be only a radio. He stared into the light fixtures until his retinas throbbed, negative ghost images floating over the surreal, white surface of everything in purple.

Tom pulled the calling card from his rucksack and studied its stark, simple text.

May 2, 1988

IV.

Admire the world for never
ending on you—as you would
admire an opponent, without
taking your eyes from him, or
walking away.

—Annie Dillard

~~86~~ 2

The weathervane showed a morning breeze, moving north-north-east at a medium clip. Tom watched the air tracing broad snakes through the shore grass. Spring currents turned balmy and floral, now on the cusp of May. Buck trotted out ahead to the pier, stopping here and there to be sure that Tom followed. She'd taken to sleeping on deck since he'd put the boat in the water, and Tom watched her scrabble up the three-step ladder, jumping over the gunnel with familiar ease.

He'd set the wooden mast, a repurposed mizzen from the *Nunavut* that he and Bradford had dragged over the sea ice, but the tackle was yet to be mounted, and the rigging all lay in coils on the wooden deck. Buck carefully placed one foot at a time inside the largest of these and lay down, resting her chin on the rim of a coil and following him with her eyes. Tom ambled around the pier, inspecting minor details, but really just admiring his boat in the water.

He lowered himself onto the foredeck, and the boat dipped only an inch or two under his weight. It felt solid and good. The deck was varnished to a honey tone and held his bare feet fast as he walked it. He put a hand on the boom and made his way aft to the helm, to look out over the harbor. A glare shone on the undulating surface, and Tom imagined tacking lazily between the depth markers that still teetered out there, chained to the earth many fathoms below.

Tom went up top, on the mast, hooking his legs around the upper rungs as the sun shone at full bore over his head. He brought up the clips and attached them, and ran halyards for the main sail and jib. He weighted the halyards with a couple of rusty machine bolts and dropped these to the deck once he'd strung them. They hit the boards below with a deep, hollow *thunk*, one and then the other.

Twenty-some-odd feet above the water Tom swayed in the wind, hugging the mast and squinting down the distance with all the light of the world on his face. From more than one hundred yards, he saw seals breach and scan the surface momentarily, upend their sleek, spotty torsos, and duck below again. Gulls swept past him, so close he could have stuck out an arm and knocked them into aerial spins. They'd catch a firm updraft and hang there at eye level, inspecting this lanky ape who'd climbed his way up to their plateau.

The wind got into Tom's hair and threw it around. He could feel sun warmth trapped in the dark mats, touching his forehead and lifting away. Touching and lifting. Touching and lifting. The bird sounds grew quiet. The slow wind. The slow current. The lazy yaw of the boat beneath him and the red-green-blue play of sunlight on his eyelids…

"Tommy!"

Tom came awake rudely and blindly, and if not for his feet hooked around the mast rungs, he would have wound up inverted in midair, having let go of the mast.

"You really 'bout fallin' asleep on a fuckin' pole, guy?" Bradford strode down the pier, yelling at him with his hands cupped around his mouth. And laughing.

"Ho, Nev," said Tom, and Jesus Christ-ed under his breath. He got a hold of the mast again and unhooked himself from the rungs. "I'm good," he reassured, while missing a step with his right foot and sliding a ways, burning his palm on an iron rung. Backward and wide-eyed.

Bradford was wiping the corners of his eyes when Tom got himself to a standing position on the deck, caught up in that short, wheezy hiccup of a man trying to stop laughing.

"Alright," Tom told him. "Lots of fun."

They got the last rigging in place, the sails raised and shipped again, and the tiller lines fastened. They loaded the cramped hold with jugs full of drinking water, which would also serve as ballast for however long they went unused. The cupboards were stuffed with MREs in half a dozen flavors. Soon the boat was visibly low in the water.

"Last vessel outa Near Haven harbor," mused Bradford, chewing on a grass blade, sitting on the pier while the sun set over their work. "Last fuckin' vessel. Period."

"You don't know that."

"Ya right, Tom. Hard tellin', not knowin'. But forgive me fa not sharin' ya optimism an' all."

"You just call me an optimist, Nev?"

"Well."

Were there something to smoke, they'd have smoked it. Instead, both men leaned back on their elbows, studying the evening redness in the east.

"You gonna name 'er or what? Bad luck ta sail an unnamed ship."

"No such thing as luck."

Tom stood up and helped Bradford to his feet, and they walked to the very end of the Stearns pier. The setting sun cut slantwise into the brackish, green water, casting mackerel stripes of reflected light over the stern of Tom's boat. Bradford held onto the furthest pylon and leaned out to read what Tom had painted there, earlier that same morning, in dark metallic blue. It said *Near Haven, ME*, the sloop's port of origin, and above that, in a swept, confident script, Tom's simple refutation:

TOMORROW

21

He pulled on some jeans. He folded his cot and rolled it off into a corner, threw a sheet over it, and did a little kind of salute to the thing. The morning was chilly, but Tom's skin burned. His heart beat like it was trying to push the tongue right out of his throat. He built up a fire, watching the still, waiting river as the flames grew, and put a pan of water on. He would brew the last of their coffee this morning.

Tom climbed the ladder and, just poking his nose over the loft edge, said, "Nev. Morning."

Bradford tossed over once and grunted. "Mmm," he said, with reluctance, "'kay, Tommy."

"You serious?" asked Bradford, noticing the scent that had by now filled the shop. He pulled at his red work suspenders, looking for his deck shoes.

"It was only enough for a small pot. Been hiding it." Tom poured them each a not-quite-full cup and looked at the grounds that swirled in the bottom of the saucepan. He tried to tip just a little more liquid into Bradford's cup, but it poured clumpy.

They sat for a while near the water, crabgrass just beginning to green again under their lawn chairs, letting the sun rise and the wind pick up. Both nursing their tiny portion of coffee, letting it go tepid. After a while, Tom said, "You know, this isn't really about Abel. I thought it was, for a long time."

"The old man tricked ya. Abel Stearns had you figured cold."

"Yeah." Tom laughed and wiped his eyes. "Shit, I guess he did."

Another pause, and then Bradford coughed and said, "Wind's comin' up a bit."

"Yeah. Good. Was dead calm at sunup."

"Jesus," Bradford said, watching Buck trot down the pier, climb aboard, and stake out her bed in the forecastle. "That mongrel thinks she's goin' along. Little stowaway." He whipped his coffee grounds across the grass and stood. "Is she?"

Tom smiled. "I guess probably."

Bradford made a big deal about double-checking all the rigging and quizzing Tom on equipment, right down to spare socks. It had come to that time when there was nothing to do but cast off the lines, and Bradford knew it.

He'd declined Tom's invite weeks before. Tom figured he'd just made up his own mind about it—about the rock—and ultimately his belief was stronger, or his doubt was weaker, or his curiosity was, at least, of a different kind. Bradford decided to stay behind, stay with the shop and the harbor and the familiar things. Decided to face whatever was coming alone.

The tide was in and the *Tomorrow* sat high, roughly even with the pier. Tom easily stepped from the one surface to the other, but it felt like a big step. He looked back at the smooth-worn pier, and then at the shore and the shop. He hadn't lost nerve, but something held him arrested as he looked at these things. It shivered in his view of Abel's shop and the stand of fir trees and the gravel drive. His mother's eyes had trembled with that something, at another point in Tom's life that saw him leaving home. His own apprehension vibrating the edges of his field of view. Maybe, in the unfamiliar water, he'd find things blacker than Fletcher's rock. Things he hadn't even thought to fear.

Bradford untied the bow and stern ropes from their cleats and threw them aboard, walking back up the pier to where the *Tomorrow*'s prow faced shore.

"Ya ready, bud?"

"Yeah," Tom answered, shrugging off his misgiving, "let's go."

Bradford leaned his weight into the bow, puffing and red of face, and got the boat moving backward, slowly, through the water. With no engine, they had to get her free of the pier and turned into the wind on manpower alone.

Tom picked up a long wooden oar and readied himself in the stern. Bradford walked the boat down the length of the pier, gaining momentum, and Tom shoved the blade of his oar hard into the last pylon, the two of them growling with the effort of the push. Bradford hit the pylon running, grabbing it with both hands to keep himself from falling into the river. The *Tomorrow* surged backward for several meters, Tom furiously working the oar through the water, drawing her into the current. She drifted easy, rocking in the outgoing tide, unbound.

He tossed the oar to the portside deck and ran forward to pull the halyards. The mainsail flapped and knocked its mast and snapped to life, spritely in light wind, billowing out like a gull's wing. The jib sheet just fluttered for a few seconds as Tom scrambled to make it fast and then held the air. The *Tomorrow* lurched into motion, picking up by fractions of a knot, sluggish with the water in her hold. Tom looked nervously over the rigging, finding nothing impeachable there. He took the helm, adjusting the sheets again, nitpicking, and then looked back toward shore.

"HEY," Bradford hollered from the pier. "WHAT HEADIN'?" His shout carried a mixture of curiosity and concern.

"DOWN EAST," Tom replied, with cupped hands. A fisherman's phrase meaning *northeast, along the coast.*

"DOWN EAST?" Bradford yelled.

"ST. JOHN'S."

Bradford nodded his understanding, hands in his pockets. It took some time for the distance to really grow between them, and then he raised his arm and waved. The knots multiplied and quickened, yet Bradford didn't seem to lose his bigness, feet set wide on the little pier and red palm held aloft. He might have been standing in that place for centuries, a monument to the English fleet. Left by Captain Waymouth himself to mark "that

Part of the River which trended Westward into the Maine."

Tom looked out and saw the channel markers coming up. He was in deeper water, now. He went below and lowered the three-foot daggerboard, clipping it into its casing. He got back to helm, put a hand on the tiller, and let his pulse slow to the easy syncopation of waves.

The sun grew high, and Tom put a cap on to shield his eyes. He had to squint down the glare, leaning toward the starboard-side gunnel and watching the hull slide along. It was easy going with a moderate wind as the *Tomorrow* shot downriver, full sail and riding the current, threading the needle past Pleasant Point and on toward the channel islands. Tom tried not to dwell on anything but the tiller, the wind, and the river. Weaving a swift course into greater Muscongus Bay, making a little over six knots. Hours passed like this and little changed. The colors as vibrant as the sounds were muted.

Around noon he passed Port Cloud, the last finger of mainland he would see and the northernmost corner of the bay. Ahead lay open water, no longer a sheltered river estuary, and Tom was nervous about his little sloop. Rounding the point, the wind kicked up considerably and he had to cut back sail. The water here moved faster, surging with the Gulf Stream force that constantly stirs the North Atlantic. It picked up the *Tomorrow* and heaved her northward into the vast maw of Penobscot Bay like dandelion fur in a gale.

He opted to stay within the barrier islands while possible, after this taste of the open-ocean current. Passing inside Isle Au

Haut, he struck the jib to slow the boat and sailed only on the main. Tom baited the hook on his stub saltwater rod with a cut of dried mackerel and set the rod in a holder at the stern. Ran some line out of the spool for a couple dozen yards, set the reel, and just let his tackle trail behind for a while. Tom left the rod and began scanning the dark, calm water in the island's lee.

Isle Au Haut crept past, a pine-crested rock of straw grass and pitched-roof shacks. The remains of small private boat docks spiked the shore, and a few wrecks could be seen littering the beaches. Before long, he saw a churning on the surface to his starboard. Tom tacked jaggedly toward it, cutting in with the rudder, trying to drag his bait through the center of the disturbance.

Only a few yards past the school, one of its number hit the bait hard and the rod bent with an archer's-bow *thwang*. Tom set the tiller and pulled the rod from its holder. He gave the fish some play, letting out a few more feet of line by hand, so the thing wouldn't snap off and disappear forever, taking his precious hook; it was the three-inch barb of proof that Tom could learn.

When the fight seemed more manageable and Tom had the fish separated from its school, he took the rod from its brass holder and knelt against the gunwale. Tom stuck the butt of the rod in the cleft of his hipbone and worked at landing the beast, tugging a couple of feet and reeling, closing the gap between them. He let the fish thrash and dive as it wanted, tiring itself—the bluefish. He knew it was a blue when he saw the school feeding *en masse*, frothing the surface with unified fervor, and he knew it when he felt the brawny thing going wild on the end of his line. Even sharks didn't have this much fight in them. Buck came aft from her nesting spot, wherever that had been, to watch the struggle. Tom spoke to her over his shoulder.

"You hungry?"

He'd reeled most of the monofilament back around its spool—tight, unbroken—but the rod was still bent comically, and the fish cut back and forth like a frustrated torpedo directly underneath the boat. Tom stood up and dragged it forward to keep from fouling his line on the rudder. He looked over the side and watched the bluefish threshing, avoiding the surface, and trying mightily to throw the hook.

Reaching out for the landing net with his left hand, Tom barely held the fish with just his right. He put the net in the water and held the rod high, giving as little slack as possible, working the net under and around. Glare bounced and jumped on the surface, and the fish flashed and wove underneath, and it was difficult to place it exactly, but at the instant they seemed to overlap, Tom lifted the whole rig—rod, fish, net, all of it—up and over the side and threw it down onto the deck where it landed with a clatter and a splash and a thump.

Panting, salt spray flying in every direction, darkening his clothes and the woodwork. The fish was over two feet, thick as his arm, and it bucked and slapped the deck under a tangle of gear. Buck watched from a defensive crouch, each of her myriad hairs standing on end, looking three times the cat. Eyes like half dollars. Tom groped around for the short bat, and once in hand, he clubbed the thing in the eyes until it finally lay still.

The two of them enjoyed a simple meal without haste or talk. Buck took sashimi hunks from where he tossed them on the deck, carried them off a few feet, and worked at each one unhurriedly before returning. The bluefish tasting oily and rich, Tom cutting translucent cubes of muscle from the fillets and happily chewing, washing it back with canned tomato juice. He allowed himself time to notice sunlight glinting off the knife blade, the susurration of wind in slack canvas. When they'd finished, he packed some fish away, out of the sun, and threw the rest to the gulls who'd besieged them. The birds dove on the carcass before it made a splash and screamed murderous, but left the *Tomorrow* in peace. Tom tossed a bucket of seawater over the aft deck, flushing the fish guts and blood out of the scuppers. Before long, they were again underway.

The afternoon's sweat had dried and cooled on his skin, and Tom decided to pull on some more layers. There was nothing ahead, as per the chart, but open water, so he tied down the tiller, keeping *Tomorrow* full and by. He went below and Buck followed, picking a spot under the bunk, turning several times in a circle, and lying down. Tom put on two sweaters and traded his ball cap for a woolen one.

The sloop cruised well enough on its own, so he went forward and forgot about the helm for a while. Tom sat himself behind the little bowsprit and just looked out over everything, looked at the sun making its long dive westward and the golden sheen it left on whatever was behind. He looked at where he'd been and where he was going. He looked north.

He'd come so many miles up the Maine coast, seeing little if anything human in all that time, and now that the sun was setting, he was heading further out to sea. It seemed like he'd broken free of humanity for good and for all, and soon the blackness would take over and any inkling of his culture would be invisible and moot. Those gutted cities and mournful towns, what good could they be? Civilization was the hind legs on a whale. Tom felt no coldness in this assessment, no anger—just acceptance and calm—the kind of bludgeoned, gun-shy objectivity of a survivor. He had parted with the conventions of his life and was now sailing directly into not-life—or between-life, maybe. This condition occupied no physical space, no location. He could sail for any coordinate and meet it there. It only mattered that he was acting when it found him. That he'd continued to act.

If they say the sky's falling, you can bet your ass they'll make sure it does.

Abel's assessment hadn't been untrue, but its truth was dependent on a framework of judgment. One had to be within the story to feel its validity. Tom had sensed this distinction. He'd gambled, like a Magellan of ontology, on the narrative having a border which one could cross. He'd departed the world as it's talked about for the world as it truly is.

Fletcher's rock was the first thing to break the eastern horizon—brighter than any of the early stars, choking out the tiny lights of the universe beyond. Tom had expected it. Regardless of trajectory, the comet would rise like any other body in the heavens, probably for many nights. He knew this from his reading, he'd prepared for the rock's physical presence, and yet he couldn't control his animal response. His limbs seized, holding him to the deck in a feline crouch, and his veins ran instantly cold.

It was drawing closer. Any illuminated object, the astronomy text had asserted, will appear blue during its approach. This was known as the Doppler Effect—a sort of light-wave compression that occurs when two objects move closer at great speed.

With its angle still low to the horizon, the rock glowed blue-white. Tom watched for maybe thirty minutes, as it climbed through the sky alone, before the familiar constellations resolved into vision and surrounded it. An ugly thing—a pale and paling thing, moving with the speed of a planet across unimaginable lengths of space—powerful as a million warheads and delicate as a pocket watch. Tom could hardly take his eyes from the comet, fear of it holding him entranced. For all the occult mathematics that had gone into apprehending it, he couldn't suppress his feeling that the rock would not be so easily reduced. He watched it like a picador sizing up a bull, waiting for it to act.

Tom moved back to the helm as the sea grew under him. The lazy chop he'd ridden for a full day was now breaking up into angry whitecaps, the boat climbing them and Tom's stomach lurching at each crest before crashing into the trough. The wind came on and it snapped the sheets with irregular, sudden changes of direction. The boom came up on his right like a propeller blade, and Tom ducked before it knocked him overboard. He got hold of the tiller and brought her about, pointing the boat into the storm and attempting to ride through it—just maintaining the heading, hoping that this squall was narrow and isolated.

It's not the rock, Tom assured himself. It's just a normal gale.

Within minutes the wind shifted again, suddenly tearing across his beam and catching the mainsail at ninety degrees. It bore down, keeling the *Tomorrow* hard on her port side. Tom watched his saltwater pole and a handful of other objects tumble over the port gunnel and plunge into the sea. Twenty feet out on the mast, a top spar dipped into the waves as the boat lay almost fully on her side. If he didn't find a way to cut sail, she'd capsize.

Hugging the tiller post with one arm, Tom reached desperately for the boom line, straining with two fingertips to unhitch it from its cleat. The wet rope was reluctant to slide, but he worked a bony finger into the half-hitch and pulled. The line sprang loose and whipped through the cleat, singing out with the force of the mainsail as the boom swung away and crashed into the waves. The boat hove to and lurched back up, onto its keel. Tom caught his breath for a moment, appreciating the feeling of gravity under his seat.

He struck both sails and battened down.

Without sail, the *Tomorrow* was adrift. Drifting in the night, where no lighthouse shone and the waves grew like dream monsters out of the nothing that lay ahead. Tom crab-walked down the companionway and sealed the cat below. He crouched there with his forehead against the woodwork as the boat pitched, and he imagined Buck inside, a tense spot of heat in the darkness.

The swells were growing and Tom considered the limits of his boat—its strong but shallow hull—its fast but narrow beam. It wouldn't survive seas much higher than those tossing it now. He realistically considered his own mortality. This sea was from a dream. This was not his Atlantic. Something was warping it and maligning it and throwing it against him. Still, if he kept a low profile, if he just kept that daggerboard in the water… Waves beat the hull, surged up over the gunnels, flooded the deck. Tom knew what this was supposed to be, and his resolve was deteriorating. It was impossible that the comet could draw tide with its small gravity, but these waves were not just hearsay. It was now in fear that Tom looked over the years he'd spent cultivating a very specific doubt, the doubt that had kept him moving, that had built this vessel now groaning and yawing beneath him. *Show me*, he'd said, challenging their God—never hearing an answer.

Tom wouldn't lose the boat. He threw himself back to the helm as she back-slid down the wall of a momentary trench, and the stars were lost behind it. That black mass of water—Leviathan rising to gulp the sky and tremble the horizon with its weight—he could have reached out and stuck a finger through its frothy skin. As the boat came around in the trench, the rudder was torn sideways, and the tiller cracked against his chest, fracturing something under his wet layers and stealing the air from his lungs. For a thrilling moment, a moment the rock owned, Tom felt the nearness of death in his heart, and he shot it back out to his extremities like lightning searching for a ground.

A great new wall of ocean rose and separated him from the world. Hands white and hard-veined on the tiller, he watched the hairs on their backs rise as though magnetized. Pale blue, radiant, the rock climbed the meridian lines, and a reaping surge followed with it.

Tom fell to the deck, pressed his body flat and tangled himself with loose rigging, closing his fists and closing his eyes. The sea came on like an animate mountain, charging, roaring, breaking at the summit, and crashing.

Over him.

At first, there was pain and cool air on his skin—a throbbing in the ribcage and a sting of wet ropes binding him. Tom opened his eyes to a sky of washy blue—and gulls. He squinted against the light and saw them high above, heard them calling back and forth, announcing all that had stirred to the surface in the storm. He wasn't far from land, it seemed, but what land? The boat rocked slightly beneath him—afloat.

As if waking from a long and vivid dream, Tom was suspicious of the world. He breathed an atmosphere that had neither boiled away nor choked with ash. The pain was real, but maybe he'd passed into some lonely, floating afterlife with his infirmities and his doubts intact. Tom coughed and shook the sleep out of his head. He looked at his hands, the lacerations and rope burns he'd sustained in the night. This was not some theological error. It was the real, living world.

The water was smooth and glassy but for those pieces which the *Tomorrow* had shed. Oak trim from the cabin roof and splinters of the boom floated out there. "Fucking hell," he whispered to no one when he discovered the mast trailing astern, tethered to the boat by its frayed halyard. He checked its former mount ahead of the cabin, just to be sure he wasn't imagining. Tom wouldn't be sailing home, but he was alive.

He was alive.

A fit of emotion overtook him, knelt there on the deck. It shook him and pulled him to the wooden planks like a great voice shouting him down. The tears came so thick he could see only colors ahead, the long green blur of land in the distance. It came in surges, each convulsion bringing up a memory to get stopped in the wet, gasping channel of his throat. John Hupper's body. A dead kitten and a street filled with fire and shouts. The empty hallways of the clinic. He rocked on his knees and wept and tallied the unbelievable litany of what had been lost.

Tom wiped the warm salt from his face and breathed very slowly. The air was dense with quiet.

Tomorrow wasn't more than two miles offshore, the storm having pushed her north as she drifted, and so back into the main. Tom scanned the shore for activity and saw a handful of small craft, only white dots in his cracked binoculars, gradually tracing the contours of the land. Salvage and rescue. He could also see spirals of black smoke rising here and there, where the storm had turned cooking fires and pushed them back into the trees, unchecked and spreading.

He pulled open the companionway hatch and Buck shot up the ladder past him, snuffing up the morning air and squinting into the light. Tom had both saved and neglected her in the bowels of the sloop. He found a jug of drinking water and three tins of sardines, dented and rolling free around the cabin, and then cleared a spot on the deck of the glass shards that glinted there.

They ate breakfast slowly, Buck watching the harbor seals who'd come to investigate their stranded vessel. Tom opened cans and tossed provisions to the seals, amused at the way they anticipated and lunged at the fish. He stripped off his damp, heavy layers and laid himself out on the deck. Tom closed his eyes and, for a long, aimless while, listened to the sea.

"Mayday, Mayday…" Through the glassless window frame, he watched the cat placidly gazing over the water. "*Mayday*. This is *Tomorrow*, requesting assistance…" With one hand he held the snapped antenna against the cabin roof while working the ship-to-shore with the other. It spat and crackled and Tom made little, arbitrary adjustments. The signal came and went. "This is *Tomorrow*. Throw me a fucking bone, would you? I'm talking to *you*, Nev…"

After testing several channels, he walked away in frustration, only to come back thirty minutes later and try again. Tom was in danger of running the boat aground. He cast a glance out, toward the nearest place he'd suspect to find rocks, still over a nautical mile off his port bow. With no power, they were at the mercy of the tide.

Lunch and dinner were both eaten on deck. Hour after hour passed as he repeatedly checked the sun, checked the shore, checked the radio. He began to worry for Bradford. With winds like that, it was possible Stearns Fiberglass, the whole shop, had just collapsed on his head in the night. Tom pushed the image aside. Surely it would take more than a windstorm to destroy Neville Bradford. The man's hardiness, after all, was maybe his last repository for what Tom could reasonably describe as faith.

Buck awoke after a post-supper nap below deck and climbed the ladder to shout something at him in her language, all emphasis without syntax. *"Aeeooow."*

"Okay," he said. "Alright."

On hands and knees, Tom swept the top deck clear of debris with a wadded shirt, the tiny fragments of glass and paint and laminate board perforating the water's surface in small, quick showers. He held a bait knife in his teeth as he crawled the horseshoe of the deck to slice any ropes that trailed into the water. As she drifted, Tom watched these severed portions of his boat gradually gain distance or else slip silently to the bottom, fodder for the rock tumbler of the tide.

The mast was still stuck by its mainsail halyard, the base end of it maybe six feet off the stern. The halyard rope alone wouldn't be enough to haul the mast by, so he went below for a length of hemp line that he dunked twice in seawater for tensile strength. Hanging his torso out over the water, Tom gradually pulled the floating mast close enough to tie. When his rope was attached, he took a couple of breaths, readying himself for any small disaster, and began to pull.

After a great deal of cursing, spitting, and hollering non-words, he'd gotten the butt end of the thing out of the water and let it rest on the wooden edge of the gunwale. Tom took a look behind, judging the space, and noticed Buck above the cabin, alert and concerned. Tom said, "Shut up," and continued to pull.

Pain flared in his chest with each full-bodied exertion. Glancing at his bare ribs, he noticed for the first time the ugly, purple bruise, like a small spiral galaxy of ruptured blood vessels growing under his skin.

He couldn't let up for more than a second's pause without the sea threatening to reclaim the mast. It squealed and shuddered against the gunwale, slipping and taking out chunks of maple with its steel rungs. There came the halfway point, more mast weight above the water than below. It teetered there on a fulcrum, dipping into the shadowy sea, holding the *Tomorrow*'s stern an even foot below her natural water line. Tom released the hemp rope and kneaded his palms together, breathing heavy, and looked back to shore.

The sun had landed itself in a comb of distant trees, and the vessel speeding toward him, quickly overtaking Tom's position, was backlit and anonymous in those last, oblique rays.

Tom panicked, realizing his "gull swatter" was below deck. He picked up the mast line and gave it one massive tug, and the mast came crashing to the deck and sliding up the portside catwalk, the boat listing to that side and him jumping backward before the thing could crush his toes. He trapeze-walked along the mast, jumping down the companionway to retrieve his shotgun.

The fast-approaching vessel threw a messy wake as it throttled down, slowing, now maybe a hundred meters off the *Tomorrow*'s stern as she sat dead in the water. Tom squinted down the oily single-barrel, keeping a bead on the other boat's wheelhouse, knowing he'd be an easy mark for an unprincipled salvager. The distance closed and he could make out the pilot's silhouette, could hear the choppy, coughing sound of their engine.

You son of a bitch... Tom lowered his gun as Mike Hupper's lobsterboat, the *Puffin*, hove to within a couple boat lengths. The familiar outline of Bradford's ballcapped head and waving arm sharpened in the gloaming.

When the business of coupling the crippled sloop to the *Puffin*'s winch had been sorted out, and Bradford had his fill of punching Tom and calling him a "shit-ass sailah," and berating him for being yet alive, the sun was full-down and they were preparing to chug south under motor.

"Mikey says I oughta give ya his apology, by the way."

"Accepted."

Bradford looked over the sloop, an incredulous smirk in his features. "Ya still bound for St. John's?"

Tom considered his work, tethered as it was to the *Puffin*'s stern cleats. The fallen mast and swamped bilge and shattered cabin. He lifted a hand equivocally, wincing at the pain this brought. "I might take another year."

"Home, then?"

"Home."

Tom sat on the foredeck of the *Tomorrow*, watching Bradford's form in the lobsterboat's wheelhouse lights, enjoying the feeling of motion once more and scanning the dark shore as it slowly moved into and past his view. The sheer mass of water moving beneath him pulled the tiller line from one side to the other as he held it, and Tom pulled back, immersing himself in this simple interrogation with substance.

In the same moment, both men saw it. Bradford stuck out an arm, pointing east to where Fletcher's rock—or whomever's—rose for its second appearance in the northern hemisphere. Now speeding away, many times faster than the sound of their hollering out, its wavelength had increased and its color shifted toward pink. A quarter of the sky was aglow with the trail, the comet outgassing and shedding mass and burning in solar radiance.

The rock traced an elliptical orbit past this world, unchanged by its gravity and deaf to the inanities its people spoke in a common, garbled tongue. Whatever spirit moved it would not be contained by their theories or their myths.

Tom's gaze drifted earthward. Muscongus Bay was narrowing before them, drawing the boats past Hawthorne Point, into the narrows, and on toward Near Haven. A small cluster of lights came into view, breaking the horizon like minor stars, paltry under the comet glow. He watched them gradually brighten, cutting a straight path through the night. They seemed familiar and yet unprecedented, these three swift beacons shooting over the land, over the George, and high above his crippled sloop. Predictable in every way the rock was not, and piloted by mortal men. Only after their passing could he quantify them, these dark machines, as the world shuddered beneath.

The author would like to acknowledge:

I would like to extend my thanks, in roughly chronological order, to those who have most helped me shape this story over the last eight years:

To my early readers Kris Minta, Roz Ray, and Joseph Stager, who slogged through piles of utter shit yet kept their comments constructive, and The Richard Hugo House in Seattle, where I burned several bridges but gained much perspective. It was in that city, with those people, that I turned my narcissistic pipe dreams into an honest craft.

To The Writer's Hotel, NYC, where I first got my hands on publishing's ropes. Specifically to Scott Wolvin, an outstanding writer and teacher, who gave several months worth of keen attention to the manuscript which would become *Near Haven*.

To all those who have read, commented, trouble-shot, and copy-edited the work since finding its home at Belle Lutte Press. Particularly you, John, you son of a bitch.

To Lance Person, who saw fit to usher this peculiar novel into existence. As an untested, argumentative, and hopelessly idealistic artist, I could not have found a better champion, or friend.

Finally, to my wife Signe, who is always my first editor. Thank you for weathering my obsessions.

— MSS, May 14, 2017

Belle Lutte Press would like to thank the following people, in connection with *Near Haven*:

Matthew Stephen Sirois
Thomas Fincke
Ravindra Banthia
Michael Patrick Dudding
John Stephens
Diane Shirk
Christopher B. Derrick
Antonio Mora

Matthew Stephen Sirois

Matthew Stephen Sirois' fiction and essays have appeared in *The New Guard Review*, *Split Lip Magazine*, *The Ghost Story*, and *Necessary Fiction*, among others. Raised in coastal Maine, he now lives with his wife and daughter in western Massachusetts, where he works as a metal fabricator. This is his first novel.

CPSIA information can be obtained
at www.ICGtesting.com
Printed in the USA
BVOW09s1803220917
495616BV00002B/243/P